BETTER THAN YOUR DREAMS

DEE ERNST

235 Alexander Street

The characters and events portrayed in this book are fictitious. Any similarity to real persons, living or dead, is very flattering to the author, but purely coincidental and not intentional.

Published by 235 Alexander Street

ISBN-13: 9780985985462

OTHER BOOKS BY DEE ERNST

A Slight Change of Plan
A Different Kind of Forever
Better Off Without Him

You can visit Dee at DeeErnst.com
or you can reach her at Dee@DeeErnst.com

Better Than Your Dreams is dedicated to my readers, particularly those who contributed to the creation of Coco Zipperelli, a character in this book.

I ran a contest, asking for readers' suggestions in three areas: character name, physical appearance, and personality quirk. The top five suggestions in each category were put to a vote, and the winners were:

Wanda Sue Jochens
and
members of the Always Re(a)d Book Club, Wheaton, Illinois
Linda Bull, Grace Chen, Carol Johnson, Dana Lingle, Kathleen Manning, Virginia Reynolds, Victoria Ryan, Debra Shipway, and Dawn Wolter.

And many thanks as well to those participants who made it into the Top 5
(in no particular order)

Michele Hopler, Robert Zitzman, Jo Elle Rybakowski, Chase Ashley,
Kay Rivera, Susan Loving, and Sandy Giden

I have the best readers in the world!

CONTENTS

CHAPTER ONE

IN THE EIGHTEEN MONTHS THAT I had been flying back and forth between LAX in California and EWR in Newark, New Jersey, I had never quite gotten the hang of it. I didn't mind the flight *out* to LA. For some reason it seemed shorter and easier. But coming back—very tough. Maybe it was because I always took the first flight out at six in the morning. Which meant being at the airport by five in the morning, which meant I had to leave my house at— never mind. It's too depressing to think about.

Then there was the time difference. I was actually flying *forward* in time. Now, maybe a sci-fi aficionado might find that exciting, but to me it just meant I'd lost a few hours of my life that I would never get back. I'd leave before breakfast and land midafternoon. Where did lunch go?

The flight itself was long. Very long. Five and a half hours. After being in a plane for that amount of time, I wanted to land in an exotic locale where people spoke a different language—or at least had a cool accent—and there were lots of fruity drinks with umbrellas sitting around. It was a bummer getting off the plane and everyone spoke English, and the most exotic thing I could look forward to was Stewart's root beer.

But every time I got off the plane at Newark airport, at the end of the seemingly endless walk from the gate, was Ben Cutler.

I had known Ben for a very long time. He had been my plumber. Four years ago he became something more. Much more. And as long as I'd known him, my first glimpse of him always took my breath away. He was by far the handsomest man I'd ever

1

known. Usually that was all people saw, which was a shame, because he was so much more than that. He was kind. He thought about things beyond his own small circle. He cared about other people, and what they thought or felt. I had found that, by and large, kindness had always been very underrated.

He was also funny and charming and smart as a whip. He loved me. I loved him. And I always ran those last few yards through security just so he could sweep me up into his arms.

This last flight, in the cold and gray of November, was no different. I threw my arms around his neck, and he lifted me off my feet in a hug, then kissed me long and hard before setting me back down.

"Welcome home, Mona. And this is it, right? No more commuting?"

I shook my head. "Nope. I'm done. I'm home. And I'm all yours."

He grinned as he picked up my tote bag and carry-on. "Good. Let's get you out of here."

We walked down toward the luggage carousel. When I had flown home in the past, I'd just carried on some makeup and my laptop and wore what I'd left in my Westfield, New Jersey, closets. But this trip, this last trip, required the purchase of two more pieces of luggage to accommodate my expanded wardrobe. The new pieces were initialed *MQ*, for Mona Quincy. The older suitcases still bore *MB*, even though I had legally ceased being Mona Berman four years ago.

"I hope you brought your truck," I said to Ben. "I bought a few things in California."

He laughed. "Of course you did. I have the pickup. Or should we get a U-Haul?"

"Ha, ha. Very funny. Well, maybe."

We stood and waited. I leaned against him, partly because I loved the feel of him—lean and strong—and partly because I liked letting all the other women waiting for their luggage know that this particular man was all mine.

He put his arm around me and kissed my hair. "So, how did you leave things?"

I had published the book four years earlier, after my then-husband Brian left me. For another woman, of course—younger, blond, and French. I was a writer of historical romance, and a very successful one at that, but I found my happily-ever-after switch had frozen in the off position. I ended up writing a very non-historical, nonromantic book about a woman of a certain age—like me—who got dumped by her lousy husband—also like me—but found herself much happier. It was called *Better Off Without Him*, and it not only became a best seller, it also won a few awards and got optioned by a Very Famous Hollywood Personage for film development.

It took a while for the whole option thing to go anywhere. After the papers were signed and the first check arrived, my assistant, Anthony, and I churned out a terrific screenplay in record time and sent it off to the Very Famous Hollywood Personage. Who read it, loved it, and promptly went on to another project. So I returned to writing, concentrated on raising my three daughters, and had generally gone about my life pretty much as I had done before.

Then, eighteen months ago, I got the Call. From Hollywood. Was I interested in working on a new screenplay for *Better Off Without Him*? Would I be willing to move out there for at least six months and work with "the team"?

Well…yeah.

The Very Famous Hollywood Personage had found a producer, director, and two experienced screenwriters who wanted me to work with them. My original screenplay had been looked over several times, and was now found wanting, but they wanted me "on board." Was I willing to get "on board?"

Yes!

That's how I ended up in the land of the Beautiful People.

I rubbed my head against his shoulder. "I won't know a thing for at least a few months. There's this strange phenomenon out there called *development hell* where all screenplays seem to land. If it can work its way up to the top of the pile, then maybe it will be a movie after all."

He laughed. "That's a very odd business."

"Oh, Ben, you have no idea."

3

My suitcases began to appear. Ben, because he was such a sweet man, did not even flinch as he hauled them all off the belt. He just rounded up a skycap, who neatly arranged all the pieces on a long cart and followed us out into the parking lot, where the luggage was then thrown into the back of the truck, and money discreetly changed hands.

The last time I'd been home was three months ago, when I'd flown in for the twenty-fourth birthday party of Ben's son David. I'd managed to drag two of my three daughters with me, and we all had a great time. Ben flew out to LA three weeks ago, and we spent the weekend skinny-dipping in full view of the entire downtown Los Angeles area. We hadn't been together since then.

"So," I said as we pulled onto the parkway, "should we stop somewhere for a bite, or just go right to my house and get naked?"

He laughed. His teeth were slightly crooked. Thank God, because I couldn't stand it if he were perfect. As it was, the dark hair, amazing blue eyes, and dimples were almost too much to take. Almost.

"I think," Ben said, "there are some other people who are also eager to welcome you home."

Probably true. Not my children, who were scattered up and down the East Coast in various colleges. Although any of them were close enough to come home at any time, even just for a day in the middle of the week to see their beloved mother, all three of them had declined my invitation, saying they'd see me on the weekend. Fair enough. They were in college. They were all grown-up, with lives and things.

But still.

"Patricia?" I asked.

Ben nodded. "And Anthony. He really missed you. And there's something up with Lily."

That was not good.

Lily Martel was seventy-eight, my father's only sister and my beloved aunt and godmother. She had been living with me since she sold her Park Slope co-op—luckily before a planned alien invasion that would have caused the bottom to drop out of the Brooklyn real estate market. Aliens never actually invaded, by the way, and she ended up very rich. She had, coincidentally, arrived on my doorstep the same day that Brian announced that he was leaving me. Lily's arrival seemed to be a sign, and she never quite left. Her position in my home was vague and ever changing. The past several months she'd kept things running smoothly during my long stretches in California, keeping the house for when the girls came home, and making sure the dog and various cats were well cared for. It was a situation that worked well for all of us. But Lily had also managed to involve herself in a few of the more, shall we say, questionable political organizations around the town of Westfield. One, I knew, supported the idea of no central government at all, but rather a series of city-states. Another had something to do with redistribution of corporate wealth. I was always afraid she'd end up in jail, or at least on a watch list somewhere.

I sighed. "Hmm. Well, okay. We'll say hello to everyone, hear what Lily has to say, then get naked?"

He glanced over at me. "Why, Ms. Quincy, are you suggesting that perhaps you missed me?"

"Ben, for the past year and a half, we've spent a small fortune flying back and forth to see each other. Before I left, we were together every other night."

"I knew it." He sighed, shaking his head. "You only love me for my body."

I laughed. "Yes. And your heart. And your soul."

"Ah, now, that's more like it. So…I was thinking…"

"Oh, Ben, you know that only gets you into trouble."

"Yeah. I do know. But I think you and I should, maybe, you know, talk about getting married."

Something hit me in the stomach, and I couldn't breathe for a second. "To each other?" I finally asked.

He swore softly. He usually didn't do that. "I'm sorry. I should have waited. I should have gotten down on one knee or something."

"No. I mean, don't be sorry. It's just…"

Just what?

"Ben, you and I have been getting along just fine."

"I know. But it's time, don't you think? We should take the next step. Listen, this really wasn't fair to you. I know how you are after these flights. Just think about it, okay? We'll talk later." He shot me a look, the kind of look that made my knees turn to water. "Maybe after we get naked?"

I nodded. That immediately put me back in my happy place.

But married? Not so much. I had been married. For twenty years. And I never, ever wanted to repeat that experience again.

"Honey, I'm home!" I called.

Silence. Did I really think my daughters would rally and surprise me with balloons, confetti, and a small brass band?

Well, yes.

I walked from the kitchen through the first floor. Nothing had changed since I'd been here last. The foyer was wide and welcoming, tasteful artwork on the walls, my quaint elephant foot doing duty as an umbrella stand. My living room was a cool study in comfortable, quietly elegant "transitional" pieces. The fireplace reflected calm dignity; the drapes hung softly, gently brushing the gleaming hardwood floors. I peeked around to the dining room—polished wood, muted colors. A woman of obvious taste and refinement lived here. A successful woman, a sophisticated woman, a woman who was, at the moment, grateful to return to her castle.

A woman who also wanted balloons and a little confetti.

"Fred?" I called. I counted silently, three...two...one...

My golden retriever bounded into the hallway from upstairs, tongue lolling, tail wagging happily. Fred, as he'd gotten older, had become much slower on the uptake, and he hadn't been too sharp to begin with. But he was always glad to see me, and he was one smiling face I could count on, even if it did take him a few minutes to realize who exactly I was.

We finished our ritual—head scratching, a little something behind his ears, the world-class belly rub. Then he licked my face one last time and wandered back into the kitchen, leaving me alone in the quiet, elegant foyer of my home.

Ben came through carrying the first round of suitcases.

"Let me help you," I said.

He shook his head. "No, I'm good. I missed the gym today. This can be my workout instead."

I followed him upstairs and began to unpack. I looked at the clothes I'd bought in California—gauzy maxi skirts, flowing linen tunics, gladiator sandals. Totally useless for New Jersey in mid-November. What had I been thinking?

I heard voices calling. Seconds later, Fred was barking happily. I ran back downstairs.

My two best friends in the whole world were in my kitchen. Patricia Carmichael, cool, stunning, and always elegant, was busy with the martini pitcher and a bottle of Grey Goose vodka. MarshaMarsha, my next-door neighbor for the past umpteen years, was unwrapping a wedge of cheese. I could smell fresh-baked bread from Bettinger's bakery. These two knew how to throw a welcome-home fete.

Patricia gave me a quick hug and a kiss on the cheek.

MarshaMarsha threw her arms around me and hugged me for a long time.

"I really missed you." She sniffed. Her real name was Marsha Riollo, but my former sister-in-law had been known as Marsha the Bitch, so my dear friend and neighbor had become MarshaMarsha, and she'd been that for so long I never thought of her any other way. She was tiny, dark, and adorable.

"I really missed you too," I said.

Patricia handed me a perfectly chilled martini glass, filled to the brim. "Weren't you here a few weeks ago?" she asked, eyebrow arched.

I took hold of the stem. "Three months ago. And only for five days. Now I'm back for good. It's different."

MarshaMarsha nodded. "Yes." She raised her glass. "Here's to being back for good!"

We clinked glasses and drank. As always, that first hit of vodka on the back of my throat had a bit of a kick, but the second sip was smooth as glass. I nibbled some cheese and took a bite of baguette, spread with fig jam.

Patricia smiled smugly. "I just texted Anthony. He's dropping everything to get here. And Lily. She said she was on her way now, and can't wait to see you. I saw Ben outside. I feel like Ringo, getting what's left of the band back together."

At that moment, Ben appeared with more luggage. He grinned at Patricia. "Chill one of those glasses for me," he called as he went through.

I closed my eyes and let more cold vodka trickle down my throat.

Anthony burst through my back door, golden hair swept off his high and artificially bronzed forehead, face beaming. He was an incredibly handsome man, and being gay, was the secret weapon for all of my love scenes—he could give me the man's perspective on pleasure, from both the giving and receiving ends.

Anthony Wood worked for me, but more than that, he was my friend, first reader of anything and everything I wrote, and my biggest fan. I had asked him if he wanted to come to California with me, but he and his partner Victor had just bought a house together, and Anthony did not want to become a long-distance bride. He had remained in New Jersey, still doing quite a bit of work for me from his new home. Although we spoke often, I hadn't seen him in the flesh in almost six months.

He kissed me on both cheeks, then did the same with Patricia and MarshaMarsha before taking a full glass from Patricia.

"I am so glad you're home," he said, taking a sip. "I need some excitement."

I raised an eyebrow. "And how am I going to provide excitement?"

He shrugged. "Not you, exactly. Your life tends to be a little dull. But between your daughters and Lily, something is bound to happen."

I did not mention the fact that Ben had asked me to marry him. All three of them, I knew, would have jumped up and down with happiness at that. But there was still something stuck in my gut, a small, sharp something that I did not want to think about, but I knew wasn't going to go away.

Ben came into the kitchen, nodded to Anthony, and grabbed the last martini glass off the counter. He lifted his glass. "A big welcome back to Mona, the sweetest, sexiest woman in the world."

We all drank. My glass was almost empty, and I would have asked Patricia for a second, but my aunt Lily chose that moment to come in the kitchen door, followed by a very handsome gentleman of an indeterminate age—anywhere from sixty to eighty—wearing a dark suit, a navy blue button-down shirt, and a pale pink tie.

"Mona," Lily cried, arms widespread. I got up to hug her, trying to hide my amazement.

I hadn't spoken to Aunt Lily via Skype or anything else that let me look at her, and when I'd been home last, she'd been off visiting in Brooklyn, so I hadn't seen her in months. She'd gone from a Miss Marple-ish lady with permed white hair and a cardigan sweater to something of a glamour girl. Her hair was cut short, but instead of her usual soft halo of curls, it was styled close to her head and straight, like Judi Dench. She was wearing a colorful woven shawl that she dramatically swept off her shoulders, revealing a long red tunic falling over dark denim jeans that were tucked into soft gray boots. Several chunky gold chains around her neck and a wide gold bangle completed the look.

"Aunt Lily," I finally managed, "what happened to you?"

She smiled. She was wearing bright lipstick and lots of mascara. "Vincent happened to me. Mona, meet Vincent DeMatriano. Vinnie, dearest, this is Mona."

Vinnie Dearest bowed over my hand and murmured something that I couldn't actually hear, because my brain was exploding.

DeMatriano? Vinnie DeMatriano? As in Joey "Two Shoes" DeMatriano? Notorious crime boss who happened to be the father of Lily's good friend Joe DeMatriano, also a notorious crime boss?

Aunt Lily was making introductions all around. Patricia, who would be unfailingly polite to one of Hitler's henchmen, was all smiles and charm. MarshaMarsha went into her Italian paisano mode, kissing and making exaggerated hand gestures. Anthony tried to keep his eyes from dropping out of his head. I kept looking at Ben for, if nothing else, moral support. The man was unflappable, and I tried to siphon off as much of his calmness as I could.

Joe DeMatriano had introduced Vinnie to Lily. Of course. It seemed that Vinnie and Joey "TwoShoes" were brothers. Lily was all smiles as she explained.

Anthony was bursting. "Are you in the family business too?" he asked.

I closed my eyes in horror. Anthony, really?

But he recovered nicely. "You know, shoes?"

Vinnie shrugged. "Retired. Retail was never my thing. Now I just enjoy the fruits of my labor."

Ben leaned back and nodded. "Retail is very tough. I'm sure you've earned every minute of relaxation."

Vinnie nodded back. "Exactly."

Ben always knew the right thing to say.

Patricia had made another batch of martinis, of course, but I waved her away, focusing on Lily. The woman looked amazing—happy and glowing. She and Vinnie sat down at the table, held hands, and gazed at each other like teenagers. Lily accepted a drink from Patricia and let Vinnie take a sip. Then they kissed.

"And how long have you two known each other again?" I finally asked.

Lily batted her eyelashes. "Only three months. And I know that's not a long time, but Vincent and I both know what we want."

"Which is?" I prompted.

She burst into giggles. "To get married, of course! Mona, please, will you be my maid of honor?"

CHAPTER TWO

OKAY, I'LL ADMIT IT. I'D devoted a great deal of my life thinking about weddings.

When I was a little girl I could spend hours looking through my parents' wedding photos. They got married in 1956, and my mother wore a tea-length dress of satin and tulle. Their wedding was small, only three bridesmaids and groomsmen, but they had a flower girl who tossed rose petals before the blushing bride, and a ring bearer proudly carried the matching bands.

I spent way too much time and energy planning my own wedding—especially when you considered how it turned out. Back then, I just cut pictures out of magazines and Elmer's-glued them all in a notebook. With three daughters, I'd found myself thinking about weddings again over the past few years. After all, Miranda was a beautiful young woman, about to graduate college. In fact, thanks to a few summers taking extra classes, she was graduating a semester early and was getting a head start on paying back those student loans. Lauren had had the same serious boyfriend since her senior year in high school. Jessica has had one boyfriend or another since the tender age of thirteen. So it was only natural for me to start fantasizing a bit.

Now, I knew that members of my daughters' generation were not that into relationships. They mostly hung out and hooked up. But there was a whole section on Pinterest dedicated to weddings, and surely that couldn't be just for hopeful mothers like myself. Somewhere people were getting married, and I was determined to be ready.

I had several Pinterest boards, all of them private, dedicated to these imaginary weddings—for Lauren and Miranda and Jessica, Jessica's being the smallest. Let's face it: it's hard to put together wedding looks that combine black leather, piercings, gauges, and tattoos. I even had a board of my own. I picked out so many mother-of-the-bride dresses I could waste almost an hour looking through them. I'd Googled bands and deejays, bookmarked favorite destination wedding sites, and even created a file titled "Wedding Words." But I never thought I'd have to think about my aunt marrying a retired wise guy.

And yet…

"Aunt Lily, really? How wonderful!" I hugged her, then turned to hug Vinnie.

He wasn't very tall and smelled of subtle and expensive aftershave. His cheek was smooth and his smile brilliant. He was a very attractive man—think Frank Vincent, but older and more dangerous looking.

"Lily was afraid you'd have, ah, reservations," he said softly.

Gosh, let's think—Lily was a very wealthy woman, introduced to Vinnie by his nephew, a known mafioso. True, Vinnie was probably filthy rich, but the extra million or two couldn't hurt. They were planning on getting married after knowing each other for just three months—what possible reservations could there be?

"If Lily is happy, I'm happy," I said. And I meant it. Aunt Lily looked better than she had in years, and I *was* glad for her.

"We see no reason to wait," Aunt Lily said. "After all, it's not like this is a first marriage for either of us. We were thinking the spring. Maybe April?"

Anthony, coming up behind me, murmured in my ear, "How appropriate. April fools?"

Very apropos. Anyone who would think about marrying a person after knowing them only a few months *was* a fool. After all, Ben and I had been together for years, and I knew I'd have a lot of thinking to do before I gave him an answer. How could Lily be so sure after just a few months?

MarshaMarsha had tears in her eyes. "I'm so thrilled for you both. Imagine, finding love again after all these years."

Dear MarshaMarsha. She really meant it. The woman could find a silver lining anywhere.

Patricia got practical. "And what's your living situation, Vincent? Are you living with family as well?"

The compound in the *Godfather* movies flashed through my head.

Vinnie smiled. "I have my own place. In Bay Ridge. There's plenty of room for Lily." He kissed Lily's cheek, and she gave him another sip of martini. How cute.

"Bay Ridge? Oh, Aunt Lily, how nice. You'll be back in Brooklyn," I said.

She sighed. "Yes. I've loved living here, of course, but I can't wait to get back to Brooklyn. First we're going to Sicily. For our honeymoon."

Patricia had miraculously rearranged the cheese and fig jam, added grapes and a few sliced pears, and unearthed a box of multigrain crackers. "Vincent, some wine?" she asked.

Vinnie shook his head. "No, thank you. I have a meeting in Manhattan later this evening. I need a clear head." He smiled. "I just wanted to come out here with Lily and meet you, Mona. I know how important you are to her. I want us to be friends."

Of course we'll be friends, Vinnie. We'll be whatever you want.

"Vinnie, I can tell just by looking at her how happy my aunt Lily is. You and I are going to get along just fine. It's just going to take me a bit to get used to the idea, you know?"

He came around and gave me a kiss on the cheek. "Take all the time you need, Mona. Until April, that is." He laughed. I smiled uneasily.

I walked with him out the kitchen door. A black Lincoln Town Car was parked in my driveway, and a young man in a dark suit jumped out of the front seat to open the back door. Lily and Vinnie murmured together, then he slipped into the backseat. The young man shut the door, nodded briefly to Lily, and drove off.

My aunt and I stood together in the chill fall air. She was beaming. "Isn't he something?" she exclaimed.

I took a deep breath. "Ah, yes, Aunt Lily, he certainly is. How did you meet him again?"

We walked back into the house. Lily sat down and scrutinized the tray before her, delicately picking up a slice of pear and a chunk of cheese. "Joe—you know my friend Joe—arranged a blind date. I told him I wasn't interested in meeting a man, not at my age, but I had mentioned that I'd felt a little lonely since you were in California. He was so insistent, Joe was, so I agreed to coffee in Park Slope. Vincent was so sweet! We went to the botanical garden. You know that's one of my favorite places." She chewed delicately, swallowed, then sipped more martini. "He quite swept me off my feet."

Patricia was staring at Lily with open admiration. Anthony had unearthed my laptop and was squinting at the screen. I didn't want to know what he had found online about Vinnie "I'll Be Here for Thanksgiving" DeMatriano.

MarshaMarsha was all smiles. "Lily, I am so happy. I'd been seeing the car, of course, and wondered what was going on."

I turned to MarshaMarsha. "You saw the car? The black Town Car?"

She nodded. "Yes. It started few weeks ago. Parked here at night, and still here in the morning."

I felt my jaw drop. "The car spent the night? As in, staying over? As in, Vinnie-spending-the-night over?"

Aunt Lily rolled her eyes. "Really, Mona, Vincent and I are both adults, you know. Surely you can't object to us spending the night together."

So many things were going through my head that for a moment I was incapable of coherent speech. Patricia continued to look astounded.

Ben threw me a wicked look. "Yeah, Mona. They're both adults," he said.

"Of course I don't object, Aunt Lily. I have to wonder, though —what about the driver? Where did he spend the night?"

She was examining a grape. "In the guest room, of course. His name is Tony. I couldn't have him sleeping in the car, now, could I? A very nice young man. He's also, I think, a bodyguard. He follows Vincent everywhere."

Tony the Bodyguard sleeping in my guest room. Perfect.

Patricia leaned forward, her eyes glittering with interest. "Does Vincent have any children?"

Lily had found the grape satisfactory, ate it, then chose another. "Yes, three daughters. And seven grandchildren. Can you imagine? He says he spoils them all rotten. I believe him. Vincent is very tenderhearted."

"I'm sure," Patricia said. She was obviously intrigued. "And he lives in Bay Ridge?"

Lily smiled. "Yes. It's a big house right across from the river. Very nice. There's a lovely pool in the back and a small garden. He grows his own tomatoes."

MarshaMarsha was still smiling happily. "Where were you thinking of getting married, Lily?"

"Vincent suggested just having a ceremony at his house, you know, something very small and simple, with wine and food afterward. We were thinking about one of those big tents, you know? With portable heaters. April has become a bit of a weather challenge the past few years. But his yard is small, with the pool and the garden, so I thought maybe we could have something here. There's so much more room; and let's face it, the backyard is perfect for this sort of thing. Mona, you have thrown some amazing parties here in the past." She smiled innocently at me.

Anthony's head shot up. Patricia's eyes actually widened in surprise. MarshaMarsha beamed. Ben tilted his head, and his mouth twitched.

I opened my mouth to speak, but, oddly, no words came out. My martini glass was empty, but Aunt Lily still had almost half a glass. I reached over, took it from her hand, and downed the contents in one quick gulp.

"My backyard?"

"Oh, Mona, it would be perfect,' Lily said.

"In April?"

She nodded.

I took a deep breath. So many things could happen between now and April. Including Lily realizing that maybe marrying this relative stranger was not the best idea after all.

"Sure," I said. "Why not?"

15

Aunt Lily, Patricia, Anthony, Ben, and I ended up all going out for dinner the night before. MarshaMarsha had wanted to come with us, but she was in various sports-related carpools involving three of her four sons and was booked for the night. The five of us ended up at the pub. I sat there listening, looking at Ben once in a while to see him leaning forward, obviously happy and excited for Lily.

Lily gushed about what a wonderful guy Vincent was as Patricia and Anthony pumped her for more info on his past.

Vincent had stepped away from the family business fifteen years before, when his son-in-law, while in the service of Joe DeMatriano, mysteriously vanished during what should have been a routine exchange of a suitcase full of cash for some incriminating information on a local politician. Vincent's daughter had been devastated, of course, and had apparently suggested the police look into the situation. Out of respect for Vincent, said daughter—along with both of her sons—was encouraged to go on a long cruise around the world, rather than just disappearing into the Great Swamp. Vincent realized that his nephew was not putting family first in quite the same way as his father, the original Joey "Two Shoes," had. So Vincent retired, taking millions of dollars and countless secrets with him.

My aunt seemed to find nothing wrong with Vinnie's previous life, and repeatedly told us all that he was nothing more than a quiet, retired businessman. All night long I thought about their wedding taking place in my backyard, in a huge white tent lit with hundreds of candles. Maybe two tents—one with a portable bar and long tables for catered food, the other laid with a dance floor and a small band tucked into a corner. There was more than enough room, and guests could use the bathroom right off the kitchen. I also kept having flashes of long black cars parked along the tree-lined street in front of my house, with plainclothes detectives taking down license plate numbers.

Isn't that what happened in the *Godfather* movies?

I slept well. I always slept well when Ben spent the night. When

I woke the next morning, very early, I was surrounded by balls of fur. The cats had all forgiven me for leaving them alone with Lily for so long, and Fred had curled up against my feet during the night. There had barely been room for Ben, but we managed. I could hear the shower going. No matter how early I woke up, it seemed that Ben was always awake just a little bit sooner.

Lana, my oldest and favorite cat, was watching me when I opened my eyes, her tail twitching. She was gold and white and very beautiful, and I had named her for the blond actress Lana Turner. The other two cats were Joan and Olivia—also very lovely —but Lana was my girl. She permitted me exactly twenty-three seconds to scratch her under her chin before she got up and stalked off.

When Aunt Lily first moved in with me, she had set up shop in the guest room. After it was apparent that she was in for the long haul, I had the attic space redone for her. The attic was originally going to be my writer's sanctuary, and for years I envisioned it as a haven against the distraction of the everyday world, a place where I could get away and reflect on my life and craft. But it finally occurred to me that I was not really the reflective type, so I had Ben call in his cadre of professionals and made over the attic into a three-room suite for Lily, freeing up the guest room for actual guests, like Tony the Bodyguard.

I glanced at the doorway at the top of her stairs on the way down to the kitchen. It was closed. It looked like she was sleeping in.

I made myself some coffee, toasted an English muffin, and sat in my quiet kitchen. When the kitchen had been redone years ago, I put in stainless steel everything and sleek granite countertops. The space was L-shaped—the kitchen, with its breakfast bar and eating area, in the long portion, and a TV room tucked into the short end. It was where I did most of my living, and I always felt most comfortable there.

I'd spent some part of last evening trying to rationalize the difference between Lily and myself, and came up with an obvious answer: Lily had been thinking about this for a while. This was not a snap decision on her part. Obviously she and Vinnie had talked things out, weighed the pros and cons, and concluded that being married made sense to them. I still didn't get how they could arrive at that conclusion after only three months, but it explained why my answer to "Will you marry me?" was still forthcoming. I had quite a way to go before finding an answer.

I opened up my laptop and began to work. I sent lots of e-mails. I read lots of blogs and went through my seemingly endless reading list to try to catch up with the current state of publishing. It did not look good. Then I went to Pinterest.

Ben came downstairs, his hair still damp from his shower. He took a cup of coffee and sat down across from me.

"That's some news about Lily," he said.

I nodded. I was not ready for a conversation about marriage. Not anyone's.

"I guess," I finally said, "that it's good to know she'll have someone to share her life with. She's been lonely."

"But it's more than that, don't you think? I mean, she seems to really love him."

I nodded again. "But how did that happen? In three months?"

He leaned across the table and kissed me. "I'll explain that to you later. Now, what about tonight?"

"Steaks? Wine? More getting naked?"

He laughed. "Mona, you've just made me an offer I can't refuse."

"Not funny," I called after him as he left.

I heard Aunt Lily come down the stairs. I poured myself more coffee and watched her as she made her usual—one egg over easy, two slices of wheat toast.

"Is that what you make for Vinnie for breakfast?" I asked.

"Vinnie has cholesterol issues. Poor man. He's also hypertensive and needs to watch his sugar. Other than that, he's in pretty good shape for his age."

"So are you. And I have to tell you again, you look great."

She beamed. "It's love, Mona. He has changed my life."

"I don't get why you feel the need to marry him," I said slowly.

"You mean instead of just shacking up? Well, we talked about it, but really, we're too old for that nonsense. When you love a person, you marry them."

"But sometimes marriage isn't such a good thing."

She was quiet for a few minutes as she ate; then she patted her lips with her napkin. "Mona, you had a lousy marriage, so I can understand why you're a little prickly on the subject. But I had nothing but happy years with your uncle Larry. I loved being married. I can't wait to do it again."

"You're lucky," I said softly, and watched as she carefully put her dishes in the dishwasher. She wiped her tiny spot on the table and took her coffee cup with her as she left.

I looked at the time. I had a bus to catch to Manhattan. I'd given up driving there after 9/11, when they closed the Port Authority parking. These days I didn't have the energy to drive in myself and spend hours looking for a place to park.

I had a late lunch with my agent, Sylvia Snow, a tough, beautiful African-American woman whom I worshiped for her ability rather than loved for her personality. Ours was not a warm and fuzzy relationship, although I could probably call her my friend.

We got the personal stuff out of the way in the first six minutes. Then she whipped out her leather notepad and started looking through her notes.

"We won't hear anything about the movie for at least another few months," she said. "But you knew that."

"Yes. I need some money. I have two manuscripts finished."

She sipped her coffee. "Tell me."

"A romantic comedy. Older protag, a little sweet sex, happy ending. The other is more women's fiction. Widow takes in a foster kid and develops a relationship with the kid's uncle. I love it. No easy answers, not really a happy ending, but hopeful."

"Sound great. And we should have no trouble getting a contract. But those sound like Mona Quincy books. What about Maura Van Whalen—what about a romance?"

I leaned forward. "Here's the thing. I'm not sure I want to continue writing as Maura."

She looked up. "Mona, Maura Van Whalen has made both of us a lot of money over the years."

I nodded. "I know."

"You used to publish one of her books every ten months. Your readers still have expectations."

I sighed. "I know that too. You should read some of the e-mails I get."

"I hate to sound like a cliché, but you'd be killing off a cash cow here."

Maura Van Whalen was a pen name, and I had written several well-received and nicely profitable romances under it. But I was pulling away from historical romance. My heart wasn't in it anymore. I wanted to write more straight fiction.

I continued. "It's not like I want to abandon Maura completely. I'm thinking about trying self-publishing. Remember last year, when I asked you to get some of my backlist back? What do you think?"

She'd been writing in her little notebook but stopped and leaned back. "Really?"

I'd discussed this in my head so many times, I felt pretty comfortable saying the words out loud. "I need the money, and I don't want to wait to get it. I have someone who can do the formatting, redesign all the old covers. I can release one every three months or so."

She looked thoughtful. "Self-publishing isn't as easy as everyone makes it sound. There's a lot of work. I could try to get you a digital-only deal, if you like."

I shook my head. "No, Sylvia. I told you, I need the money, and I'll make more on my own—and faster—if I do it myself. I don't mean to cut you out, but there it is."

She shrugged. "You know I want what's best for you, which is why I've worked to get those titles for you. As you know, I've gotten eight titles back so far. And you also know I always want a piece of whatever you do, but I understand."

I nodded. "Yes. I know. Are we good?"

She nodded. "Certainly. I'd love more Maura titles, but let's face it, you haven't released anything new in almost two years. In the world of romance, that's a death knell. Women's fiction can get away with one book a year, and after the sales of *Better Off Without Him*, we should be in a good place. Let me get to work on a contract for the new stuff. And I'll e-mail you those titles so you can start to do whatever." She looked at me. "This is a surprise. My younger writers are doing this self-pub quite a lot. I had no idea you were so savvy."

I laughed. "I'm not. But I spent over a year in the land of impossible dreams. I learned lots. And not just about screenwriting."

She smiled. "Smart lady."

My cell phone rang. I would have ignored it, but I saw that it was Ben.

"Ben, what's up? Can you still make it?"

"Yes, of course I can. But David just called. He's on his way down and says he has something important to talk to me about. He asked if he could have dinner with us."

David was a very good-looking young man who had graduated from Yale last year and taken a job in finance right outside of Boston. I liked David—a lot. Besides being smart, he had Ben's sweet temper and kindness. And I knew that the two of them were very close. My desire to spend an evening alone with Ben collided with my parental understanding that when a kid wants to talk to you about something important, you drop everything and listen.

"Of course. I'll get extra steaks."

"Thanks."

"Let's hope David's problem is something that we can talk out before dessert. Is it money?"

"I don't think so. God, I hope not. What if he lost his job?" Ben sounded worried. I pictured him, his wide forehead wrinkled in a frown.

"Maybe he's met a girl," I teased.

"You know, maybe he has. He's been pretty silent on that subject for the past few months."

"Ah, true love. See you tonight."

I hung up and glanced at Sylvia. "Sorry."

"No problem. I completely understand." She grinned. "True love."

Indeed.

When I got home, Miranda's car was parked in the driveway. So was Jessica's.

Okay—it *was* a Friday afternoon. Miranda, I knew, had no classes at all on Fridays, and she had been known to drive home to Westfield just to do laundry for free. Jessica had physics lab on Friday morning and often started her weekend by noon. But neither of them told me they were coming home. Something else had prompted their appearance. I thought for a moment that I had died in some alternate universe. Why else would they be home without telling me?

As I raced in through the kitchen door, my heart fell even more —I heard Lauren laughing. Lauren's presence required a train trip, then a bus trip.

I turned into the den, and there they were, my three beautiful, loving daughters. I stared at them, barely breathing.

"Who's pregnant?"

They all turned and stared at me like I was totally insane.

"Mom?" Lauren said. "Why would you say that?"

My purse slid from my hand to the floor. I shrugged out of my jacket, and that, too, fell to the floor. "Three days ago I asked each of you to come home this weekend. Each of you said no. Something has happened in the past few days to change all of your minds, and it would have to be big. Really big. One of you has news. And it can't be good. I know a wall of solid support when I see it."

Miranda got up off the couch and hugged me. "It's my news, Mom. And it's wonderful, really. Sit."

I allowed her to lead me to the couch, and I sat down next to her.

"You're not pregnant?"

She shook her head. "No. But I want to get married."

My jaw dropped open. She was glowing with happiness, her smile wide and open and beautiful.

"Miranda, honey, I didn't even know you were dating anybody!" Silently I sighed in relief. Of course she wanted to get married. She'd wanted that since she was old enough to realize that a wedding was the ultimate in dressing up. "How did this happen?

How did you meet somebody, get to know him, fall in love, and decide to marry him without ever telling me about it? Oh, God, this isn't another three-month miracle, is it?"

She looked startled. "Okay, that's scary. How did you know?"

"How did I know what?"

"That we've only been dating three months?"

"Seriously? I was joking. Lily just announced that she's getting married. To someone she met three months ago."

Was this an epidemic? First Lily, whom I could almost excuse, because let's face it, Lily did crazy things sometimes. Now Miranda? She was barely twenty-two. What did she know about men and love and life that she could fall in love so fast? It seemed like every woman around me couldn't wait to get hitched. And here I was, dragging my feet because I was so afraid of getting stuck in the same kind of marriage I had with Brian.

"Ah, Mom?"

I grabbed both her hands. "Okay, so tell me. Who is this guy?"

Her smile returned. "Oh, yes. He's so sweet, Mom. Really. One of the nicest men ever. And he's handsome."

"*Really* handsome," Jessica said.

I glanced over at her. "You've met him?" I asked.

Jess nodded. "Well, yeah."

"Me too," said Lauren. "And Miranda's right; he's very nice."

"How did you all manage to meet him in three months?" I asked. Now I was really confused, not to mention just a bit pissed off about being so obviously left out of the loop.

"Oh…" Miranda looked casually around the room, anything to keep from looking me in the eye. "Well, we met briefly about four years ago. We kind of kept running into each other, and I thought he was cute, but you know…and then three months ago we met again and things started to get serious. Fast. Not just for me, but for him, too. We were thinking about moving in together, but then thought hey, we love each other, we're good together, why not get married?"

My mind was racing. Okay, she was just about the same age I was when I got engaged to Brian. She was graduating in a few months and had a good chance of getting a job. That was all good, right? Besides, they wouldn't be getting married right away. A two- or three-year engagement would give me plenty of time to properly vet this person.

"Will he be graduating too?" I asked. After all, whoever this guy was, he'd better be able to pull his weight.

Miranda nodded happily. "He graduated last year. He's got a really good job, and he's already saved a bunch of money for a condo."

"Great. So tell me more, like his name, where he's from, when I can meet him—all the good stuff."

"His name is David Cutler," Miranda said.

Wait.

My three daughters were all watching me carefully.

"And he's from Montclair," she continued.

Ahhh…

"And he'll be over tonight. He and Ben are having dinner with us, remember?"

That David Cutler?

So…my oldest daughter wanted to marry Ben's son. She barely had a boyfriend in high school, spent her college career "hooking up" with one boy or another—not that I even *wanted* to know the details—but now she was serious enough about David to think about marriage? And she had decided this after being with him for just three months?

And what exactly did that say about me, and the fact that I had to think hard about marrying Ben after four *years*?

CHAPTER THREE

I WAS GLAD I WAS already sitting down.

"David Cutler?" I asked.

Miranda nodded.

I looked over at Lauren. She was supposed to be the sensible one. Or at least, the one least likely to do something outrageous or illegal. I could usually count on her to be a voice of reason.

Lauren smiled. "Wait until you see them together, Mom. They are *so* in love."

Jessica, my resident cynic, smiled crookedly. "Even I have to admit they're adorable."

I took a long, deep breath, held it, and then exhaled slowly. "Tell me."

Miranda bounced closer to me on the couch. "It was at his birthday party. I mean, every time I'd seen him, ever since we first met, I though he was just about perfect. But at the party we just started talking, you know? And then he told me he was living right outside of Boston, so I suggested we meet for coffee, and he said okay, and when we met again we talked, like, forever, and, well, then we saw each other again…" She blushed. "I love him, Mom. Completely. He's not like any of the other boys I hang around with. He's the real thing."

I wanted to say something, but my throat closed up. I fought back tears. That was what I had always wanted for my daughters— a certainty that, whoever they chose, he was someone special. That was Ben. Ben was the real thing. But Ben and I had known each other for years. We had been friends, then good friends. We had grown into each other. We knew everything about each other. And while I had no doubt that David was enough of his father's son as to be the best man possible for any of my daughters...three months? They were practically strangers. I'd have to talk them into a *very* long engagement.

I cleared my throat, trying to figure out what to say next.

"Mom," Lauren said, "we all know what you're going to say. That Miranda and David don't know each other very well. That they need time. That this is just lust."

I had not wanted to think that at all, but she was right.

"But, seriously," she continued. "You need to see them together. They fit. They really do. Just like you and Ben."

I glared at Lauren. The thing about her being the sensible one was that she always knew the exact thing to say that would totally shut me down. "Three months," I said finally, "is not a long time."

"But we've been together every day," Miranda said. "And practically every night."

Ouch.

"So, if you figure how most people date each other, and see each other maybe twice a week, David and I just kind of crammed the same amount of dating into a shorter time frame. So, if we were, like, a normal couple, we'd have been dating for almost a year." Miranda smiled brilliantly.

"Even a year," I said, "isn't a long time. You don't know him, honey. People are complicated. Sure, everything is hot sex and goo-goo eyes now, but things change." I took a deep breath. "If you're determined to get engaged, all I can say is congratulations. We'll have a celebration tonight. I'll run out and get more steaks and lots of champagne. Maybe lobster. What the hell, we'll even call your father and invite him. It isn't every day my oldest daughter gets engaged to be married!" I leaned over and hugged her tight. "I'm so happy for you, honey. I really am."

She kissed me on the cheek. "Oh, Mom, thank you for understanding. Can I really call Dad? You are awesome. But..." She pulled back and looked at me. "We aren't getting engaged, Mom. We're getting *married*. I'm done with school in December, and I've already started looking for a job, so a winter wedding?

Late January? Can we put together a wedding in that short a time?"

"No."

She frowned. "No? I was afraid of that. Well, maybe we'll just have something small—"

"*No.*" I could feel a pounding right behind my eyes. "No, you are not getting married in January. Are you out of your mind? It's one thing to fall in love and be all happy and crazy and want to spend the rest of your life with a total stranger. It's another thing to actually get *married.* Not happening."

Her eyes narrowed. She rearranged her features into something I recognized and had always hated—the yes-I-will face. "And how, exactly, are you going to stop me?"

Good question.

"Can't you accept the fact that even though I'm your mother, I'm also a fairly smart person who has seen a lot of the world, and I know that three months is not long enough to know a person before marrying them?"

"That's how long David's mom and dad knew each other before they got married," Miranda said.

That was true. "Yes, honey, but that was because Ellen was pregnant, and Ben felt he had to marry her."

"But they were very happy and loved each other right up until she died," Miranda countered.

Damn. That was also true. Ben had often described his first marriage as practically perfect. "Miranda, please. Listen to me. There's nothing wrong with spending time getting to know somebody. Live with him, if you want, but please wait to get married."

"We are going to live together," she said stubbornly. "For the next two months. And then we're getting married."

Aunt Lily, with her usual perfect timing, swept into the den. "Girls! What a surprise! Yes, I'm getting married; is that what you're all talking about?"

Jess jumped up to give Lily a hug. "We just heard, Aunt Lily. You have to tell us all about it. But it's Miranda we're talking about."

Lily clapped her hands in obvious delight. "Miranda, really? Why, I had no idea you were even involved with anyone. So, spring

27

for you too?"

"Miranda wants to marry David, Ben's son," I explained slowly. "They've been dating for about three months."

Lily's eyes opened wide. "David? Why, he is a divine young man. Aren't you the lucky one. To think, we'll have two of those fabulous Cutlers here in the family." She poked Jessica with her elbow. "There's still one more floating around out there," she teased. "I'd start in on young Ethan now if I were you, Jess, darling."

Jessica blushed, rolled her eyes, and slouched back down into her chair.

"Aunt Lily," I said, "did you hear me? They've only known each other three months."

Lily crossed the room to give Miranda a kiss on the cheek. "I know exactly how you feel," she murmured to my daughter. "That's how long Vincent and I have known each other. Isn't wonderful when you've found the right person?"

Miranda beamed. Aunt Lily was not going to be much help here, obviously. After all, Lily had made the same snap decision in roughly the same amount of time. But Lily, at least, had a long life going for her—she must have picked up a bit of wisdom along the way, right? Lily had been happily married for a long time, as well as having lived a very successful widowhood. She at least knew what she was getting into. But Miranda was a baby—my baby—and had never even had a serious relationship before. How could Miranda be so sure? I'd dated men, married, divorced, and dated a few more men before I finally found Ben, and after all that, I still had doubts.

Lily waved her hand at me, an annoyed, swatting motion, so I got up off the couch, and she settled in next to Miranda. "Tell me, dear, is the sex good? Believe me, that's a very important part of marriage. You want to be sure the two of you fit, if you know what I mean."

I swallowed hard and fled.

I ended up in my living room. Fred was stretched out in his favorite patch of sunlight. Lana was perched on the back of the couch. Joan and Olivia were tangled together in the window seat. It warmed my heart that my animals got so much use out of this room.

My parents had been happily married up until the time my father died, and it was from them that I learned what marriage was supposed to be. When I married Brian, our own marriage was very different from theirs, but I made it work because I loved him. And because I wanted it to work.

But being in love wasn't enough. It was never enough. How to explain that to Miranda, especially if she was in that first-love–induced haze of extreme happiness and lust?

I sat and tried to figure out an angle until Lauren came looking for me.

"Mom?"

"Hi, honey. How long have you known about all this?"

She shrugged as she sat beside me. "She called me right away. She fell fast. So did he, I think."

"How serious is she?"

Lauren snuggled beside me and rested her head on my shoulder. "They found a place to live. And she's sent me pictures of about forty possible wedding dresses."

"You realize this is crazy, right?"

She sighed. "Wait until you see them. They light up together. It's like they're in some sort of shiny bubble."

"But you realize this is crazy, right?"

"Maybe. But there is such a thing as love at first sight, isn't there?"

"No, honey. Not really."

Now, anyone who's read any of my books would probably be surprised by that answer. After all, hadn't Lady Beatrice Whitcomber taken one look at filthy and exhausted Will Markham and known at once that beneath all that grime and pain was the perfect man? Didn't James, Earl of Chestmont, know from the very first glimpse that sweet young Daphne Nethers would grow into the woman he would most certainly marry? Yes and yes. In fact, love at first sight was as common a theme in my books as hate-at-first-sight-turning-to-love. And both scenarios always had a happy ending. But that was why it was called *fiction*.

"Daddy once said that you told him on the very first date that the two of you would end up married."

"Yes, and we all know how that turned out." Brian had looked to be my ideal—big, handsome, charming, and on the short road to financial success. Our first date was spectacular—he had ticked off all the must-haves on my list, and many of the desirable options. I learned, however, that being a good boyfriend is one thing. Being a good husband is something entirely different. Brian had been a spectacular boyfriend. He had been a lousy husband. He'd been cheating on me for years, and I never knew it. In fact, I thought our marriage was going along just great. I loved him with all my heart, and I thought he loved me. We'd celebrated our twentieth anniversary just months before he walked into our kitchen and told me he was leaving me for another woman. Maybe if I'd seen signs of trouble, it wouldn't have hit me so hard. It was painful for me to find out that our marriage had been something of a sham all along. And I didn't even realize it until after he had walked out the door.

I put both arms around Lauren and hugged her. I could hear Miranda and Lily laughing in the next room. I sighed.

"Do you want Jess and me to run to the store for you?" Lauren asked.

I nodded. "Yes. More steaks. And baking potatoes. I have more than enough salad and broccoli. Something for dessert, maybe?"

"Are you really going to invite Dad and Dominique?"

My shoulders slumped. "Do I have to?"

"Well, it would be fun to see Tyler," Lauren said, a little wistfully. I glared at her. "Not fair playing the little-brother card."

She made a bit of a pouty face.

My ex-husband Brian never did marry the woman he left me for, but he did live with her, and they had a son. I guess I should have felt grateful about the fact that Dominique was not just a casual fling like the other women he had slept with over the course of our marriage. It was hard to feel warm and fuzzy toward the woman who took your husband away after twenty years of what I had thought was wedded bliss. But after I realized he was going to have to go through sleepless nights and poopy diapers all over again, and at a more, shall we say, advanced age, I began to feel downright friendly about ol' Dominique. And when the fabulous Hoboken condo he bought with her was traded in for a McMansion in suburbia, it gave me a bit of the shits and giggles. My daughters were thrilled about their baby brother, but even they appreciated the irony of their father, after leaving a conventional home and family for the possibility of a new, exciting adventure with a younger woman, was ending up having to live a complete do-over.

"Oh, all right. Get enough for them. Why the hell not? If I know your sister, she's going to marry that boy no matter what I say, so we may as well start this off with a bang."

She kissed my cheek and got up off the couch, calling for Jessica. A few minutes later the kitchen door slammed. I could still hear Miranda and Lily. They were probably comparing bridesmaid's dresses.

Lana leaped down next to me and arched her back. I stroked her a few times before she jumped back up to her perch. She stared at me.

"You realize this is crazy, right?" I asked.

Lana yawned.

Just the kind of advice I'd learned to expect from her.

We had enough prime Angus beef to feed the entire defensive line of the Green Bay Packers. The salad was in a bowl roughly the size of your average kiddie pool. Lauren and Jessica put the extra leaf in the dining room table and laid out the good china. There was even champagne chilling. Ben had already texted me that he'd do the grilling. Lauren had splurged—with my debit card, of course—on designer cupcakes and a fabulous-looking lemon tart. Miranda had even offered to rinse the potatoes and put them in the oven.

Brian, Dominique, and baby Tyler would be there by six thirty. Ben and David would arrive around the same time.

What a warm, happy family gathering this had turned out to be.

Sadly, Vincent was stuck out in Brooklyn—some sort of business social club event. I imagined a Retired Gangsters' Dining and Gun Club meeting, so I just lied and told Lily how disappointed I was he wouldn't be joining us.

I texted Ben: *Did David talk 2 U?*

He answered back: *Yes—thrilled.*

What? He was *thrilled?* How could he be thrilled? Our children were about to make a huge mistake. What if they were miserable together? What would that mean for Ben and me if our two oldest children ended up hating each other? I wanted Ben and me to be together. I wanted our mutual families to feel comfortable together. And this rushed marriage had disaster written all over it. All I could imagine was Miranda, six months down the road—or worse, six *years* down the road—coming home in tears because she realized she'd married the wrong man.

Ben apparently didn't have the same reservations, which made me feel a bit uneasy. He just assumed they would make it work. Just like I knew he assumed that I would marry him, and the two of us would also make it work. How could he know that?

But just making it work…was that enough? What about being happy? Because I was pretty sure that if I got married again I would *not* be happy. At all. Even married to Ben.

It wasn't like I was against marriage. I just knew that, for me, it was not an ideal state. I had failed terribly the first time around. I had no interest in trying again.

I slipped into the downstairs powder room, sat, then tried to breathe deeply.

This was the bathroom that had started it all. Years ago, one of my then interchangeable toddlers had flushed something down this same toilet, causing the entire sewage system of Westfield, New Jersey, to back up into my house. I had called a plumber. That plumber turned out to be Ben Cutler. And now, many years later, Ben Cutler was the love of my life, and his beloved son was about to ruin our future together by marrying my beloved daughter.

I took a few more cleansing breaths.

I tried to analyze my thoughts. Maybe my initial knee-jerk reaction was wrong. Maybe Miranda and David *were* meant for each other. Maybe theirs was a love story written among the stars. They would beat the odds. They would make it work. In years to come, there would be songs and poems written about their undying love.

Maybe a TV movie. At least an article in *People* magazine.

After all, these were two very smart young people. David had gone to Yale, for God's sake. Miranda, although she sometimes acted like she didn't possess a lick of common sense, was graduating—early, mind you—with a degree in computer something. Coding maybe? I don't know, but hey, you had to be smart to do *anything* with computers, right?

I knew my daughter. I knew that when she wanted something, she went after it one hundred and fifty percent. So if she was determined to marry David Cutler, I had to figure out a way to be okay with it.

Ben and I really needed to talk. We needed to be on the same page with this thing. Maybe his whirlwind marriage had ended well —except for her dying, of course—but let's face it, the odds are against all marriages. Ones entered into without a long period of thoughtful consideration were doomed. Maybe if we both came at Miranda and David with the same thought…

But…why was he thrilled?

Fred started barking. By this time I recognized all of his accents —that was his Brian bark. Oh, joy.

Brian and I had decided to act like adults about our now-separate lives. We had our moments, of course—like four years ago, on the morning of our court appearance to finalize our divorce, when he told me he had made a mistake, and could we give it another try. (My answer, FYI, was no.)

Some folks say that living well is the best revenge. That may be true, but in looking at Dominique, I held to another theory. She had my ex-husband. Brian was still an attractive man, although his hairline was starting to move backward while his waistline was starting to move forward. She also had the knowledge that Brian had commitment issues. I don't know when he had started cheating on me, exactly, but Dominique had not been the first. So, what did that say about his loyalty to the woman he was currently living with?

I, on the other hand, had Ben.

Snap.

Because our daughters tended to celebrate everything they could think of—college acceptances, National Honor Society inductions, beating a speeding ticket—Brian and Dominique had become fairly regular guests. And their son, Tyler, was adorable: big brown eyes, curling blond hair, and dimples all over his little face. He was also approaching two years old, and rapidly turning the corner from enchanting to a real brat.

The din outside the bathroom door rose, then fell, as Tyler stopped screaming at the dog, and Fred stopped yapping in response.

I leaned against the wall of the powder room and sighed.

On the other side of the coin, Dominique had not lost what we in the motherhood sphere call "baby weight." In fact, we can call it that for a whole five years after the actual delivery. So, stick-thin Dominique had been replaced by stuffed-sausage Dominique, because she refused to buy clothes any bigger than her original size double zero. I only weighed about twelve and a half pounds more than I did the day I got married. Would I have liked to lose the extra pounds? Sure. But since I already lost the largest and most significant weight that I acquired at my wedding—that is to say, Brian—I was happy to just let the extra pounds sit there. I'd prefer it to sit in my boobs instead of my butt, but you can't have everything.

There was a gentle tap on the door.

"Mona?"

It was Ben. I threw open the door, wrapped my arms around his neck, and gave him a big kiss. A long, sloppy, wet kiss.

"Hello again," I said when my mouth stopped being busy.

He grinned and ran his hands down my back. "Hello again to you. Isn't it great about the kids?"

Oh, boy. Were we going to have this conversation now? Couldn't we just enjoy a few minutes without this impending doom hanging over our heads?

"Ben," I started. Then my shoulders slumped.

"What?"

"It's just…" I looked over his shoulder, and David and Miranda were standing there together, looking like they were under their own private spotlight.

"David! Hi." I broke away from Ben and hurried over to give David a hug. He was a bit taller than Ben, and thinner—still a young man's body—but so handsome.

He kissed my cheek. "Mona, hi. Listen, Randi said you had some initial reservations about us getting married. We really want you to be with us one hundred percent."

"Randi?" I glanced at my daughter. She had, since she was old enough to speak her own mind (which, I believe, was roughly sixteen months of age), resisted any effort to shorten her name. She was and always had been Miranda. Yet here was this young man referring to her as Randi, with no sign of lightning being hurled down from the sky.

"Listen, everyone," I said, "this is a very big deal, but now is not the time to talk details. Now is the time for someone to start the grill and someone else to start steaming the broccoli and making the cheese sauce—and since you're of age, could you open the wine, Randi?"

She did not give me a withering look, but rather nodded happily. "Sure, Mom. David, you can help." They trotted off.

I turned to Ben. "And you'll light the grill?"

He was frowning. "Reservations? Really? Mona, this is such amazing news. What reservations?"

Oh, Lord. I needed someplace quiet. And secluded. I needed to try to explain to Ben why it was not his son that I was worried about—I wouldn't want my daughter to marry *anyone* after only three months. In the middle of my hallway an hour before dinner was not the time or place.

"Ben, listen. I'm sure the kids are crazy about each other, but —"

"*Nona!*" That would be Tyler Whitman Berman, half brother to my three daughters, almost two-year-old son of my ex-husband, an adorable child I was not related to in any way, shape, or form, and who, for some reason, loved me with all his heart. He was hard to resist.

I scooped him up as he ran to me, his fair hair in ringlets, big brown eyes wide with excitement.

"You know my name is Mona, right?" I asked him.

He giggled as he gave me sloppy kisses. "*Nona!*" he shouted again.

"Mmmmm…"

He squished his nose against mine. "Na-na-na-na…"

"Say monkey."

"Monkey!"

"Say motorcycle."

"Motorcycle!"

"Say mountain."

"Mountain!"

"Say Mona."

"Nona!" More giggles. More kisses.

"You're killing me, kiddo," I told him. "Are you going to eat steak tonight?"

He nodded and was already squirming out of my arms and down to the floor. He looked up at Ben. "Hey, Ben!"

Ben squatted down. "Hey, Tyler. What's new?"

Tyler shrugged elaborately. "Nothin'." Then he ran off.

Ben straightened. "Almost makes you want to have another one, doesn't he?" he said, somewhat wistfully.

"Ah, no," I said. "That's what grandchildren are going to be for. Listen, let's get the steaks started. We can talk about all this, I promise, but let's get everyone fed."

Ben went through the kitchen and out the back door to light the grill. I turned right and went into my living room, where Brian and Dominique were getting the good news from Miranda and David.

Brian looked shell-shocked. Well, to be honest, he'd kind of had that look ever since Tyler was born, but his jaw was slack, his mouth open, and a slight glaze was over his eyes. Dominique, ignoring her son's not-too-subtle demand for attention, was lit up like a Christmas tree.

"Married?" she squealed. "Really? Oh, how exciting. I love weddings." She turned and looked pointedly at Brian. "Don't you, dear?"

Brian remained silent. Tyler was chanting, "Mom, Mom, Mom."

"Do you have a date?" Dominique asked.

Miranda glance at me, squared her shoulders, and nodded.

"January sixteenth. About two months from now."

Dominique frowned. "That doesn't leave you much time to plan a wedding. In fact, you probably won't be able to find anywhere halfway decent in just two months."

Lily had never thought much of Brian when he was married to me, and cared even less about him now. But she loved being in the same room with him and Dominique, and she was known to say things in French that none of us could understand, but that often caused Dominique to blush, turn white, or storm off in anger. Lily's floor show was worth any price.

She spoke up from her chair in the corner. "Vincent's daughter Carmella is a wedding planner. I'm sure she could help out. She's already been very helpful in planning my wedding."

Brian's head whipped around. "Lily, you're getting *married?*"

She sniffed. "Good heavens. Brian, it's not like I'm going to the moon. It's quite easy, actually. I did it before, quite successfully, in fact." She smiled sweetly. "Why, I believe even you did it once."

Brian was frowning. "When did all this happen?"

"Just this week," Lily said.

Dominique managed to get her lower jaw back in its proper place. "Congratulations, Lily. Anyone we know?"

Lily shrugged. "My girl, I have no idea who you know. His name is Vincent DeMatriano. He's a very nice widower, from Brooklyn."

"How lovely," Dominique managed.

Brian, still frowning, looked over at me. "Why is that name familiar?"

I shrugged innocently. "Can't imagine. I just met him myself the other day."

Miranda went over and perched on the arm of Lily's chair. "Do you really think this Carmella person can help?"

"Wait a minute," I said. "I think we need to talk about this a little more before we start enlisting help."

"Talk about what?" Ben said, coming up behind me.

"The wedding," I said brightly. "Is the grill heating up?"

He nodded, so I grabbed his hand and pulled him back into the kitchen and pointed to a huge platter of rib eyes that had been sitting on the counter. "Take it away, chef," I joked.

He leaned forward and kissed me. It was one of those kisses that sent little bolts of lightning to various places in my body. One of those let's-go-somewhere-soon kisses. "How soon can we get them all out of here?" he asked softly.

"Depends on how fast those suckers can cook," I said, slightly giddy.

He grinned, grabbed the platter, then left. I leaned against the counter and took a deep breath.

He still did that to me.

CHAPTER FOUR

WE HAD A LOVELY DINNER. Miranda and David looked so happy, I almost started thinking they might be together for more than six months of wedded bliss. Lily was reveling in her new role as bride-to-be, trading centerpiece ideas with Miranda and Lauren, insisting that Jessica be her flower girl.

The kids did not want a big wedding. Something small, David said, just family and close friends. Brian looked relieved when David said he and Miranda would be paying for it all themselves. I shot a quick look at Miranda to see if she was rolling her eyes or biting her tongue at that statement, but she just nodded happily at David's pronouncement. And then Miranda said she didn't *really* care about a dress either, which I found incredibly difficult to believe. This girl took better care of her clothes than some people took of their children. Who was this new Miranda who was talking about grabbing something nice off the clearance rack at Macy's? And who was not expecting a huge to-do paid for by her father? This girl had had a sweet-sixteen party that rivaled a New York society debutante ball.

I sat and watched, my mind going in a million directions at once. David was obviously a great influence on my daughter. He was following in his father's footsteps in the kind, sensible, and thoughtful department. Miranda appeared to have dialed down her "me" meter and seemed genuinely happy with all of David's practical suggestions. Her blind selfishness had always been the one thing about her I did not find at all endearing. This Miranda was a much nicer person. And Lauren was right; they lit up together.

But right across the table from the happy couple sat Brian. I vividly remembered the first time I had met him. I thought he was going to be the answer to all my dreams. He seemed to be every single thing I wanted and needed in a husband. It took me until he left for another woman to realize how wrong I'd been. Did I want that for my oldest daughter?

Ben sat next to me and contributed to the wedding discussion only when directly asked a question. He was his usual charming and funny self, but I knew we had a hard conversion coming up. We had never actually disagreed about anything before. Not anything important, that is. But I knew that at some point I was going to be up against a very hard wall, and I wasn't sure what to do about it.

Thank God for Tyler. He did not eat any steak. He chewed a piece and spit it out, ate three forkfuls of baked potato and half a leaf of lettuce, gave his one floweret of broccoli to the dog, and inhaled two cupcakes. He was bouncing off the walls by the time coffee was served, prompting a hasty retreat by Brian and Dominique.

Lily arched an eyebrow after they left. "Where did her accent go?" she asked.

Good question. Her accent had faded to almost nothing as Tyler got older. Was that something that chasing after a toddler did?

"I think," Lauren said wisely, "that her accent was more profound when she was in her seduction mode. She's in her mommy mode now, and nobody says *Vat is zee mattier?* in playgroup."

Lily sniffed. "Whatever," she murmured. "Brian looks very old and tired these days. You were good to be rid of him, Mona."

I had no say in getting rid of him, but I never argued with Lily where Brian was concerned.

Despite the coziness around the table, I was becoming increasingly uneasy. Not just about finally getting Ben alone so we could talk, but (just as important) getting Ben alone so we could continue along the path we'd started on *last* night. But our children were everywhere. I know they all knew that Ben and I had spent our nights together, but he'd never stayed over with all of my girls home. Usually one or more of them was off somewhere. We mostly went to his place, because David had been away and Ben's younger son Ethan, before going off to college himself, never left his bedroom. I had never worried about that awkward breakfast conversation with the offspring.

But here we were. How could I gracefully suggest anything that would not make it obvious that I was looking forward to some really great sex and would everyone please get out of the way?

Maybe everyone else could figure it out for me.

"Ben, walk the dog with me?"

He smiled and nodded. It had turned much cooler in the past few hours, so I bundled up with a few adorable scarves, snapped the leash of the now ecstatic Fred, and Ben and I left the house.

It was one of those crisp fall nights where the stars were close and you could see your breath. I loved this weather—any excuse to dress in long, flowing sweaters and roomy ponchos. As we came down the driveway, I saw David's little Fiat parked on the street, right behind Ben's truck. Ben was always thinking ahead—he made sure that if he stayed the night, David would be able to get home on his own. What a guy. It made me feel all warm and smushy inside, knowing we were both thinking alike.

But…we weren't thinking alike about everything.

"Mona, what are your objections to David marrying Miranda?"

I took a deep breath. "I have no objection to David marrying Miranda. I have lots of objections to my daughter marrying someone she barely knows."

"We're talking about two very smart, sensible kids," he said gently.

"No, we're talking about a smart, sensible young man and a smart young woman who, until six months ago, didn't realize that if your credit card bill wasn't paid on time, it could be taken away from you. She has some real gaps, experience-wise. Miranda has never been in love before. How can she know this is the real thing? How can she be willing to risk her future happiness on something that may be as fleeting as dropped-crotch pants for women?" I shook my head. "Listen, Ben, David is a great kid. How could he not be? He's your son. But is he great for Miranda? And as much as I love my daughter, she can be a real piece of work. Do they even know what they're getting into?"

He chuckled. "Come on, you saw them together. They practically sparkle."

"Yes, they do. But married? I mean, isn't theirs the generation that doesn't believe in marriage? If they want to live together, fine. They have my blessing."

"Some people," he said slowly, "believe that marriage means something. It means a promise of more than just waking up together in the same bed. It means having faith in the unknown."

I was glad it was dark, so I could not see the hurt that I knew was in his eyes. I hated this. If we were so far apart on what we thought was best for our kids' future, how were we going to agree on our own? "Yes, well, I had a marriage once, and it may have meant something to me, but it meant squat to my husband."

"Does that mean you aren't willing to try it again?" he asked. "I gotta tell you, Mona, I really expected your reaction yesterday to be a little different."

There it was. Right in front of me in the cold night air.

Fred had stopped to ruthlessly destroy a particularly nasty leaf. It gave me an excuse to also stop and carefully think about what I was going to say next. This was the man I loved. I could not imagine what my life would be like without him in it. But the very thought of being married again brought on an automatic reaction —I felt cold; I couldn't breathe—surely my subconscious was trying to tell me something.

"Ben, it's not that I'm *not* willing to try again. Yesterday you just caught me off guard. I mean, it came right out of the blue."

"Really, Mona? We've been together for almost four years now, and we love each other. What is the next step, if not getting married?"

"I don't know why we just can't continue on the way we are now," I said. "We're so good together."

"But you don't think David and Miranda would be good together?"

Fred was tugging on the leash. I turned and started walking back to the house. How could I explain myself to Ben? "Look, I fell for Brian in the first ten minutes of our very first date. I married him based on that, without even bothering to look at the kind of person he really was, because I was blinded by that first impression. I wanted to have the perfect marriage. So I made one. But it wasn't perfect, not at all. And I spent a long time not being happy because I refused to face the truth. That's what happens when you make a mistake but refuse to admit it."

I stopped and turned to face him. "We have something different. It's taken me a long time to settle into the idea that yes, we *are* a good couple. And I want to be with you for as long as we can keep this going. But I also know that marriages fail all the time. Even the good ones. I can't go through something like that again."

"For somebody who's made it her life's work to sell happily ever after, you sure aren't much of a believer."

"You're right. I'm not. I used to be, but having someone you trusted for almost half of your lifetime betray you with no warning cured me of that. That's also why I think David and Miranda are making a huge mistake. Because I know from experience that just because you meet someone you *think* is perfect, love at first sight is not real. It's not possible for two people who've only known each other a short time to have a love that lasts."

"And I know, from personal experience, that it *is* possible."

We were back in front of the house. "Are you willing to bet our kids' future and happiness on that? Because I don't think I am," I said.

"Are you willing to bet on *our* future happiness? Because I fell in love with you, Mona, the first time I saw you. Ellen had just died, and I was so grief-stricken I didn't think I'd ever be able to be happy again. I came into your house, and the girls were running around screaming, and there was crappy water everywhere, and I looked at you and thought, yeah, maybe there is another chance for me."

I stared at him in the darkness. I thought of all the years he had been in and out of my house, all the casual conversations, the moments shared over cups of coffee. I had just been admiring the scenery. He had been in love. And he never let it show. I felt suddenly choked with guilt. "You never told me that before."

He shrugged.

"But you remarried," I said.

"Well, you were married, remember? I didn't think it would be terribly healthy to be alone, mooning over someone I couldn't have for my entire life. So I found someone I really liked and thought I could live with. And we got along pretty well, until she started talking about having more kids. But it was you, Mona. All those years. When David told me what had happened to him, it was no surprise." He shrugged again. "It's what we do, we Cutler men. We fall fast and hard."

I didn't know what to say.

"Do you trust what David feels for Miranda?"

I shook my head. "I don't know," I muttered.

"Do you trust what I feel for you?" he asked.

"Yes, of course."

"But you aren't willing to marry me."

"It has nothing to do with our loving each other."

"And how can I know that? You've just told me you don't believe in the very thing that has been the backbone of my entire relationship with you."

"But I never knew that!" I blurted.

Ben let out a long breath. "Yes, but I did. And I always thought…" He bowed his head. "Mona, I'm not sure what I'm supposed to be feeling right now."

"Ben, I love you," I said.

"I know you do. Being married is important to me. That's why I asked you. We're adults, Mona, and I would have no qualms about continuing things just the way they are. We could continue to see each other indefinitely; I know that. But I want more."

He was silent. He was waiting for me. And I didn't know what to say to him. I realized, in a sudden rush of fear, that I could easily lose him. I couldn't bear to think about that. "Ben. Listen, about the kids—"

"No, Mona." His voice was sharp. "Forget the kids. David and Miranda are going to do exactly what they want to do, whether you and I support them or not. I, for the record, do support them. I happen to believe that two people can have a strong and happy marriage, even if one of them is a romantic, headstrong fool who's willing to trust his first instincts and take a chance on the unknown. You obviously don't."

I felt tears. I couldn't breathe. Fred nuzzled my leg.

"Ben—please. There's so much going on right now. The kids, Lily, the holidays are coming up—I need to be able to think. About you and me. I want us to be together. Can we just take a break from talking about this?"

"Maybe we should take a break, period. I think we could both benefit from a little time apart."

"Oh?" Time apart? I felt my heart start to race, and I couldn't swallow. How much time apart was he talking about? Not anything...permanent, right? Please, God, don't let him mean something permanent.

He leaned forward to kiss me on the cheek. "Let's face it, Mona. We're going to be seeing an awful lot of each other in the next few months. Which is great, because spending time with you is my favorite thing to do. But I think you and I need to put our, ah, more intimate relationship on hold. Just to see how things shake out, you know? And when things calm back down, we can sit and talk this all out." He smiled in the darkness. "We are destined to be together, Mona. I really believe that. And a bit of distance won't change that."

He was right. I took a deep breath and nodded. "Okay." A bit of distance? I could live with a bit of distance if I had to.

I watched Ben as he pulled his keys from his pocket. "Tell David I'll see him at home," he said quietly.

Then he got into his truck and drove away.

My family did not say anything to me when I returned to the house with only Fred and announced that Ben was on his way home, and I was going up to bed.

The next morning I seriously thought about just staying in bed all day, sparing me the inevitable questions and dark looks. But someone—probably Lily—had made breakfast. I smelled bacon and waffles and coffee. I grabbed my favorite old robe from the closet and padded downstairs.

Lily was at the stove, wearing a red kimono-type robe with a golden dragon down the back, instead of her familiar pink housecoat. She flashed me a brilliant smile and handed me a plate, bacon still sizzling, syrup dripping from a golden stack.

"I knew you wouldn't be able to resist," she said. "Have a seat."

I slid next to Lauren, who gave me a quick kiss on the cheek.

"Did you and Ben break up?" she asked.

"Lauren," Miranda said sharply. "We agreed to wait until she at least ate something."

Lauren rolled her eyes. I sighed heavily.

"Ben and I just need a little time to think about things," I told them. I took a huge bite of waffle.

Miranda's eyes filled with sudden tears. "Is this about me and David getting married?"

I swallowed quickly and shook my head. "No. Absolutely not. I mean, we disagree on that, but..." I took a quick sip of coffee. "Ben asked me to marry him. And I didn't say yes. I didn't say no, actually. Well, maybe I did. It's just that we look at marriage very differently. We're just coming at it from two completely different places."

"Where are you coming from?" Jessica asked.

I looked at her in surprise. She rarely asked what I thought about anything. "I happen to believe," I said slowly, "that two people can love each other and have a great life together and not be married." I looked at Miranda. "I also believe first impressions can be deceiving. I believe that in order to know a person, I mean *really* know them, you have to live with them for a while. And not just a few months, because you're naturally on your best behavior when you first get together. You have to see how they treat people when they're *not* on their best behavior. When they're tired or angry or disappointed. You have to see how they treat *you* when you disagree or disappoint." I played with my bacon before taking a bite.

Miranda sniffed. "So this isn't my fault?"

I shook my head again. "No, honey. Ben and I would have had the same conversation even if you and David had never met. With everything that's coming up in the next few months, Ben and I aren't going to have the time we need to figure our situation out, so we're going to slow things down. That's all." I pointed my fork at Miranda. "As for you and David, I just want you to be happy. That's all I've ever wanted for any of you girls. So if you think David Cutler can make you happy, I'm behind you. I don't particularly like it, but I since I couldn't stop you anyway, I promise I'll try to get with the program, okay?"

She got up and gave me a hug. "Thank you, Mom. And I'm sorry about Ben."

"Don't be sorry yet. This isn't the end for us. It's just a little time-out." I stuffed more bacon into my mouth and prayed my words were true.

Lily dropped another waffle onto my plate. "I invited Carmella Ciavaglia over for lunch," she announced. "I'll make chicken pot pie."

I inhaled deeply and reached for more syrup. "Who?" Not that I really cared. Lily's chicken pot pie was worth the most boring of lunch guests.

"Carmella. Vincent's daughter. She's a wedding planner, remember?"

"Aunt Lily, David and I can't afford a wedding planner," Miranda said.

Lily waved a hand, coral nails flashing. "My gift to you," she said airily. "She's already hard to work on my plans. Besides, it's going to be tough to throw this together on such short notice, especially with you up in Boston until December. Mona, you won't mind the help, will you?"

I shook my head, my mouth too busy chewing for speech. My oldest daughter was getting married in two months. I needed all the help I could get. Even from someone named Carmella.

"Thank you so much, Aunt Lily. But like I said, it's not going to be a big deal," Miranda said. "We want something small."

"True," I said. "But you still need bridesmaids and rings and a dress and a place to get married. And food. Maybe music."

"No bridesmaids," Miranda said. "Jess and Lauren will be my maids of honor, Ethan is best man, and Tyler will be the ring bearer."

I raised an eyebrow. "Tyler?"

Miranda grinned. "Well, Dad called this morning. Dominique's idea, of course. She wants him in a tiny tux."

I pictured his sturdy little body wrapped in a cumberbund and almost smiled. "He'll look adorable. But remember, he's going to be two. You'll probably have to hold his hand as he walks down the aisle." I glanced at Lily. "Are you planning on a ring bearer too?"

She shook her head. "No. We're going to be more streamlined than Miranda. Just the two of us, with you and Joe standing up for us."

"Joe? Your buddy Joe?" The well-known Mafia don?

"Of course," she answered. "After all, it was Joe who brought Vinnie and me together in the first place."

"With a priest?" I asked. As far as I knew, Lily had a very flexible relationship with God. She and my father had both been raised Catholic, and she once confessed to me that she had thought about becoming a nun. She also went to temple with her Jewish husband, spent time in India studying with a guru, and most recently had been frequenting the Center for Spiritual Purity off Route 22.

She leaned her hip against the counter. "Actually, yes. Vincent is very old-fashioned that way. You know I don't believe in organized religion, but he seems to have a friend who's a Catholic bishop."

"Nice friend to have," I said. Surely there would be no wedding violence with a bishop on the scene, right?

She nodded. "Yes. I don't mind him being at the ceremony, really. I'm just hoping to avoid lightning and possibly brimstone."

Lauren giggled. "Really?"

Lily winked. "I've lived a long life, ladies. Well, must get dressed." And she sailed out of the room.

Jessica started loading the dishwasher. "She has got to be the coolest old lady ever."

I had to agree.

Carmella Ciavaglia arrived exactly on time. She parked her shiny Mercedes in the driveway and knocked on the kitchen door. Like family. Which, I guess, she would be.

She did not look like a Mafia don's niece. She looked like a Mafia don's daughter, as played by a very sexy forty-something actress. She was stunning—glossy black hair, red lips, big, dark eyes, high cheekbones. She was short but built, as we used to say, like a brick shithouse. Underneath a mink coat, she was dressed in a clingy blue dress. She was wearing stilettos, no stockings, and had a thick gold cross hanging from an equally thick gold chain around her neck.

She also had a gold watch with a dial the size of a dessert plate on one wrist, and several chunky gold bangles on the other wrist. She clanked faintly as she shook hands with me. Lily got a hug and kisses on both cheeks. How cozy.

She stood in front of Miranda, grabbed her by both hands, and sighed. "You'll be such a gorgeous bride," she cried. She dropped her hands, sat down, then hauled a large purple handbag onto the kitchen table. "Let's start. We need ideas."

Since I'd never worked with a wedding planner before, I was naturally curious to see how this would play out. I sat next to Miranda and watched as Carmella pulled several things out of her tote, which was the Coach version of the classic clown car. She finally grabbed a fat silver pen and opened to a page in a bright pink moleskin notebook.

"Tell me," she said.

Miranda blinked. "Tell you what?"

"Your perfect wedding! Every single dream you've ever had."

Miranda glanced at me, then frowned, thinking. "I always thought the beach in Bermuda would be a good place to get married. I'd ride in on a white horse, barefoot, wearing a raw silk slip dress with pale pink roses in my hair," she said slowly.

Carmella scribbled furiously. "Excellent! We can do that!"

"No," I said quickly. "We can't. They're getting married in two months, are paying for it themselves, and want small."

Carmella frowned and drew big slashes in her notebook, then turned the page. "Okay. Forget perfect. Forget dream. Are you knocked up?"

"No," Miranda said quickly.

"Then what's the rush? Listen, honey, weddings take time," Carmella said.

I fought down a smile. Could this woman possibly change my daughter's mind about this whole thing? After all, she was a stranger. Her opinion would matter much more to Miranda than mine.

Aunt Lily sat down. "Young love," she explained. "And that's why we need your help. A mere mortal could never pull off a spectacular wedding on such short notice."

Carmella smiled smugly. "Yes, well, I am considered a miracle worker. You want to stay in Jersey?"

Miranda nodded.

"How many in the bridal party?"

"My twin sisters are my attendants. David's brother will be his best man. Oh, and my baby brother as ring bearer."

"Oh, how adorable. How old?"

"He'll be two."

Carmella shook her head. "Are you sure? 'Cause I gotta tell you, little kids in a wedding are a real pain in the ass."

Miranda lifted her shoulders and let them drop with a sigh. "I'm sure."

"Weighed against the adorable factor," I said, "it's pretty much a draw."

Carmella was scribbling again. "What's the parent situation?"

"My mom, David's dad, my dad, and his, ah, person he's living with."

Carmella threw me a glance. "She the baby-mama?"

"That's one way to describe her," Lily said, "though not my preferred—"

"Aunt Lily," I said sharply.

She smiled sweetly.

Carmella stopped her scribbling. "Okay. So, we need a venue for the reception. What about the ceremony. Church, temple, what are we lookin' at here?"

"David is speaking to his priest."

Carmella nodded. "Good. So how come the groom isn't here?"

Miranda glanced at me. "He and his father will be here in a little bit. For lunch."

I didn't know that. I wasn't quite ready to see Ben yet. I was still absorbing our decision to "take time."

Carmella, watching me, must have seen something cross my face. She tapped the pen against her cheek. "So, what's the story with the groom? Or is it the father?"

"Nothing," I said quickly.

Carmella leaned forward. "Listen, honey, I've been doing this a *long* time. Families are very complicated things, and the parents usually provide more drama than the bride and groom. Tell me now. You can't shock me. There is no bizarre situation I haven't seen. Forewarned is forearmed in this business. The more I know now, the fewer embarrassing moments there will be later on."

I cleared my throat. "David's father, Ben, has been…well, that is, we've been…you know—"

"Good for you, Mona," Carmella said. "Glad to know you're getting a little."

"She didn't get any last night," Lily said.

"Aunt Lily!"

"Well, you didn't," Lily said.

I leaned forward. "We were," I said to Carmella. "But not now."

Carmella sighed. "See," she said to Miranda, dropping her voice. "Drama."

Miranda glared at me.

"Mona, take a little advice from a seasoned pro." Carmella leaned toward me, and as she did, her boobs kind of jumped up into the low-cut neckline of her dress. I stared, waiting for them to roll out onto the table, then moved my eyes to meet hers. "Weddings, even the simplest and, you would think, easiest, bring about great changes, and I'm not just talking about the two people getting married. It makes everyone involved rethink love, commitment, all that happy crap. It looks like you're confused about this guy. Are you? Because if you are, planning this wedding is not going to make things easier for you."

Lily rose from the table. "Oh, dear," she said.

Miranda smiled brightly. "So…"

Carmella went back to work. "How many people were you

thinking?"

Miranda shrugged. "No more than fifty, I would think. Mom?"

"Well, it depends on how many friends you and David want to invite. I know that the Cutler family is rather large, but since most of your cousins would never think to come, fifty sounds right. This is a you-and-David decision."

She nodded.

"Let me know ASAP," Carmella said. "Since we gotta find you a room." She frowned, her perfectly plucked brows coming together. "Instead of a hotel or someplace like that, there are a few small museums around with nice space. Something like that sound okay?"

Miranda brightened. "That sounds great. Instead of a sit-down formal dinner, we'd like a buffet. And a wine bar."

Carmella went back to scribbling. "'Kay. Great. Band? Deejay? What about flowers? Favors?"

Miranda put on her thinking face. "Deejay. White roses with lots of green ferns, for me to carry. And for the tables, maybe potted ferns in little white pots, clustered around big white candles. The ferns could be the favors."

"Cute idea." Carmella glanced up at me. "You crafty?"

"When I have to be," I said.

"Whatev. So, this is good. We'll wait for the groom, what's his name—David. And Ben." Carmella sat back and smiled.

That was when the back door opened, Miranda sprang up to give David a hug, and in walked Ben, looking so handsome and sexy in a dark blue sweater and faded jeans that I almost choked. Yesterday I would have wrapped my arms around him and known he was all mine. Today I had to smile and nod. It was the hardest thing I had had to do in a very long time.

Miranda was introducing Carmella, and there, right before my eyes, the current in the room completely changed. Carmella lingered over her handshake, touched Ben lightly on the shoulder, and had him laughing in under twenty seconds.

The woman had a certain style. Lucky for me, I knew that Ben would never fall for her charms.

Right?

CHAPTER FIVE

YES, AUNT LILY'S CHICKEN POTPIE was delicious. So was the salad of mixed baby greens with homemade vinaigrette. And the flakey apple tarts from Bettinger's bakery were to die for.

It was the most awkward and uncomfortable luncheon of my life.

Ben was charming (as always) and funny (as always) and had Carmella completely in his thrall. He didn't know it, of course. In the years I'd known him, he had been completely oblivious to the effect he had on woman. One deep, sexy laugh, a few nods of that handsome head, a casual wave of those strong, beautifully formed hands, and they fell at his feet.

Carmella Ciavaglia was obviously enjoying the view from down there.

Lauren and Jessica joined us. I had to hand it to Carmella; she worked all through lunch, taking notes, her silver pen flashing as often as her brilliant smile. Guest list—up to seventy people. Tuxes for the guys—downgraded to navy three-piece suits. Dresses for the twins—their choice, just simple and matching in whatever color they chose. Miranda's dress—off the rack at a great place Carmella knew of, where we would be treated, she assured us, like royalty.

Lily beamed. "I'll go with you. I need something too, you know. After all, I'm a bride-to-be as well!"

Heavens. I kept forgetting that.

I couldn't look at Ben. Here I was, surrounded by the most unlikely brides-to-be, when, in a world where I did not feel so afraid, *I* should be the bride. I felt that tightening in my chest again.

"What kind of dress are you looking for?" Jessica asked. Of all my three girls, she was enjoying Lily's upcoming nuptials the most. "I say go for something bold—how about red?" Jess had a rather warped sense of humor.

Lily, dressed today in a multicolored blouse tucked into black pants with orange ballet flats, looked thoughtful. "No, not red. But for spring, I was thinking pink? And an armful of white tulips. Can we do that, Carmella?"

"Of course. We can do anything." Carmella put down her pen and sat back. "I imagine the best time to go dress shopping would be during your Thanksgiving break, Miranda. Not Black Friday, of course. Saturday would be more bearable. Shall I set something up?"

Miranda nodded. "That would be perfect."

"And what about the gentlemen?" Carmella said, her voice dropping to almost a purr. "I'd be happy to set something up for you too. Just say the word. I know a fabulous shop in Bay Ridge. Dad gets all his suits there. We could make a day of it—fittings, then lunch."

David frowned. "Fittings for what?"

"David, I know you're on a budget, but I'm sure I could get you a great deal on a suit."

"Can't we just go to the mall?" David asked.

Carmella raised her eyebrows and turned to Ben. "Surely you want to look your best on your son's wedding day?"

Ben chuckled. "I do. There's actually a little men's shop right here in town. We're good. But thanks for the offer, Carmella. It's very generous."

She leaned forward, allowing her boobs to bounce up like matzo balls bubbling to the surface of chicken soup. "Generous is what I do," she said, smiling.

Ben smiled back. "I'm sure."

Oh, my God. Was he really falling for that? It hadn't even been twenty-four hours, and strictly speaking, we hadn't even broken up, and already he was letting this woman sharpen her claws instead of warning her to draw them back in. Maybe I shouldn't have been feeling quite so sure of myself.

Miranda kissed David on the cheek. "You'll look amazing no matter what you wear," she said.

David kissed her back. "You too."

They were so sure of themselves, so confident in their feelings for each other. Just like Ben and I had been just yesterday. I finally looked over at Ben, and he was watching David and Miranda too, with a wistful, slightly sad expression on his face. Was he thinking the same thing? I hoped he was.

"Speaking of Thanksgiving," Lily said, "we need to figure that out."

I'd been stabbing what was left of my tart with my fork. "Figure what out?" I asked.

Lily shrugged. "Well, there's Vincent and his family now. I'd love to spend Thanksgiving with him, naturally, as well as with you and your usual crowd." She waved a hand at Carmella. "Mona always has the most fun dinners here. Very unusual guests. How do holidays work in your family, Carmella?"

Everyone at the table looked at Carmella. Yes, how did a known organized-crime family celebrate the most American of all holidays?

"Everyone comes to my house," she said. "But there's not a big crowd. My sister Assunta is in Santa Monica, and Vincenza is down in West Palm, and their kids are scattered everywhere. So there's just Dad and me and my boys. There's the occasional cousin, but we usually keep it small. This year, of course, Dad asked about inviting Lily. And, of course, Mona, and your lovely daughters." She smiled. "Would you all like to come out to Brooklyn for Thanksgiving?"

"But, Mom," Miranda said, "I thought David would be *here* this year. And Ben and Ethan."

The year that Brian left me, I had invited Ben to share Thanksgiving with my recently broken family. Since then we had not shared the holiday again, for various reasons. The next year, Ben and the boys went down to spend the weekend with the boys' grandmother, because she had just been diagnosed with cancer. The year after that, my ex-mother-in-law invited the girls and me out to Brooklyn. Then Dominique had a baby boy, and the girls all wanted to spend Thanksgiving with them, and I had been invited. I didn't want to appear to be a bitch, so I said yes. Last year David got an invitation to ski out in Colorado for the whole week, and Ben and Ethan went along.

I looked at Ben. "Of course you're invited," I told him.

He smiled. "Why, thank you, Mona. The boys and I will be delighted. What can we bring?"

Why was he being so polite? Almost formal? Like he hadn't eaten dinner in my house hundreds of times before, always bringing wine or flowers or a box of cookies from my favorite bakery? And then I saw, quite clearly, that he was detaching himself. He was no longer making assumptions about his place in my life. He had said he wanted distance. And this was his way of doing that.

"I'll let you know," I said carelessly, trying to hide my sudden jolt of sadness. I glanced at Carmella, who was watching Ben and me like she would a tennis match, her eyes shifting from one side of the table to the other.

"What about Dad and Tyler?" Lauren asked. "I thought they'd be with us this year."

"And Grandma," added Jessica. "And Aunt Rebecca."

"Well..." I started. I glanced at Carmella again, who was not jumping up to invite my entire extended family out to Brooklyn.

"Obviously," Lily said to Carmella, "you all will have to come here. It only makes sense, right, Mona?"

I stared at Lily, then at Carmella, who was smiling like the Cheshire Cat.

"Right."

I woke Monday morning alone. Except, of course, for Fred and the cats. The girls had all left by Sunday afternoon. Lily got picked up by Tony and was whisked off to Bay Ridge.

I lay in bed as long as I could, then dragged my lonely butt out of bed, took a quick shower, and walked to work.

There was a big detached garage behind the house, and over it was a small studio apartment. The chauffeur probably lived there back in the twenties when the house was first built. Now the space was my office, long and narrow, with a half bath at one end and a kitchenette at the other. It was there that I originally went to get away from my husband and kids to write alone and in peace.

Now I could pretty much write alone anywhere in the house I wanted, but old habits died hard.

Besides, Anthony was coming over, and we had to get my career back into high gear. It could take Sylvia months to get a contract on my new books, and months after that to actually cash any checks. I needed some royalties, and fairly quickly. I sat back on the overstuffed couch and drank coffee until he arrived.

He climbed the stairs, unwrapped three scarves from his neck, shrugged out of his tweed jacket, then sat down next to me.

"Tell me all the wedding plans."

"We have a wedding planner." The good thing about that, I'd told myself, was that since I didn't have to worry about details of the wedding, I could concentrate more on tearing my hair out with worry and frustration. "Vinnie's daughter Carmella."

"As in Carmella Soprano? Oh, I just might die from happiness right here and now. What's she like?"

"Think Sophia Loren. In anything."

"Oh, my. What has she planned so far?"

"Pretty much everything—where to get the dresses, flowers, finding the place, food—she's very good at her job. Both Miranda and Lily are in capable hands."

"What has Miranda got to do with anything?" he asked, clearly confused.

"Oh, right. I haven't talked to you since Friday morning. Miranda is getting married."

He was silent, then broke into a crazy grin and hugged me. "Oh, Mona, how wonderful! But I didn't even know she was dating anyone seriously."

"Me neither. It happened pretty fast—like, in the past three months."

He pulled back. "Well, that's certainly not a very long time."

"No, I don't think so either."

"I'm assuming you're not over the moon with excitement?"

I sighed. "No, not really."

"Hmmm. So, who's the lucky young man?" Anthony thought all of my daughters were the smartest, sweetest, most special girls on earth.

"David Cutler."

He started to laugh. "Oh, how funny is that? Ben's last name is Cutler."

"Yes. And his son's *first* name is David."

He stopped laughing. "No way."

I nodded. "Way."

"Wait a minute. Your daughter and Ben's son are getting married?"

I nodded.

He took my coffee mug, got off the couch, walked over to the coffeepot, then returned with a steaming cup for himself and a refill for me. I could tell he was thinking hard.

"You do know, don't you, how extraordinary it is that my favorite family of women is marrying into my favorite family of men. I bet that Ben is going to propose any day now."

"He already did."

"What! Oh Mona, how wonderful! Why didn't you tell me right away?"

"Because I didn't say yes. In fact, Ben and I are taking a bit of a break." It was hard to say the words. They caught in my throat. "Just to, you know, sort things out."

He put his coffee mug down slowly, staring down at the floor. Then suddenly he started to cry.

"Oh, Anthony, please. It'll be okay, honest."

He covered his face with his hands, shoulders shaking.

Anthony had been with me as my personal assistant for more than ten years. And for most of those years he had a deep and unwavering love for Ben Cutler. His crush was so intense that he used to become completely tongue-tied in Ben's presence. Eventually they became friends. Now, even though Anthony had been with his partner Victor for some time, there was still a bit of lust in his heart. And he had great expectations about Ben and me being together.

I put my arms around him. "Anthony, listen to me. Ben and I still love each other. We're just having a difference of opinion about the kids getting married, and well, marriage in general. But it's just a wrinkle. We'll work it out."

"What difference of opinion?"

"He thinks that it's perfectly fine to get married to someone after knowing them a few months, and I don't."

He jerked his head up. "Seriously?"

I nodded.

"Well, it's not perfectly fine." He sniffed. "In fact, it's almost stupid. And he's okay with it? I guess it's good to find out there's at least *one* thing wrong with the man. But you won't hold it against him forever, will you?"

"No."

"Promise?"

I patted him on the shoulder. "Anthony, I can't make promises like that. But I'll try, okay?"

He sniffed. "And what about you?"

"As much as I love Ben, I don't want to be married again. It's not about him; it's all me. And that's how I feel right now." I gave him a quick hug. "But do you really think I'd just let Ben go? I mean, he's one of the best people in the world. I'll never give him up without a fight."

He wiped his face with his palms and took a long, shuddering breath. "The two of you belong. You're perfect together. I can't imagine you being with anyone else. And it's not just because he's so damn good looking."

"I know."

"Although that's kind of part of it."

I smiled. "I know."

He twisted his lips. "Is she pregnant?"

"Nope."

"That's good. They are going to make beautiful babies. You know that, right?"

"Right. But not anytime soon."

"You and Ben could also make beautiful babies."

If I had been drinking my coffee, I would have spewed it all over myself. "Are you crazy? I'm going to be fifty, Anthony. Not right away, but in the next few years."

He smiled slyly. "It's been done before."

"And may very well be done again, but not by me."

He had calmed down enough to reach for his coffee and settle back against the couch. "I trust you, Mona. I have faith that you and Ben will soon be back to your happy couple hood. And I'm sure that Miranda will be happy. I mean, come on—Ben's son? What's not to love there?"

I sighed. "This is kinda hard."

He put his coffee mug down again and took both of my hands. "I'm sure it is," he said very seriously. "You do know, don't you, that whatever you decide, I'm behind you one hundred and ten percent?"

I squeezed his hands. "Thank you."

"Now, I read your new stuff, and it's great, but we have to start working on this backlist thing," he said, letting go of my hands and putting on his business face. "I found formatters and a few cover artists. We need to start preparing ourselves. This self-publishing is a lot more work than I thought. And you need to get going on this so you can make some money and give me a raise."

"What have you done to deserve a raise?" I asked, smiling.

"I want to put in an in-ground pool at the house."

"Of course. Okay, let's get started."

I came of age in the land of feminism. I had always scorned the woman who felt so insecure that she felt the need to use her sexuality to get what she wanted, rather than her brains, strength, and will. I had made a career for myself—and a very successful one —without having to sleep with anyone to get what I needed. I never even used sex as a weapon—or enticement—in my marriage. I knew that I was the type of woman certain men found attractive, and I had been known to shamelessly flirt with waiters to get faster service, but I never thought of myself as a femme fatale, using my feminine wiles to prey on unsuspecting men. I was better than that.

So I wasn't sure what I was thinking, exactly, when I went into Bloomingdale's and bought one hundred and sixty-seven dollars' worth of black lingerie. I did know that when I got home and tried everything on, I was satisfied enough to call Ben and ask if he was busy, and if he wasn't, could I drop by? Maybe for a drink? After all, we were both adults, and we had things to discuss. It was perfectly natural for me to want to see him, right? And if I managed to remind him of what the two of us once were and could be again, well, that was all right too.

He said yes.

I found the only pair of black spiked heels I owned, a pair that I had worn once in California but never again because of the sharp pain they inflicted on all ten of my toes. But I didn't care—I wasn't planning on keeping them on for that long. I threw my camel hair coat over my black lace bustier, black satin tap pants, black stockings held up by a black garter belt with tiny red bows, and headed out the door.

I pulled into his driveway with my heart pounding. I had spent the entire drive over running scenarios in my head. Since I was a romance writer by trade, you can imagine that the ground was pretty fertile, so I arrived in a state of what we romance types like to call "heightened arousal." I was ready to jump his bones. I checked myself in the rearview mirror, fluffed my hair, got out of the car, then went up to the front door.

He answered right away, handsome and smiling. "I'm glad you called," he said. My heart jumped into my throat. Right inside the foyer, I knew, was a nice oaken coatrack, the kind with a bench for sitting and pulling on winter boots. It could also be used for other things that could be done in a sitting position, and I was walking through the first few steps in my head when he reached back to that selfsame coatrack and brought forth a coat.

"I thought we'd walk into town. That jazz piano player you like is playing; you know the one? We can have a few drinks there. It's a great night for walking. What do you think?"

He was already in his coat and closing the door behind him. What did I think? I thought that he was taking this whole "take a break" thing a lot more seriously than I was. I felt suddenly foolish, thinking I could just walk in, flash some skin, and make everything all better. I also felt that it didn't matter how great the night was;

walking eight blocks in those heels was going to kill my feet. But I smiled and linked my arm through his. "Perfect!"

We took a few steps. "You're taller," he said. "Are you wearing heels?"

"Oh, yes," I said, laughing a little. "Breaking them in, you know."

He shook his head. "No, I don't know. But I'll take your word for it. Do they hurt?"

"Just a little," I lied.

Ben wasn't a big talker under the best of circumstances, and since the air between us was so unsettled, we mostly made comments about the weather and local politics as we walked. It took only three blocks for my toes to start hurting, and by the time we arrived at the bar, my entire left foot was in agony, and the right foot was not far behind. Luckily there was a small table by the door, so I could sit down right away.

Ben was still standing. "Do you want me to hang up your coat?"

"Ah, no, thanks. A bit chilly right here."

"Do you want to stand by the bar?" he asked.

I shook my head. "No, This is fine. Really."

I scooted under the table, turned in my chair to cross my legs, then felt the coat open to my thigh. I looked down. The top of the stocking and the tip of the garter belt were in plain view. Damn. I tugged to close the coat and smiled brightly as the waitress came by.

"Vodka martini," I told her. "Straight up, with an olive. And keep them coming."

"Ah, Mona," Ben said gently. "Don't you have to drive home?"

Ooookay then. I lifted my chin. "You're right. Make that a white wine. Pinot."

Ben ordered a beer and sat back. "I'm glad you called. I want to give you a heads up. I gave David Ellen's engagement ring before he went back to Boston. He's having it resized. He'll give it to Miranda at Thanksgiving, I think."

I felt a rush of emotion that pushed aside all the confusion and disappointment I had been feeling about Ben. Ellen had been David's mother, Ben's first wife. The very first woman he'd ever loved. The woman who had made him believe in love at first sight. And my daughter would be getting her ring. "Oh, Ben, how lovely. Miranda will be so excited. She hadn't expected a ring."

When Miranda had mentioned quite calmly at the breakfast table the previous Sunday that she didn't care if she got an engagement ring or not, Lauren and Jessica had joined me in staring in utter disbelief. Miranda, for all her amazing qualities, had a few less than admirable traits, and her blatant and unapologetic materialism had always been one of them. This was the girl who took a second job one summer so she could buy UGG boots in every color. And she didn't want a ring?

Ben grinned. "David and I had quite a conversation about Miranda. He's well aware of all her, well, shortcomings, and realizes that she's trying very hard to change for his benefit. She knows he's saving all his money for a house. But *he* knows she'd do anything for a big, bright diamond ring. He was getting ready to sell his Corvette." David had a classic '63 Corvette that he had bought when he graduated high school and had been taking years to restore it. Last I heard, it was almost finished. "That's why I offered him Ellen's ring."

I was getting teary. "That is so sweet. I mean, both of them. Kind of a 'Gift of the Magi' thing."

"That's what happens when two people really want to spend the rest of their lives together. They're willing to make sacrifices without even thinking about it." The waitress had arrived with our drinks. Ben took a sip of beer, watching me over the rim of his mug. "Know what I mean?"

I stared into my wineglass. The door opened, and a blast of cold air shot up the hem of my coat and hit the bare skin of my left thigh. I shivered. "Yes, Ben. I know." I took a quick sip. So, my plan for a quick and spontaneous seduction was obviously off the table. Even a slow and carefully planned seduction was out if he'd already decided I wasn't going to spend the night. Now I felt really stupid. I should have known better. Ben never said anything that he didn't mean, and he had said he wanted distance. I tightened the belt of my coat.

"When does the piano guy start?" I asked.

Ben nodded slightly. "Pretty soon. Nine, I think. Are you sure you don't want to take off your coat?"

Despite the door opening and closing, and the semi constant breeze going up my legs into just-one-man's-land, the place was getting warm. In fact, there was a thin line of sweat along the back of my neck where the wool collar was rubbing. "No, thanks. I'm good."

"Carmella seems nice. I bet she's very good at her job," Ben said very casually, but my radar went into overdrive.

"Yes. And she's very attractive, if you like the black-widow type."

"Yeah, what's the story there? Lily started telling me her husband was knocked off?"

I shrugged. "Apparently. He was on a routine assignment for his wife's family, and he disappeared for a week. When they found him, there was concrete and an oil drum involved."

Ben shook his head. "It must have been tough, raising two boys alone."

"How do you know she has two boys?" My grip tightened on the stem of the wineglass.

"She called me Monday night."

I almost snapped the wineglass in half. "Oh? About the wedding?"

"Yes. She just needed some info, you know, names for the guest list. We got to talking."

"And are her sons in the family business?"

He shook his head. "No. Trevor is in cooking school, and Paulie is over in France, studying art."

"Paulie?" Wait. Ben was calling her kids by their *nicknames*?

"Her oldest. She wanted them as far away from her father and uncle as she could get them."

"Well, bravo for her for good parenting skills. I'm sure if my father were an underworld impresario, I'd want my girls off doing something else with their lives."

Ben looked at me shrewdly. "Underworld impresario? Hmmm. And just think, he's marrying into your family."

"True. But I trust Lily to keep him in line." I finished off my wine. A bead of sweat was running down the middle of my back, and the underwire of that fancy lace bustier was poking a hole in the skin under my right arm. The door opened, and two couples crowded the door, holding it open while they spent at least three hours looking to see if there was a place to sit, letting in another chilly gust.

"Are you sure you don't want to move?" Ben asked.

"No, really. Besides, I've got a great view of the piano," I lied. I did, provided about thirty people, seven tables, and a few dozen chairs moved out of the way.

I flagged the waitress and asked for water, and Ben and I sat in silence. It was a good silence—we had always been able to sit together without talking, enjoying looking at the people around us, relaxing in each other's company.

"How's the Basking Ridge project coming?" I finally asked him.

He made a face. "The homeowner is a lunatic. Changing his mind every five minutes. Then the wife screams at him about money. I'm having both of them sign off on every change, because it's costing them a fortune. The good news is, her nephew is on staff at *Architectural Digest*, and she wants a cover story."

"Wow, that's great. Hitting the big time."

He chuckled. "Maybe."

"No, really. Think of all the higher-end clients you could get!"

"True. But the higher-end clients I've got now are a pain in the ass to work with, and I can't wait to get out of there. I'm not sure I want too many more like them."

I laughed; then the spotlight hit the piano, and a scruffy young man sat down to play. Ben and I had heard him a few times before, and he was a delight. Unfortunately, as I crossed my legs, I snagged my expensive stocking on something and felt a run climbing up the back of my leg. The garter started to dig into my thigh, and the sweat drying in the middle of my back was starting to itch. I kept my head fixed resolutely in the direction of the music, even though I couldn't see much more than the backs of just about everyone else in the bar. Ben, a head and a half taller, smiled throughout, his head nodding gently to the music.

I finally slipped into the ladies' room and collapsed into a stall. I shrugged out of my coat, letting the cool air wash over my semi-naked body. I closed my eyes for a few minutes, enjoying the feeling of relief. Then I cautiously opened my eyes.

I had not one, but two runs in my stocking. Both garters holding up said stockings were digging into my flesh. There was a rash on both arms from the heat, and the lace under my boobs was damp from sweat. My satin tap pants had rearranged at the back seam, giving me the world's biggest wedgie.

Boy, was I a picture of irresistible booty or what?

I eased my foot out of my left shoe. A blister roughly the size of Duluth was on my little toe. How was I going to walk back to Ben's? I clenched my teeth and forced my foot back into the shoe. Maybe I could snap off both heels—hadn't it worked for Kathleen Turner in *Romancing the Stone*? But Michael Douglas had done it with his machete—all I had was a nail file in my purse, and it didn't look up to the job.

I made my way back to the table and forced a smile. "Ben, I think I need to start home. I'm more tired tonight than I thought."

"Oh, sorry." He drained his beer.

"I'm the one who's sorry. I should have just stayed home."

He smiled. "No. It's always good to see you, Mona."

I silently thanked him for saying that. At least I didn't feel like a complete idiot.

We got up to leave. I thought I was walking just fine, but Ben grabbed my arm.

"Why are you limping? Are you okay?"

"It's just the shoes."

He stared at my feet. "Do you want me to get the car?"

Gratitude pushed embarrassment out the door. "Please. Would you? That would be great."

He steered me back to our table. "Give me fifteen minutes."

Not wanting to appear totally incapacitated, I was waiting for him outside when he returned. I hobbled over to his car and got in gratefully. As I did, the coat opened up to my thigh, flashing black nylon and little red bows. Ben stared at my leg as I rearranged my coat and calmly fastened my seat belt.

"What exactly are you wearing?" he finally asked, putting the car in drive and heading back to his house.

I cleared my throat. "Just some black underwear."

He shook his head. "No, Mona, really. What are you wearing under that coat?"

"I told you. Black underwear. Just black underwear."

We pulled into his driveway. He shut off the ignition and turned sideways to look at me. "So I'm guessing you had some sort of definitive plan for this evening?"

I cleared my throat again. "Possibly. Or I could have just forgotten to put on clothes before I left the house."

He took a deep breath. "I thought we agreed we were taking a break. If I had known you were planning something like this—"

"I know. And I feel really stupid. And I do apologize for not taking your wishes, well, very seriously."

"But?"

I swallowed. "I miss you. I was going to walk in the front door, drop my coat, and you'd be so overcome with lust that you'd forget about everything else."

He laughed softly. "Mona, I've got to hand it to you; that probably would have worked. Which is why I wanted us to go out instead of having a drink in the house. I'd eventually be overcome with lust no matter what you were wearing."

"Well, that's good to hear."

"I still need to clear a few things in my head before we go any further. Okay?"

I nodded. Then I got out of his car, got into my own, and drove. As soon as I was around the corner, I pulled over and sat in the car, eyes closed, until my hands stopped shaking. Then I drove home.

CHAPTER SIX

FOR YEARS, REBECCA BERMAN HAD arrived at the crack of dawn on Thanksgiving morning with a pan or two of her homemade, ready-to-bake cinnamon rolls. All I had to do was pop them in the oven, and within minutes my house was filled with a sweet and spicy scent that made being married to her brother Brian for twenty years worthwhile. Rebecca was one of my favorite people in the world—an elegant hippie with long, beautiful gray hair and a clear, lovely laugh. My divorce from Brian did nothing at all to our friendship, or her long-standing tradition of arriving with cinnamon rolls. She did not, just as a point of information, bring rolls to anyone else's house where we might be gathering for Thanksgiving, something that Dominique had commented on more than once.

Julian was with her again this year, he of the rakish good looks, silver hair, and pierced ear. I was alone in my kitchen when they arrived, sipping coffee and trying to decide between sausage scramble casserole (recipe found on Pinterest) or egg-and-cheese on English muffins for breakfast.

"Mona, love, how are you?" she cried, sweeping in with her usual swirl of long skirts and silky scarves. We hugged. She was taller than I and smelled of her signature patchouli.

"I'm so happy to see you," I told her. I kissed Julian on the cheek. "You too, of course. Here, let me take those." I grabbed the pans from Julian's outstretched hands and popped them in the oven. "Today may be a three-martini day," I told her.

She raised both eyebrows. "It's barely eight o'clock. Have you developed the sight?"

Rebecca was a practicing Wiccan, and took those sorts of things very seriously.

I sighed as I poured them both coffee. Rebecca and I had had a long talk the weekend before, and she knew about all the drama, but she needed to be brought up to speed on the events of the past few days. "Carmella called to ask what she could bring."

"How nice," Rebecca murmured.

"I suggested sweet potatoes or green beans or pumpkin pie. She's bringing lasagna and a few dozen cannoli. Vincent is bringing homemade wine and Tony the Bodyguard. Patricia won't be here—she's down in Boca, at her aunt's, who's not doing well at all. I haven't talked to Ben in over a week. It's the longest we've gone without speaking in four years. Lauren broke up with Justin, and she's taking it really hard. Tyler's potty training is not going well, and I'm told he pees on anything blue. One of the cats has an issue and has been throwing up all over the house, but I haven't been able to find out which one it is. Just watch where you walk. Oh, and Jess's new tattoo might be infected. She can't sit down."

Rebecca sighed. "Oh, dear."

"Perhaps you should start drinking now," Julian suggested. "Rebecca and I can handle dinner."

"Thank you," I said sincerely. "But I have to stay sharp. Carmella wants Ben."

Rebecca smiled gently. "We all want Ben."

"True. But she may be in active pursuit."

"Then may I suggest you change before your guests start arriving?" Rebecca said.

I looked down at myself. I was dressed in my usual make-Thanksgiving-dinner outfit—sweatpants and a T-shirt. In deference to the drop in temperature, I was also wearing a very chichi flannel shirt, unbuttoned, sleeves rolled up, with the pocket torn off. I sighed. "Maybe one of my California outfits?"

She shrugged. "Anything, Mona. Really."

"I will. Your sister is still in Chicago, right?"

"Yes, thank God."

Brian and Rebecca's other sister, generally referred to as Marsha the Bitch, had finally divorced her incredibly boring husband—or perhaps he divorced her—and moved out to Chicago to be near her daughter, and her presence would no longer be a threat to any family holiday.

I heard the girls coming downstairs. I quickly decided on the English-muffin idea, which I could throw together before the parades started, and they became transfixed in front of the flat screen.

Rebecca pushed her coffee mug aside. "How can I help?"

My daughters think Rebecca is the best aunt ever, and I have to agree with them. After hugs and kisses, Rebecca immediately insisted on seeing Jess's tattoo, which Jess showed her without asking Julian to look in the other direction. Julian, a born gentleman, averted his eyes anyway. Rebecca immediately rattled off several DIY options for improving the situation, sending Jessica off in search of the tea tree oil. We all scrambled eggs and toasted muffins, and by the time Lily came down, the girls were happily eating in the den.

Lily was wearing a shimmery bronze tunic over a wine-colored maxi skirt.

Rebecca stared at her. "My God, Lily! You look amazing. Love certainly does agree with you!"

They played kiss-kiss, and Lily gave Julian a peck on the cheek; then she settled in at the breakfast bar. "I can't wait for you to meet him. I had always thought that you'd captured the last handsome rogue over sixty-five, but I think *I* may have!"

"Lily," I asked. "How old is Vinnie?"

"Seventy," she said, sipping her coffee.

"Does he know how old you are?"

She shot me a very cold look. "No. And it's nobody's business. Is it?"

"Of course not," Rebecca soothed. "Tell me all about him."

I left them to it and went upstairs. My dinner had been ready for two days now—everything chopped and precooked, mashed, sliced, and peeled. It was mostly a matter of getting the two turkeys in the oven at the right time, then finishing off the sides. I took a shower, blow-dried my hair, put on some makeup, then opened my closet.

During the time I'd spent in LA, I had noticed that most of the people were beautiful, rich, and thin. And young. Oddly, I had not met one person who admitted to being alive during man's first walk on the moon. In fact, nobody asked your age; the unspoken agreement being that no one should deliberately provoke a lie. It took me a while to get used to.

The east coast, on the other hand, had a different outlook. Nobody here said that fifty was the new thirty. Most of my friends in New Jersey felt that fifty was the new Spanish Inquisition. It was best to run like hell in the opposite direction, but if caught and threatened with torture, admit everything.

Just as a point of information, I'm barely forty-eight. So it's really not a concern of mine.

At all.

While in LA, I had a chance to meet those beautiful thin young people at a variety of functions that required me to buy outrageously expensive outfits, along with ridiculous shoes. One of those pairs of shoes, the ones I wore to Ben's a few weeks ago, had been donated to my local consignment shop, because I'd never, *ever* wear them again.

I grabbed several outfits and started trying them on. Nothing that was appropriate for drinks on a terrace overlooking the Hollywood sign was going to fly during a family dinner in Westfield, New Jersey, in November.

Maybe I'd just come downstairs in my black bustier, satin tap pants, and garter belt.

I was finally pushed into a decision by the sound of Fred barking. Someone was here, and as hostess I should at least make an appearance in something other than my robe. So I grabbed dark-wash jeans, a cashmere V-neck sweater, and a long scarf that I spent several precious seconds trying to tie around my neck in a way that suggested a fashion-forward sensibility. Then I gave up, because it would probably dangle over the stove while I was cooking, catch fire, then burn down my house with my entire family trapped inside.

I pushed my feet into black Minnetonka mocs and ran

downstairs.

Carmella Ciavaglia was wearing the perfect outfit for a family dinner in Westfield, New Jersey, in November: skinny jeans tucked into black booties, a silky tunic that fell past her hips but hugged every curve, and a long draped cardigan. She also had with her a very tall and striking young man who was arranging foil trays on my countertop.

Rebecca, bless her heart, had taken coats and was introducing everyone. I smiled broadly at Carmella. Were we at the hugging stage yet? Would we ever be? Apparently yes, because the tall, striking young man swept me into his arms.

"Mona, thank you for having us," he said, his voice very deep.

I detached myself politely. "A pleasure."

"Yes, thanks. You have no idea how nice it is to not have to cook!" Carmella said.

I looked at my countertop. "You call this not cooking?" I asked.

She laughed. "This is Trevor," Carmella said "He did most of this. He's at the CIA."

Jess, hearing the commotion, had torn herself away from the TV. "CIA?" she asked. "Are you going to be a spy?"

Trevor shook his head. He had Carmella's dark eyes and Vincent's beautiful head of hair, although his was dark brown instead of steel gray, of course. "No. I'm going to be a chef. Culinary Institute of America."

Jessica looked disappointed. "Oh. Well, that's cool too, I guess. How do you feel about marching bands and floats?"

His eyes lit up as he followed her into the den.

"My daughters love the parades," I explained to Carmella. "It's kind of a tradition."

She waved a perfectly manicured hand. "Sure, I get it. We too early?"

"Not at all," I assured her. Where had Aunt Lily gone?

Rebecca smiled. "Coffee?"

Carmella nodded and perched her shapely butt on the stool in front of the breakfast bar. "I thought Ben would be here already."

I glanced at the clock. It was not even ten. How long was I going to have to be talking to this woman? "Soon," I told her.

"Ethan likes to sleep in."

She was drinking her coffee with lots of cream and sugar, and as she stirred, the spoon clinked against the side of the mug. "Ethan, yeah, the one at Penn State?"

I smiled. She wanted me to know that she and Ben had talked about things—things other than the wedding. Was she expecting a reaction? Because she sure wasn't going to get one. "Yes. He's prelaw."

"Right." *Clink. Clink.* "Ben says he's a bit shy."

"Maybe with strangers," I said, still smiling. "But he and I get along fine."

"It's nice when you get along with the kids, ya know?" *Clink. Clink.*

"True. Especially now that we're going to be family. Ben mentioned that your other son was in France?" It was my turn to let *her* know that Ben and I talked as well. Regularly. About her.

"Paulie? Yes. He's studying art, of all things." She shrugged. "I don't know how these kids today think they're going to make a living. Cooking? Painting? Whatever happened to good, old-fashioned kinds of jobs, ya know?"

Right. Like money laundering and prostitution.

Aunt Lily came in. She had added a fabulous scarf tied around her neck, perfectly looped and draped. I felt a pang of jealousy.

"Carmella, hello!" she said, planting a kiss. "And Trev? Did the girls kidnap him already? I have to say hello. He's such a wonderful young man." She hurried into the den.

"Lily is quite a character," Carmella said. *Clink. Clink.*

"Yes," I agreed. "She's a very, ah, forceful personality."

Julian made a noise, possibly from choking on his coffee.

Rebecca looped her arm through his. "Let's go watch the parade with the young folks," she suggested, dragging him into the den.

Carmella finally took a sip from her mug and smiled brilliantly. "Lovely home."

"Thanks. And you live in Brooklyn?"

She nodded. "Right around the corner from Lily's old place."

"Imagine."

"Yes."

Lily came back in and looked at me, then at Carmella. She put her arm around Carmella's shoulder. "I know this isn't technically a workday for you," she said, sounding very apologetic, "but could I steal you away for a few minutes? I found the most wonderful flowers online."

Thank you, Aunt Lily.

I cleared the table and loaded the dishwasher for the first load of the day. I poured another cup of coffee. I opened my full-size freezer, the one I had installed right next to my full-size fridge, and gazed longingly at the two bottles of Grey Goose on the bottom shelf.

It was going to be a long day.

The rest of the cast, in order of appearance, was as follows:

Brian, Dominique, Tyler, and Brian's mother Phyllis.

Vincent DeMatriano and Anthony Lorenzo. (Or, as he was more affectionately known, Tony the Bodyguard.)

Ben, David, and Ethan Cutler.

Anthony Wood and Victor Shapiro.

And finally, unnamed pizza delivery guy.

Phyllis Berman, who was still my favorite mother-in-law ever, had had a series of ministrokes the year before. Prior to that she had lived quite happily in the sprawling Brooklyn apartment she had raised her family in, renting out the spare room—with its adjoining bath—to a series of students attending Brooklyn Law School. But last year Brian talked her into selling the homestead and moving to the 'burbs, where she could be closer to him. She was now living in a fabulous assisted-living facility, complete with bingo night, trips to Broadway shows, and Walmart Day. She was happy as a clam. She could also spend every Sunday with Tyler and was much closer for all holidays.

I knew Dominique was thrilled.

Phyllis bought her usual pecan pie. Dominique's contribution to the festivities was a five-pound bag of gourmet coffee, two bottles of Amaretto, and Cheerios. I assumed the cereal was Tyler-specific. Rebecca and Julian came back in, and they all sat at my kitchen table, Tyler crawling off the chair looking for the dog, and

Dominique chasing after him, muttering in French, while Brian and his mother and Rebecca trash-talked Marsha the Bitch.

Vinnie came into my kitchen like Caesar entering the Roman Senate. He had a gorgeous bouquet of roses in one hand, and bakery box of cookies in the other. Behind him was Tony, carrying two large jugs of what I assumed to be homemade wine. Tony mumbled as he put the jugs on the counter, then started to back out of the door.

"Ah, Tony?" I said.

He stopped dead, looked at me, then looked at Vincent.

By then, Aunt Lily had fluttered in from her deep discussion with Carmella. "Oh, darling, you can't make poor Tony sit in the car all day. It's Thanksgiving. We'll just add a chair at the table, right, Mona?"

Vinnie was nothing if not smooth. "Lily, my love, of course." He then made introductions all around. My daughters, sensing drama, tore themselves away from the television to shake Tony's hand. Trev, of course, was an old buddy, and he and Tony performed some sort of complicated handshake, hopefully not involving gang signs. Tony then asked, very politely, if there was someplace he could just sit and read. I sent him into the living room.

Seconds later Carmella appeared. "What's Tony doing in here?"

Lily blinked. "Why, Carmella, it's Thanksgiving. We have more than enough food, heaven knows. Besides, I feel like he's part of the family."

I'm sure that, technically speaking, Tony *was* part of the family, but there was an obvious line where the help was concerned, and Tony must have fallen on the wrong side of it.

Carmella may have been gearing up for an argument, but Ben and his sons came in.

Ben and I hugged. His body felt so good against mine—lean and strong, his arms fitting perfectly around my shoulders and waist, my head tucked under his chin. He kissed the top of my head, and I stepped away from him, my heart racing. I was proud of myself for keeping my hands under control. The kitchen was getting very crowded, so I shooed everyone into the living room, where the silent Tony relocated himself to the window seat, Kindle in hand.

I watched as David and Miranda went upstairs and hoped they would not be having sex.

I could hear Ben laughing—Carmella had turned on the charm. I felt something tighten in my belly as I imagined her leaning toward him, her breasts pressing against his arm, flipping her long shiny hair around.

I peeked in to the den—Trev was sitting between the twins, conjuring up another unwelcome visual.

I felt something warm under my left moccasin—I had stepped on something that had once been in a cat's digestive tract.

The kitchen door opened—again—and Anthony and Victor came in, arms full.

"Mona, did you know that there was a black Lincoln Town Car parked on the street, totally blocking your driveway?" Anthony said, giving me a quick kiss.

I sighed. Escape was impossible.

He gave me a hug. "Don't worry. Victor and I are here. Let's get these turkeys on the oven."

"Before you do that," I said, "let's see if we can crack open one of these jugs of wine."

I was not drunk for Thanksgiving. Perhaps if I had been, I could have rationalized some of my behavior. Not that I embarrassed myself in front of my family and friends, mind you. But I made an error in judgment that, when I think about it now, may not have been the wisest of choices.

Things were going along fine. More than fine. About the time Anthony (not Tony) served his appetizer, Miranda and David came downstairs looking flushed and very excited. Miranda was wearing a brilliant emerald-cut diamond ring. I almost cried, she was so happy. Vinnie made a few congratulatory noises, then pulled out a little surprise of his own—a ring for Lily. It was a gorgeous sapphire—her birthstone—surrounded by diamonds. It was not huge, gaudy, or in any way overdone. It was simply perfect.

I had already sampled a bit of Vinnie's homemade wine. The

first glass upon the successful transfer of two turkeys into their respective ovens, the second when Dominique asked for towels because Tyler—although he had made it into the powder room to go peepees—had not quite gotten to the bowl. After the third glass, where we all wished good luck and long love to the happy couples, I could not have stopped smiling if you paid me.

Tony offered to light the grill outside to heat up the lasagna, because I had run out of oven space, even though I had two full-size ovens. Three trays of lasagna took up a lot of room. Tony was joined by Trev, which did not bother me, and Ethan, which did a little, and Jessica. That bothered me a lot. But who was I to pass judgment on Tony's choice of career? When I had asked him earlier what he was reading, he showed me—*Finnegan's Wake*. Really? What kind of goombah hood reads James Joyce? Obviously this was a young man of many facets. Who knows—maybe he was bodyguarding his way through a degree in comparative English literature.

I almost felt sorry for Dominique. Phyllis made no secret of her attitude toward her potential daughter-in-law. Although I no longer harbored any ill feelings toward the woman, Lily certainly did, as did Anthony and—by extension—Victor. My daughters had grown to appreciate Dominique for her fashion sense and organizational skills, particularly when it came to throwing together a party, but there were no warm and fuzzy feelings there. So she was never completely relaxed or happy when in my home. But I have to hand it to her—she was one tough broad. She put on a brave face, was polite and sometimes charming, ignored all of Lily's less-than-subtle digs, and kept Tyler from climbing furniture, writing on walls with his crayons, or otherwise being an obnoxious brat.

Anthony was so fascinated with Vinnie that he barely drooled over Ben. Lauren and Jessica were having a field day. Ethan—the known entity—was almost as good looking as Ben, very shy and geeky. Trev, also almost as good looking as Ben, was outgoing, funny, and snarky. There was also Tony, silent, dark, a total mystery man. Let's face it—when you're young, mystery men are hard to resist.

Brian somehow worked his way to Carmella's side, and they had a long and intimate conversation under Dominique's icy glare.

Rebecca and Julian sat, wide-eyed and obviously amused.

Fred had disappeared, hiding from Tyler, but emerged to try to grab a cannoli off the counter. Dogs and Italian pastry. Who knew?

Carmella remained a respectful distance from Ben most of the time, but if I left the room, I'd return to find her slithered in and around him like a python.

I had never written anything as complicated as this.

I'm a great believer in plot twists and surprise endings, but there was so much going on in my house, I could not have fit it all into a five-part series.

I had added a long folding table to the end of my dining room table and had retrieved folding chairs from the basement to accommodate the extra guests. I mixed china and crystal and cloth napkins. Instead of a centerpiece, there was a line of small lit votive candles down the center of the table in little red glass holders, alternating with single stems of gold-colored mums in amber shot glasses. Very Martha Stewart.

The dining room was barely big enough for us all. When I announced dinner, there was a bit of a bumper-car moment as everyone tried to figure out where to sit. I stayed in the kitchen, carving with the help of Anthony, and when I finally carried the turkeys into the dining room—to actual applause—I was gratified to see a space for me left at the head of the table, with Ben seated to my right and Carmella at the far end. We all stood and held hands, and then went around the table, each of us saying what we were thankful for. Tyler, of course, beat us all—he was thankful that Christmas was coming, and he would be getting lots of toys. You've got to love the honesty of the young.

One advantage of a table that could double as a bowling alley was that I didn't have to talk much to Carmella. The downside was that the food took so long to get around that some people were almost finished eating before the rest of us had been passed the cranberry sauce. But everyone was smiling and talking, always a good sign. Ben reached over and squeezed my hand.

"This could have been dicey," he said. "But it looks like one big happy family."

I looked at our hands together and felt a tiny burst of happiness. I nodded. Yes. A bit bigger than I had ever imagined, and much more complicated, but *happy* was the operative word here. Everyone was smiling and laughing—even Dominique, who actually looked relaxed as she watched Tyler cuddle on Jessica's lap. Brian had assumed his familiar king-in-his-castle pose, one leg thrown over the other, leaning back, arm draped casually over the back of the chair, even though it wasn't his castle anymore; it was mine. Surprisingly, he got up to help clear the table, and even carried out the dessert dishes. Six pies. And the cannoli. And Vinnie's cookies—I was going to have to eat nothing but salad for the rest of the week.

Dessert was finally over. When people began to migrate from the dining room, Lily suggested taking Carmella out to the backyard so they could start planning a few things. That was fine. I got why Vinnie went out with them. And I could even understand Miranda and David offering to take Tyler out there as well. Tyler's Thanksgiving dinner had consisted of two bites of turkey, a spoonful of stuffing, half a green bean, a piece of pecan pie, and several bites of chocolate chip cookie. He was sugar-loaded.

Tony followed them out, of course. You never knew when a well-paid hit man would come bursting through the dormant forsythia hedge.

But I didn't quite understand why Ben had to go out there with them.

Anthony was helping me load the dishwasher and kept looking out the window to give me a running narrative.

"They're out by the fountain, and Lily is waving her arms. I bet they put the dance floor there.

"Tyler is on the ground, rolling, and Vinnie is taking pictures of the back end of your garage with his phone."

"Carmella is leaning against Ben and taking notes. I do love that pink notebook, but her booties are hideous.

"Tony is walking the perimeter of the property. I bet he's pacing out footage for barbed wire."

Rebecca was carving up what was left of the turkey and putting the meat in neat piles. "Are you really letting them marry here?" she asked.

I lifted my shoulders, then let them drop. "Why not? After all, this has been Lily's home for almost five years. And it will be better than driving out to Bay Ridge."

"I don't know," Julian said. He was packing Rebecca's piles into Ziploc bags. "Bay Ridge is probably quite something in the spring."

Phyllis, carefully portioning out the leftover veggies, made a noise. "I've seen Bay Ridge in the spring. Believe me, it's nothing special. That Carmella person is quite attractive, isn't she?"

"I think she's overdone," Victor said.

"I was thinking ripe," Julian said.

Rebecca raised her eyebrows at Julian. "Ripe? Really? I didn't think you would notice."

"Rebecca, please," Anthony said. "Even I noticed. And believe me, she is *so* not my type."

"Who's not your type?" asked Lauren, coming in with the last of the wineglasses.

"Carmella," Anthony said.

Lauren lowered her voice. "Trev said she sleeps around a lot."

Rebecca grimaced. "Ew. Her *son* said that?"

Lauren's eyes were wide. "I know, right? I mean, gross."

Julian nodded. "Very."

I handed Lauren the platter I was drying off. "Finish this for me, baby. I just want to check out what they're saying about my yard."

I went out without a coat, which I immediately regretted, because it was getting dark and very cold. I trotted over to where they were all huddled.

"So, what did you all decide?" I asked, sounding bright and innocent.

Carmella had opened her notebook. "Can we put the buffet and bar in the garage? We'll cover the walls and ceiling with white fabric —it will look spectacular. There's already electricity in there, and getting running water in will be easy. We'll put the band on the deck to discourage people from going in and out of the house. The Port-A-Potties will be behind the garage."

"Oh?" I said. "Port-A-Potties?"

"Honey, I can get ones that look like bathrooms at Buckingham Palace. We'll have one tent for tables and one for the dance floor. Lots of candles on stands. We'll have a few of the boys park cars, and a few more making sure no strangers wander in." Carmella flipped a few pages. "Would you like new azalea bushes? We can have yours dug up and replaced with blooming ones."

"Oh, Mona, wouldn't that be marvelous?" Lily gushed. "I love azaleas."

"I know that, Aunt Lily," I said, "but I'm kind of attached to the ones I have already. Please. Let's not do any major landscaping if we can help it."

"Of course," Vinnie said. "We so appreciate your allowing us the use of your yard. We'll keep any disturbance to a minimum." In the darkness, I could see he was not looking at me, but rather his daughter.

"Of course." Carmella slid her arm through Ben's. "And Ben had this fab idea about lighting up this fountain. Something that one of his clients did. I really didn't understand it, so would you mind if he took me to check it out?" Her smile gleamed in the night.

What? Was she really asking me if it was okay for her to poach my boyfriend under the pretense of lighting up a fountain?

"Why would I mind?" I shot back. I could feel the spot behind my eyes start to burn. "Ben is a grown man. He can do what he likes."

"Oh, good," she cooed. "Then maybe we can make a whole day of it, Ben. After all, I'll be driving all the way in from Brooklyn, and we're going where? Chester? I've heard it's a charming town. I bet we could do a great lunch while we're there."

I clenched my teeth. Ben was looking in my direction, but I could not read his expression. Where was he with this? Did he want to spend time with this woman?

Lily and Vinnie had wandered off. Tony was out of sight, possibly seeing where the land mines could be buried. Miranda and David were leading a sniffling Tyler back inside. It was just Ben, Carmella, and me, standing in the dark.

I fought to keep my voice even. "There are also some fun shops right on Main Street." Did she really think I would pull the jealous and insecure act? Like I was in any way threatened by her?

"Excellent. Ben, I'll be sure to give you a call." And she slunk away.

"If she tries to make a pass," Ben said, "I'll make sure she calls you first. For permission."

He turned and walked back to the house.

Damn. It was then that I thought that I might have made a mistake. Maybe I needed to grab Ben and make it clear to him that although I had no right at all to tell him what he could and could not do, I really didn't *want* him hanging around with Carmella any more than absolutely necessary.

I counted to twenty before I followed him into the house. No reason to appear needy. As I entered, there was some shouting. Not happy post holiday shouting. I ran into the foyer.

The front door was open, revealing a skinny, long-haired young man in a red Domino's shirt who had obviously just delivered a pizza, and who was wearing an expression of complete terror, eyes bulging, mouth hanging open in a silent scream. Ethan was standing in the foyer, holding a pizza box, yelling, "Stop, stop," his own face a mixture of confusion and utter disbelief. Lauren was also shouting at Tony, who had pulled out a small firearm and assumed the position, legs spread apart, arms straight in front of him, both hands holding the gun that was pointing directly at the pizza delivery guy.

Ben walked slowly up to Tony. "It's pizza," he explained quietly.

Tony lowered his gun, looking embarrassed. "Sorry, but he was just standing here, alone, with the door open. I didn't know."

"I went to get some money," Lauren explained. "And left him with Ethan."

"You were getting a pizza?" I asked. "You just finished Thanksgiving dinner."

Ethan blushed. "We wanted it later," he mumbled. "When we were playing *Call of Duty*."

I gawked at Ben, who shrugged. "Video game," he explained.

Vinnie came up, put his arm around the pizza guy, and leaned in to speak softly into his ear. No one heard what he said. Then Vinnie reached into his pocket, turned his back to us all, and stuffed what I can only imagine was a wad of cash into Pizza Guy's hand. Pizza Guy backed out, shutting the door behind him.

Vinnie turned to Tony with a broad smile. "No harm done," he said smoothly. He glanced around. "Tony was just looking out for me. He's very protective around strangers. After all, that kid could have been anybody."

Right. Like a deadly ninja wearing a Domino's pizza shirt.

Carmella was shaking her head. "So excitable! Listen, everybody, it's no big deal!"

Maybe not in her world.

Ethan and Lauren went back into the den with the pizza. Lily, Vinnie, and Carmella went into the living room. Ben and I stood alone in the foyer.

Fred came lumbering in from somewhere, barking hysterically.

I looked at Ben. His mouth was in a tight line from trying to keep a straight face. His eyes were blazing.

"Whenever I'm with you," he said, his voice shaking with laughter, "the most interesting things happen."

"It's not like I plan them," I told him.

He nodded a few times. "I know. That's the best part," he said.

And then we walked back into the living room lights, and the sound of Carmella's laughter.

CHAPTER SEVEN

WHEN CARMELLA TOLD US THE time and place to meet her for wedding-dress shopping, I had a few concerns. First, it involved driving into Brooklyn. I didn't want to do that, but taking public transportation was out of the question because, as anyone who's tried to take a bus or subway from the easily accessible Port Authority building in Manhattan will tell you—you can't get there from here. At least, not without a local Sherpa to guide you on the way.

So we drove. Miranda, Aunt Lily, and I set off bright and early Saturday morning armed with a GPS, a MapQuest printout, and an old-fashioned street map.

My other worry was the shop itself. It was called Dressed to Kill. Not only did the name throw me off just a little, but also I imagined a thick, battered door with a peephole, where you had to know the secret knock and password to enter. Then you'd follow a one-eyed mute (with a limp) to the showroom, where all the dresses would have had the labels removed.

I was surprised—and relieved—to find Dressed to Kill was a simple storefront in a crowded strip mall. Sadly, under the name of the shop was the tag line "Formal Fashion to Knock 'Em Dead."

Lily got out of the car, took a long look, then shook her head. "Subtle."

Miranda frowned. "What?" She was still rather clueless about Vincent and the other DeMatrianos, and I was very grateful.

We entered the shop, and I must say it was impressive. There were a dozen mannequins standing around, all beautifully dressed in bridal and ball gowns, including a stunning cocktail dress in royal purple that I immediately wanted for myself.

Carmella came out of the back all smiles. Hug-hug, kiss-kiss. A few seconds later, a tall woman in a plain black dress appeared, hands held prayer-like to her lips.

"Ladies," Carmella said, "this is Coco Zipperelli."

Coco was a striking woman—big, dark eyes, high cheekbones. And her jet-black hair was swept up off her face in a pompadour. Not an Elvis Presley look. Think Lyle Lovett, 1986.

"Welcome," she murmured. "Any client of Carmella's gets my personal attention. Now, who are the brides?"

Miranda and Lily both beamed. Coco clapped her hands together. "Perfect. Now tell me what you think you want; then I'll tell you what you really want."

Aunt Lily wanted tea length, with a tulle skirt, in the color of spring. Maybe that new orchid color? I had to admit it made sense. Since her fashion metamorphosis, I could see her in something vibrant and playful.

Coco raised her eyebrows. "Radiant Orchid? Yes, that would work well for you. It's a great color for your skin tone." She scurried over and pulled out a beautiful dress, not quite the style Lily wanted, but the color was amazing. There was a tall brass coatrack in the middle of the room, and she hung the dress on it. "Or maybe a bit deeper? A bit more hyacinth? Or how about Vivid Violet?" She found two more dresses and hung them up as well.

Lily frowned. "What's the difference, exactly?"

A small cloud passed over Coco's face. "Well, this is the precise color of grape juice in a clear glass, with the sunlight reflecting off the ice cubes. This is a bit pinker, almost as though some red wine —a merlot, actually—was mixed in with the grape juice. And this last dress here is about fifty-fifty wine and juice. Subtle, I admit, but very important."

Lily took a deep breath and glanced over at Carmella, who was hanging on Coco's every word.

"Anything in this general grape family," Lily said at last. "At my age I have no patience for nuance."

I glanced at Miranda, who was trying very hard to keep a

straight face. Thank God, she only wanted white.

Coco looked disappointed, but squared her shoulders as she turned to Miranda, who whipped out her cell phone and proceeded to show Coco a complete slide show. Coco was looking over Miranda's shoulder, shaking her head at some photos, nodding at others. Finally, after a few minutes of intense whispering and pointing, Coco nodded. "Fine. I can totally understand your style. Now, do you want white-white, like a flat, snow white? Or maybe something with a bit of shine, like a frosted ice cube? Of course, we could always go with the lovely white of antique lace."

Miranda cleared her throat. "I'll leave that to you."

Smart girl.

Finally Coco turned to me. "And you, Mona. I saw you eyeing that deep lilac."

"For what?" I asked.

"Mother of the bride? Unless, of course, you want a more traditional taupe or gray."

I glanced at Carmella. She was wearing wine-colored skinny jeans, black heels, a clingy knit tunic in black and wine, and a camel hair swing coat.

I turned to Coco. "Size ten."

Coco nodded, grabbed all the dresses, then hurried toward the back of the shop. "Lottie," she barked as she turned a corner.

We sat in comfortable wing chairs, listening to chamber music, and waited. A squat woman, also in black, hurried out, locked the door, then turned the sign from Open to Closed. Then she lowered the shades.

Lily leaned over and whispered, "Should we be worried?"

"Only if Lottie pulls out a machine gun," I whispered back.

Lily smirked.

Carmella smiled at the woman. "Thanks, Lottie. Coffee?"

"Sure. Ennybuddy else want some?" Lottie, to my complete delight, had the voice of a merchant marine. If only she had a half-lit cigarette hanging from her lower lip…

Miranda asked for bottled water, Lily for herbal tea. I declined and watched Lottie shuffle away.

Carmella had whipped out her notebook. "Lily, you first. I

confirmed Bishop Micheline, and catering is set. Tents are ordered. All the rental pieces are confirmed: chairs, tables, and linens. Daddy picked a band, and he's taking care of security."

Of course he was.

"Randi," Carmella continued, "I found three spots, all in Bergen County. If you can make time to see them tomorrow, we can get a contract. All three places were, or still are, private homes."

Wait—first of all, she was calling my daughter *Randi?* And a private home? *Still* a private home? Was she muscling innocent people out of their houses?

I cleared my throat. "Private homes?"

Carmella nodded. "WestWind House is the best. All the ground-floor rooms are public and beautiful, and they let you use the kitchen. The other two are your basic conversions, but they aren't quite up to WestWind as far as style goes." Carmella smiled and patted Miranda's knee. "And I know how much style means to you, Randi."

I knew the WestWind House, high on a hill overlooking the best part of the New York City skyline. I never realized it had public rooms.

She went back to her notebook. "The caterer your mom suggested is good for your date, and so is the deejay. As you know, David and his family have belonged to the same church forever, and the pastor there is thrilled to marry you both. Now, the big question—do you want a rabbi as well?"

Miranda frowned. "What for?"

"The ceremony," I said. "After all, even though we aren't as religious as David and his family, you may want to bring some Jewish tradition into your marriage ceremony."

Miranda blinked. "Hello? Have you *met* me?"

Carmella made a notation. "Forget the rabbi."

Lottie reappeared pushing a sleek bar cart in front of her. She parked it in front of us, then retreated.

Carmella served as hostess, and we waited some more. "Thanks again for a terrific Thanksgiving," Carmella said. "Trev had a blast with your girls."

I forced a smile. "The pleasure was all mine. Welcome to the family."

Lily sipped her tea. "I imagine Christmas will be a little more complicated," she said. "Vincent said something about Aruba."

"Yes," Carmella said. "We spend Christmas week at Dad's villa down there. He flies in the whole family from wherever, and we have a whole week to catch up. The weather is perfect, and we have our own private beach."

"Sounds lovely," I said, inwardly breathing a sigh of relief.

"It sure does," Miranda said, a little wistfully.

"It is. Listen, Randi, why don't I ask Dad about letting you and David use the place for your honeymoon? It's always staffed, but empty most of the time. I'm sure he wouldn't mind. You'd have the whole place to yourself."

I sat up. "I was going to give the kids a trip to Paris for their honeymoon."

Miranda jerked her head around. "You were?"

My shoulders slumped. "As a surprise, yes."

I could see my daughter was torn. Paris had always been on her to-do list. But a week alone in a seaside villa with hot and cold running staff and a private beach?

Carmella waved a hand. "No hurry to decide. Talk to David. Ah, she's back."

Coco turned the corner, pulling a clothing rack behind her. Lottie appeared in the rear, pushing for all she was worth. A long sheet covered the rack.

"Here we are," Coco announced, and with a magician's flourish, pulled the sheet away.

I had been expecting a row of white, but that wasn't what I saw. My purple—excuse me, deep lilac—dress was in front, followed by bright and subtle colors, fading into ivory and finally white.

She held out the purple dress. "We'll start with you, Mona." She pulled the first three dresses off the cart. "Take these to the dressing room, and try them on. The brides and I need to discuss. Let Lottie help you." I followed Lottie. The dressing room was about the size of my bedroom at home, with a few comfortable chairs, plenty of empty hangers, and a three-way mirror. I didn't need much help getting undressed—after all, I was in black pants, a gray sweater, and ballet flats. She did help me with the purple dress. Then she pulled a pair of black heels that almost fit out of a dresser, and combed my hair up in a messy but quite sexy bun that looked perfect for a wedding.

When I walked out, everyone stopped talking. Carmella's eyebrows shot up.

"Wow, Mom, you look amazing."

The mirror in the showroom was bigger, and the light was better, and Miranda was right; the dress fit like a glove. It pushed my boobs back up to where they used to sit before gravity became my enemy and outlined my butt just right. The heels made me appear taller, and the updo gave the illusion of a long and graceful neck. I tried not to look too smug.

Coco sighed happily. "That's made for you. Now, how about something for Lily's day? You're matron of honor, right?" She looked at me critically. "Forget any of the colors. You won't be able to compete with Lily. But you might be able to get away with ivory. Try on the one that looks like white satin seen through a glass of very expensive champagne."

I went back into the dressing room. "White filtered through champagne?"

Lottie was grinning broadly, showing coffee-stained teeth. "Coco is a bit of a nutcase when it comes to color."

"So I noticed."

"It makes me crazy, but she knows what works. You'd be surprised how the slightest variation in white can change the way a woman looks," she said, unzipping the purple dress.

"Really?"

"Her real name is Henrietta," Lottie went on. "Can you imagine? Who names their kid Henrietta?"

This from a woman named Lottie.

"She and Carmella go way back. They went to high school together or something. Carmella is kind of a tramp."

"Ah..."

"So is Coco. They go trolling for men together. You'd be surprised how many men go for a woman with a pimp's haircut."

"This is all very interesting, but how do you know I'm not a good friend of Carmella's?" I asked, by way of conversation.

"She don't got no friends. She got clients and men she sleeps with." Lottie slipped the ivory dress over my head, careful of the updo. She handed me ivory slingbacks.

I went out again, twirling like Loretta Young in front of the mirror. The dress looked lovely, loose and draped on the top, hugging my hips, and floating down to my knees.

"Perfect," Lily declared. "Simple, classic. We'll need to get you some killer shoes."

"Aunt Lily, aren't you the one who's supposed to be in ivory?"

"Not ivory," Coco corrected gently.

"Right. Filtered champagne?"

Coco sighed.

Lily smiled. "No, Mona. I'm going to be in something way more spectacular. Don't worry. No one is going to confuse you for the bride."

Coco was smiling. "I think you're done. You can walk out right now with both of those—they're a great fit. We could alter this one, if you like—a bit tighter around the hips, maybe. Here, let me —"

"No," I interrupted. "The hips are fine. I don't think anything has to be altered."

Coco shrugged. "Whatever you say. Now we can work on our two brides. Unless, of course, you're in the market for a wedding dress as well? I have a great discount if you buy three."

I shook my head. How many people walked in here and bought three wedding dresses? "No, thanks, Coco. When it's my time, I'll probably just run off and elope." I turned away from the mirror and looked Carmella straight in the eye.

I went back with Lottie, who eased me out of the dress and handed me my clothes.

"You *could* get married in either of these dresses," she said. "If getting married was something you were thinking about doing. Just saying."

Coco was calling her name. Lottie sighed and trotted back out. I finished getting dressed alone.

The purple dress shimmered. The ivory dress glowed.

Lottie was right.

I could be married in either of those two dresses.

Patricia Carmichael had moved from her rather grand twelve-room Victorian to an equally grand eight-room town house. Actually, two four-room town houses that she combined, because she wanted two guest rooms and a room for Letitia, her maid, who had been her live-in for almost fifteen years. She also wanted extra parking spaces, so she could keep both her cars and still have designated spots for her guests. It had taken almost a year for the renovations. Ben had done the kitchen and all four bathrooms, so I had seen pics of the project while it was still in progress. Her place was magazine-worthy. Of course.

I didn't have to drive over—she was now right in the center of town, so I could walk there with Fred whenever I wanted. She called me when she got home from Boca, and Fred and I headed over early Tuesday morning, armed with corn muffins and a cell phone full of photos.

"I love your dresses," Patricia said, staring into the phone and flipping through all the pictures. "The purple is perfect for you, and it fits like a dream. You don't even have to fool with the hem. And the ivory? Very classy."

"I know. I love them both. And look at Miranda." My daughter had settled on a very traditional dress—no bias-cut or creative neckline. Simple white satin, off the shoulder, the train embroidered and embellished with seed pearls.

"Oh, Mona. She's stunning."

"I know. When she came out in it, we all got choked up. She needs a few alterations, but she's buying off the rack, so it will be ready on time. Carmella has it all under control."

Patricia was swiping my camera roll. "What kind of place sells stuff this beautiful off the rack?"

"Carmella's kind of place. She takes all her brides there."

Patricia was still looking at my phone, smiling until she came to my Thanksgiving Day pictures. "Is that Carmella?" she asked.

I nodded. "Yep."

She gave me a very long, measured look. "Mona, should we be

worried about Ben?"

My throat suddenly filled, and I felt tears. "I don't know," I blurted. Patricia knew all about Ben's proposal, of course, as well as our decision to take a break. "I thought the whole *get a little distance* idea was fine, but he's moving away a whole lot faster than I am."

"Of course he is. You wounded him, Mona. He wanted you to come rushing into his arms and say, 'Yes, let's get married,' and you didn't. Then you pooh-poohed his idea of love at first sight. Now, I'm with you on that one, but I can see his point. Everything he wanted for the two of you, everything he believed to be true, has been thrown back in his face. By you."

I swallowed hard. "You're right."

"Yes, of course I'm right," she said impatiently. "My being right was never an issue. What are you going to do about this?"

"I don't know." I related my feeble attempt to seduce him via designer underwear, and being the true friend that she was, she did not laugh or even roll her eyes.

She had made tea, and we were sitting in her beautifully decorated living room, sipping from fragile Lenox teacups. She looked at me intently. "Why don't you want to marry Ben?"

I looked into my tea. "It's not that I don't want to marry Ben. I just don't think I want to get married. To anyone. Ben and I had a terrific relationship before I went to LA—we had our own lives; we had our lives together; I was completely happy. So was he. I like my life just the way it is, Patricia. It's so much better now than when I was married. Being single suits me. I feel freer and more in control. I have a great career, great friends, and my daughters are successfully making their own way. Except for Miranda, who may be making a huge mistake by marrying a total stranger, even if he is the best total stranger she'll probably ever meet."

"She and David are not strangers, Mona. They're two young people who fell in love. What else do they need to know about each other?"

"Why can't they just shack up, like all the other twenty-somethings in the world?"

"Because Ben believes in true love, Mona. And David is his

father's son." She looked at me shrewdly over the rim of her teacup. "You and Brian did not have the only kind of marriage that's possible, you know. There are other options. I should know; I'm still trying them out."

"Yes, you are. Why is that?"

She smiled. "Because I believe in true love, too. And I'm willing to divorce as many men as it takes to find it."

"What do I do about Ben?"

"He knows you love him. Make sure he doesn't forget. And go easy on yourself. You have nothing to prove. We all know you don't need a man. But spending the rest of your life with Ben is not such a bad thing." She leaned forward. "He will never diminish you. He will only add to your happiness."

"I know. So what's the plan?"

She settled back against the couch and raised her eyebrows. "I have no clue. You're the expert in romance. I'm sure you can figure something out."

She was right. But the first thing I had to figure was what I really wanted.

Anthony and I had work to do. Lucky for me, he had no outside art commissions pending. Anthony was a very successful painter of what he liked to call "interior landscapes," usually involving whole walls painted over in the style of the great muralists. He had graduated with a degree in fine art, and it was his passion. But he loved my romance books, and me, and was my most faithful fan as well as employee.

He had already looked the list that Sylvia had sent him, ten titles in all. It had taken her more than a year to get the rights back, and I really appreciated her hard work for no commission. He arranged them in somewhat chronological order, and now all we needed to do was update the manuscripts, get them formatted, have new covers designed, and boom—the money would come rolling in. That was what Anthony told me, but I had a feeling there was more to it than that.

Sylvia had gone forth like Don Quixote, trying to sell my newest manuscripts, two books about women over forty who were not knitting, quilting, or solving murders on a senior cruise ship. She said she was surprised by the interest—could it be that editors were finally getting the message that women didn't stop reading at thirty-nine?

"There's a buzz," she said.

"That's good. How's the backlist coming?"

"I'm still working on it. I should have a few more titles for you by the spring. What are you working on now?"

"My daughter's wedding, Lily's wedding, Christmas, finding a cover designer for the self-pubbed stuff, and a possible nervous breakdown."

"You do know I meant what are you *writing*?" Sylvia asked patiently.

I sighed. "Yes, of course I know that's what you meant, but did you really want me to answer *nothing*?"

"You're supposed to be working, Mona. The LA vacation is over."

"It wasn't exactly a vacation, Sylvia. After all, I did manage to write two manuscripts while I was out there. I have ideas, but it's really hard to focus right now. I'll have something started by the new year, I promise."

I hung up the phone and sank back onto the couch.

"Liar," Anthony called from the other side of the room.

We were in my office over the garage and had been since early that morning. We'd spent most of the time on a conference call with the tech guys who ran my website. Did I want an online store, where I could sell my books directly? Separate pages for the older backlist titles? Did I want to link Maura Van Whalen with Mona Quincy? By now all my readers pretty much knew we were the same person. Anthony had lots of ideas, most of which involved redoing my entire site. I was hoping for more of a cut-and-paste approach, adding in the new stuff with as few billable hours as possible.

When Sylvia called, we were just finishing a very late lunch, and I was ready for a nap. "I was not lying," I said. "I do have lots of ideas."

"About centerpieces and favors and white daisies, which I think are adorable and perfect for Randi."

I glared at him. "Her name is Miranda."

"Not any more, baby cakes. Show me her dress again."

I threw him my phone. He'd been rather hurt that he hadn't been invited along to go wedding-dress shopping, until I told him it involved going through Staten Island.

"You look pretty hot in that purple, you know. Ben won't be able to resist you."

"Wanna bet? Patricia says I need to remind him how much I love him, but how am I supposed to do that if I never get to see him?"

"A gesture."

I frowned. "Gesture?"

"Yes. Name a forest in Bulgaria after him or something."

I sat up. "Can I do that?"

He immediately went to the laptop. "Let's find out."

The phone rang again, and it was Miranda. "Mom, guess what? David just closed on a great little place, and I'm moving in with him this weekend. My last final is Thursday, so the timing is perfect. You should see it, Mom. Adorable. It's a real mess right now, a fixer-upper for sure, but I know it can be perfect."

"Oh? You two found a place already? Tell me."

"Well, it's three bedrooms, bath and a half, and even has a tiny backyard. It's a row house, so it's pretty old, but it's got these great moldings and some wonderful original details."

That's love for you. She was obviously parroting David. She wouldn't know a great molding if it fell out of a Victoria's Secret bag. "Oh, Miranda." She was moving in? Already? Didn't she just meet this boy? "Do you have pictures?"

"Of course."

"Send them. Do you need help moving?"

"No, thanks, we've got that covered. Oh, and I got a job."

"*What!* Oh, thank God. Where?"

"Right in Boston. IT work at a local bank. Not much money to start, but it's close, and I'll get benefits."

Listen to her—talking benefits! Just like a grown-up!

"Mom—I gotta go. I'll send you the pics, okay?"

I hung up. They'd found a house. That would bring them even closer together.

Anthony sat next to me. "How's my girl?"

"Got a job. With benefits!"

"See, I knew she'd get something right away. She's very smart, you know." I did know, but even if Miranda were stupider than dirt, Anthony would never say otherwise.

"She's moving. David bought a row house, a fixer-upper with great moldings and some wonderful original details."

"Does she even know what moldings are?" See, it wasn't just me.

"Probably not. She's sending me pictures." I closed my eyes. "We need a nap. Miranda living in a fixer-upper is too much for me to get my head around. She's killing me."

"I'm sure she is, but I need to see where she's going to be living." I heard my phone make text-receiving noises. "Can I look?"

"Of course," I said.

I felt myself relaxing.

"Oh, Mona. Look."

I opened my eyes. There were eight pictures in all, two of what I assumed was the living room, a few of the bedrooms, a narrow staircase, and a furnace that looked like it was leaning into a dirt wall.

The main living area was tiny, with peeling paint and dark, ugly wood floors. Pale sunlight filtered through grimy windows. The kitchen ran the length of a short wall, and the stove looked caked with filth, the cabinets cracked and hanging crooked above ancient Formica counters. There was a shot of what may have been a backyard, or it may have been a Superfund site—piles of garbage, broken furniture, and large rusty barrels leaking plutonium. The bedrooms were carpeted in what looked to be avocado-green shag, badly stained. No bathroom pictures. I don't think my heart could have taken it.

"This is no fixer-upper," Anthony said. "It's more like a teardown-and-start-over."

I sat up, not sleepy anymore, and called Miranda back. "Honey, when are you moving into this place?"

"Next weekend. But I told you, I don't need help moving."

"Yes, but…Miranda, this place looks awful. Has it at least been cleaned out and painted?"

"Mom, I told you it was a little rough. That's how David could afford it in the first place. We're getting some some people together to help us paint and clean up weekend after next. Honest, Mom, it will look great."

I remained unconvinced. "Are there things in that basement?"

Miranda laughed. "Yes, but David says he's killed them all. I have to go, okay? Don't worry. We'll be fine."

I hung up and stared at Anthony. "She says people are coming to help them paint and clean."

"Then you should go up there too. Help them. That can be your grand gesture."

"What are you talking about?"

Anthony got that look in his eye, the one he always got when he had a great idea that required me to do something I wouldn't be happy doing. "Go and help Miranda and David paint their new home. That will show Ben that even though you are philosophically opposed to their marriage, you are in total support of their love and commitment to each other."

"Anthony, I haven't painted so much as a fingernail in years."

"Come on, Mona, how hard can it be? People do it all the time on HGTV."

Now, I am not a princess. I spent many years cleaning and hauling garbage and clearing out piles of crap. But that was before I could afford to pay other people to do those things for me. Which would make my contribution to the cause that much more significant.

"That might be a good idea, Anthony."

"Of course it is. And when David tells his father how hard you worked and how selfless you were, Ben will know that you did it for him as much as for the kids."

"Will he?"

"Of course. I'm telling you, Mona, it will be a piece of cake."

Famous last words.

CHAPTER EIGHT

I HAD MADE THE TRIP up to Boston before, of course. I had tried several different routes, and left New Jersey at different times of the day, all in desperate attempts to avoid the deadly traffic in and around Boston proper. Route 95 or Route 93, seven in the morning or three in the afternoon—there was always a stretch where traffic stopped dead for at least a half an hour. At least I got to read for a while, listen to the radio, do a little online bill paying. I never made the trip without my Kindle being fully charged, a few water bottles, and a bag of trail mix.

The GPS got me to their little row house with no trouble, but sadly, could not find me a parking space. I finally found one that seemed less than a ten-minute walk away, so I grabbed it, hauled my overnighter out of the trunk, then walked briskly to my daughter's new home. It was in the middle of a long block of identical houses—six steps up to the stoop, two narrow windows beside the front door, two-storied with a tin roof. The block was well lit, and I didn't see any drunks huddled in the gutter. The cars parked on the street were all fairly new, and none of them were minus the tires and up on cinder blocks. All good signs.

Miranda hugged me long and hard, and welcomed me to her home. She was obviously proud and happy, as she was bouncing like a new puppy in her eagerness to show me around. Which took less than six minutes. This house was without a doubt the smallest three-bedroom, bath-and-a-half property in all of New England. And possibly the mid-Atlantic states as well.

The first floor tour was not bad, because David had taken a few days off the week before they'd moved in and gone through the place like Sherman through Georgia. The floors had been sanded and stained, and the windows had been cleaned to let in the December sunlight. Everything in the kitchen had been scrubbed, and the refrigerator looked, if not new, at least clean. The walls were still awful, but they had at least been scraped, so there was no physically peeling paint anywhere. The back door led to what had probably been a covered porch. Now there was a neat new powder room and a washer and dryer in the space. The yard, however, looked even worse than in the picture. I immediately decided to focus all my efforts on the interior.

On the way back through the house, I saw the door to the basement. "We don't have to go down there, do we?" I asked.

Miranda shook her head. "I never do."

The second floor had two fair-size bedrooms front and back, with a bathroom and a tiny bedroom sandwiched in between. I had been right about the carpet—fresh from the seventies, and smelling of cat pee.

The bathroom, fortunately, was not old and gross. It was clean and had a quaint retro feel. The tiny bedroom did not have a window.

"So I take it this will be your closet?" I asked.

She beamed. "Yes! David said it might just be big enough!"

"Does this mean you'll finally move all of your clothes out of my house?"

She rolled her eyes. "Maybe the summer ones."

"No, Miranda. All of them. If you're going to be a married woman with a home of your own, you can't store six months' worth of your wardrobe with me."

She tilted her head. "So, if I were just a woman living in sin, I could?"

"Yes?"

"Good try, Mom. We're still getting married."

"But if you did want to just live together, you know I'd be completely okay with that, right?"

"Mom. We've got the church. We've got the reception hall. I bought a dress. *You* bought a dress. It's happening."

I sighed. "I know."

The front bedroom was the designated guest room and office combo. It had a futon, a floor lamp, and a desk with a printer and laptop. A file cabinet served as an end table, and there was a small dresser in the closet.

"The first thing I'm going to do," I told Miranda, "is tear up all this wall-to-wall."

"Yes, that's on our list. David says there are very nice hardwood floors underneath. Did I tell you how much I appreciate your coming up here? Really. Thank you so much."

She hugged me again. I felt tears start. Or maybe it was the scent of cat urine.

Whatever.

I ignored the awful carpet, unpacked in five minutes, then went downstairs.

As I came to the foot of the stairs, I stopped and stared in disbelief. My oldest daughter was chopping onions and scooping them into a Dutch oven like this was something she'd actually done before.

"You're cooking?" I tried to keep the shock out of my voice.

"Very funny, Mom."

"Miranda, honey, you could barely make grilled cheese at home."

"That was a choice. Just like I chose to try to do better once I moved in with David."

"That was only eight days ago."

"I usually spend the morning watching YouTube videos on how to cook stuff. Then I go to the store, buy what I need, and make it. I figure if I can learn to cook a dozen different things, I'll be good for a year or two."

I gave her a kiss on the cheek. "You are one smart little girl. I'm particularly impressed, because this kitchen looks about fifty years old."

She made a face. "Yeah, it's pretty bad. But Ben is putting in a new kitchen for us as a wedding present."

"Oh? How nice. So he's been up here already?"

She nodded. "He was with David when he bought it. Ben knows

a lot about houses, and David wanted his opinion." She glanced at me. "How are you two getting along these days?"

"Fine. Great. We're both really busy, of course. Taking a bit of a break has been a good idea. Really."

"That's good. David was kinda worried that you two were...I don't know, not speaking or something. I told him you guys were fine. So you'll be okay with sharing the futon?"

I stared at her. "Sharing what futon?"

"Upstairs."

"Why would I need to share?"

She stopped stirring the onions. "Because he's coming. Ben. To help paint and stuff. I told you we were calling in all the reserves."

"But I thought you meant your college friends," I sputtered.

"Well, yes, but also you and Ben." She frowned. "Mom? Is that a problem? You just said you two were fine."

"We are. I'm just, well, surprised, that's all. So he'll be here tomorrow?"

"No, he's coming tonight. He's between jobs, and he's staying until Tuesday or Wednesday to do the kitchen."

"How good of him. I don't suppose you have anything to drink?"

"Yes, of course. Sorry. There's wine in the fridge."

No vodka? Heavy sigh...

Her refrigerator contained more food than I imagined—salad stuff, bread, bowls of things, milk, orange juice—and three bottles of wine. I pulled out a promising-looking red.

"Corkscrew?"

"Here. And the glasses are up there. Are you sure this is okay?"

I forced a smile. "You want a glass? What are you cooking, anyway?"

She frowned. "Chicken something? With onions and peppers... I'm serving it with polenta."

I took a big gulp of wine. "Really? Wow, I guess you really can cook."

She shook her head. "No, but I really can follow directions."

I spent another forty-five seconds basking in the warmth of this priceless mother-daughter moment, then excused myself, tried not to run upstairs, and threw open the tiny closet I had filled just minutes before.

Ben was coming for the weekend. And I had packed my grubbiest, most shapeless clothing. Of course I did—I was planning on painting, cleaning, and emptying out a dirty, disgusting backyard. I took another gulp of wine. For sleeping, I had my "What, me Query?" T-shirt from the Passive Voice, and gray leggings with the knees bleached out. I didn't pack any makeup, well-fitting jeans, or cute shoes. Would it look odd if I ran out to the nearest mall?

My wineglass was empty.

Grand gesture, I kept thinking. *Remember the grand gesture. And Ben will now be able to witness it in person.*

I needed more wine. I went back downstairs.

David, when he came home from work, gave me another tour of the house, this one with all pending renovations explained, and I must say the boy had vision. He may have graduated with a degree in finance from Yale, but he was his father's son, and knew his way around a hammer and wrench. He showed me the work done so far—refinishing the floors, rehanging all the doors, stripping off wallpaper in Miranda's closet, as well as replacing the vanity and toilet in the powder room, which explained why it was the best looking room in the house. Then he showed me all he was planning to do—he had paint chips, stains for the floor, tile for the upstairs bath, and pavers for the backyard. The kid had lots of plans, and Miranda not only had helped him make them, she had even lent a hand in practical ways.

"I scraped off the peel-and-stick tile that was in the laundry room, and David did the sanding. I'm also good at scraping paint. But I hate wearing those stupid masks."

Of course she did. What was a little poisoning from lead paint compared to looking silly in a mask? But I had to hand it to her—her nails hadn't seen polish or topcoat in a while, and she had blisters on her palms.

Miranda had always been a very organized person—anyone with as many clothes as she had needed to be, if for no other reason than to make sure an outfit wasn't repeated in the same month. She had put together a nice little spreadsheet in her iPad, a schedule of work, and the estimated costs. She had penciled me in for taking up the carpet on the second floor, removing all the furring strips, and pulling out any stray nails or staples. That was Friday. Saturday was painting the downstairs, because David would be sanding the newly revealed floors upstairs. Sunday morning was simple, helping move all the furniture downstairs so the floors could be stained and finished on Monday. I had planned on leaving Sunday afternoon. But now, knowing that Ben would be there all weekend as well, should I stay the extra day? You know, just to help out? Or should I suddenly receive an emergency call from my agent and run like hell back to New Jersey immediately?

I looked closer at her spreadsheet. Ben was taking apart the kitchen on Friday. With Miranda. Saturday he was painting the downstairs with Miranda and me. Cabinets would arrive Monday morning, and he and Miranda would be installing them, with David taking Monday off from work to help.

Their other friends, including a few names I recognized from Miranda's time at Boston U, would be spending the entire weekend emptying out the backyard into a Dumpster that was due to arrive Friday morning.

"Where are you putting a Dumpster?" I asked. We were sitting at their dining room table after dinner, another bottle of wine half empty.

"We'll have to move our cars," David explained. "We have two spaces at the end of our lot, on the alley, to park. The Dumpster will go there. Not ideal, but good enough."

I liked David. I always had. He was a very relaxed and confident young man, and I always thought he'd make a great husband. And I'm sure he was worthy of my Miranda. I just wished they'd known each other three years instead of just three months.

There was a knock on the door, and I immediately felt butterflies. It had to be Ben. I had not seen him since Thanksgiving, more than two weeks ago, although we had texted and spoken on the phone a few times.

David opened the door and hugged his father. Ben looked down at the floors.

"Nice job, David. You went with the dark stain? Good choice. Upstairs too?"

David nodded as he took Ben's coat and overnight bag. "Yes, we're doing that this weekend."

"Oh? Has the carpeting been pulled up?"

I pasted on a bright smile. "That's my job. Hello, Ben."

He looked past David. His face did not change, except for a slight twitch around the mouth. As always, the sight of him hit me in all those private places, resulting in the unlikely combination of heat and shivers at the same time. I immediately reeled that in. True, I might be here partially to score points, but this was my daughter's first home, and now that I'd seen it, I realized she really needed my help. I was not going to let anything get in the way of that, even my feelings for Ben.

"Mona, I didn't expect to see you here."

"Yes, well, when I saw the pictures and Miranda said they needed help, I couldn't just sit around and do nothing. So here I am. Ready and willing."

Ben sat down across from me. He was smiling, his voice even. "To do what?"

"Oh, you know—pull up furring strips, paint...whatever."

Ben chuckled. "Do you even know what furring strips are?"

Miranda had gotten him a glass and was pouring wine. "I do! David explained it all to me. They're the things that the carpet is attached to. You'll probably need a crowbar, Mom."

"Crowbar?" I knew what that was, of course. I just never knew what it was used for.

David sat down with us. "Yes, and then just use pliers to pull up the stray nails and staples," he explained patiently.

"From the floor?" I asked. I was trying to imagine what the whole process looked like without giving away the fact that I had no idea what David was talking about.

Ben was practically laughing now. I couldn't read how he felt about my being there other than his obvious amusement at the idea of me on my hands and knees, pliers in hand. "Yep. Did you bring something to cushion your knees? Being down on the floor all day is murder on your joints."

"No, but I'm sure I'll be fine."

"Ben, did you eat? I can heat something up," Miranda asked.

Ben waved a hand. "I grabbed something on the road. I'm good, thanks." He shifted his gaze back to me. "And painting, too?"

I had calmed the butterflies just enough to relax a bit, but now I was getting a little annoyed. "You know, Ben, I couldn't always just pick up a phone and call someone to do work around the house. I've painted."

He held up both hands in quick surrender. "I'm sure you have. I apologize. I just never realized how handy you were. It's nice to know you can still surprise me, Mona."

I met his eyes. "I'm full of surprises."

There was a brief silence.

"So, Dad, you and Mona are sharing the futon," David said, sensing the tension in the air. "That's okay, right?"

Ben nodded slowly. "Of course it is."

His gaze was making me a little short of breath. He narrowed his eyes just enough for the lines around them to crinkle a little and tilted his head. "Right, Mona?"

I gulped. "Of course. I told Miranda, no problem at all."

I saw David and Miranda looking at each other. David raised his eyebrow and moved his head and shoulders in a complicated motion, the universal gesture for *WTF?* Miranda responded with a gesture of her own—*No clue.*

Ben reached over and slapped David on the shoulder. "Listen, guys, Mona and I are in a complicated place right now. But we are adults, and we love each other. More important, we love both of you. Very much. We can work out our own stuff. We'll be fine."

Miranda looked at me with wide eyes. "Are you sure?"

I nodded. "Yes, baby."

She took a deep breath, then smiled brightly. "Well, then, I know it's early, but I think David and I will go on up and maybe watch some TV in bed. See you both in the morning."

She and David left. I stared into my wineglass. Ben reached over with his foot and nudged my leg. I looked up.

"Do you want me to stay in a hotel room?"

"Are you kidding? Have you *been* up there? It smells like a litter box. If anyone's staying in a hotel, it's going to be me."

He threw back his head and laughed. "Yes, I suppose that makes sense. It is a little rough up there right now." He leaned back, his arm stretched out over the top of the chair. "That futon is pretty tight. I'm not too sure I'd be able to resist you."

I was staring down at my hands. "Why would you need to?" I asked, very proud that my voice remained steady and did not tremble or hit one of the higher registers.

"Well, Mona..." He was frowning.

"Listen," I said, "sex between us was always great, and it was never something that we used for a reward or a bribe or a Band-Aid because something was wrong. It was always about the fact that we loved each other. And we still do. Do I want you now because I'm also lonely and confused, and I need to feel safe? Yes. But I also still love you, and I miss you. I miss feeling that connected to you."

He nodded. "I know how you feel. Not touching you is hard. But you kind of threw a few things at me all at once, and I'm still figuring out what to do with it all. I'm still angry, I guess. And I'm disappointed in you, because I always thought we were so much in sync with the important things in life, you know?"

I took a deep breath. "I'm disappointed too. I was so shocked about their getting married, and I had this long argument all thought out in my head, and I just assumed you'd back me up, and when you didn't, it, well...it kinda hurt."

My wineglass was empty. He reached over and poured what was left in the bottle into my glass. Then he got up and put the empty bottle in the sink. Instead of coming back to the table, he stood, arms folded across his chest.

"Mona, what are you afraid is going to happen if we get married?"

The question was so unexpected that my jaw dropped open. I had to take a deep breath to collect my thoughts. "I'm afraid that we'll change," I said at last. "We're so good together, you and I. And that's why I don't see why we have to get married. Why change something that's working so beautifully? Marriage is a… thing. It's called an institution for a reason."

"Oh? So you're comparing marriage to what, a prison?" His voice was light, but his eyes were dark and serious. "You really think that being my wife will be like being in prison?"

"Oh course not," I said quickly. "Ben, no. But I don't know what it *will* be like. And right now that scares the hell out of me."

His eyes were sad. "And do you think that's bound to change?"

"I sure hope so, because right now I want you so badly I feel like I could wrestle you to the floor, you know, do things."

The tension broke a little and he laughed. "As far as wanting you goes, that never changed. For me either. At all. But I need to separate plain and simple lust from all these others feelings I've got."

"Feelings, huh? That's about right. Every other man on the planet would be, like, 'Feelings? Who cares; let's get naked,' but, no, not Ben Cutler. Not my guy."

"Would you really want it any other way?"

"No. Absolutely not."

"So?"

"So, I promise to keep my hands to myself. I will not run around naked in front of you, talk dirty in my sleep, or do a pole dance with the floor lamp."

He laughed. "Thank you. And I will not parade around, flexing. Or sing you romantic love songs."

"Ben. You have a lousy voice."

"And I bet you can't pole dance to save your life."

We started laughing. He stretched, looked at his watch, and yawned. "It actually is kind of late. We can watch a little television down here, and then go up in an hour or so."

So we sat on the couch and watched a documentary about whales, and I sat close to him, head on his shoulder, drinking in the smell of his skin, and it was enough. And later, when we were both lying on the futon and he curled himself away from me, I could still feel the heat of his body warming me, and his gentle snoring lulled me to sleep, and that was also enough.

As I said before, I'm no princess.

But tearing up filthy carpeting that smelled like cat pee and had years of dust and grit and possibly dead insect bodies within its avocado-colored strands was not a job for the fainthearted.

Ben had patiently shown me what to do. First, you dragged the furniture to one side of the room. Starting in a corner, you pulled the carpet up and away from the furring strips. (By the way, a furring strip is a narrow piece of wood with little spiky things that stick up and grab onto the carpet, holding it in place. Those little spiky things also hurt like you would not believe if they come in contact with unprotected skin.) Then you took the utility knife and cut a notch in the carpet, sectioning off a piece about three feet wide. The carpet should tear neatly, leaving a long, narrow strip that can easily be rolled tightly, wrapped with duct tape, and thrown out the back window into the yard, where it could then be thrown into the Dumpster.

Once the carpet and the rubber pad underneath were gone, you simply had to pry the strips off the floor with a crowbar (Ben showed me how) and had to make sure there were no nails or staples left in the floor. If there were any, you removed with pliers.

Then you moved the furniture from one side of the room to the other, and did it all over again.

Repeated in other bedroom, Miranda's closet, and, finally, the hallway.

It took Ben about six minutes to show me what to do before he went downstairs to tear out the old kitchen. It took me the better part of an hour to tear up one side of the guest room. And that was without throwing the old stuff out the window, but instead leaving it in a pile in the hall.

I was coated with filth, my knees were aching, my neck was stiff, and I was starving, despite pancakes and bacon for breakfast.

I crept down the stairs and peeked around the corner. There was no one in sight on the first floor. All that was left in the kitchen was the fridge and stove, standing on the old linoleum. The walls were bare, but looked moldy. I could hear voices out back.

The Dumpster had arrived, and Ben was helping get it into position, which involved lots of waving and shouting. Miranda, bless her little heart, was carrying the old cabinets to the back of the yard.

They were working. Hard. And they had accomplished so much. I found my purse, popped four Advil, then went back upstairs.

When I finally pulled up all the carpeting and padding from the front bedroom and pried up all the furring strips, I began to haul it all to the back window. I was careful to look down before I threw, in case Ben or Miranda was below me—death by falling wall-to-wall was too absurd a possibility to ignore.

By one in the afternoon I had finished a single room. I was exhausted. I sat on the edge of the futon and leaned back, closing my eyes. I breathed deeply for a few minutes and tried not to completely zone out.

"Sleeping on the job?" Ben asked.

I didn't move. "This is hard."

"Yes, it is. And you've done a great job so far. Miranda and I are coming up to help you, but we all need to eat first."

My eyes opened. "Thank God." I held out my hand, and he pulled me up. He must have put a lot behind it, because he pulled me right into his arms. His mouth was so close, all I had to do was lean in just a little, but I didn't.

"I thought we weren't going to do this," I said.

"We aren't. The sight of you engaged in manual labor was almost more than I could resist."

"Quick, where's my hammer?"

He laughed and let me go, and we went downstairs.

There were sub sandwiches and chips for lunch. Anything that had been in a cabinet was now in one of several boxes in the middle of the floor. The Sheetrock in the kitchen area had been replaced.

"When did that happen?" I asked, pointing with my ham and salami with provolone on a hard roll.

"While you were busy swearing at the crowbar," Miranda said. "Ben can do anything."

"I was not swearing at the crowbar," I corrected her gently. "I was swearing at all those stupid staples sticking out of the floor. Shouldn't there be that annoying drywall dust everywhere?"

Ben nodded. "This evening we'll sand. That way we'll be ready for painting first thing tomorrow."

"First thing?" I asked, feeling wimpy and old.

He grinned at me. "Look how much we accomplished today by starting so early. Same thing tomorrow. And Sunday."

"Sunday," I reminded him, "is a designated day of rest."

"Not for us."

I took more Advil, prayed for my kidneys, and went back upstairs. By the time David came home from work, armed with pizza and beer, the entire upstairs was finished. We proudly showed him our work. The floors really did look to be in great shape, and Ben said none of the wood would have to be replaced.

I would have been in a very good mood if I hadn't been so exhausted. I think Miranda was exhausted as well, which may have been why the fight started.

Miranda had gathered up the few remaining slices of pizza and wrapped them in foil, opened the refrigerator, and sighed. "I can't wait," she said wistfully, "until we get rid of this thing. Besides being old, there's never any room."

David got up and stood beside her. "There's plenty of room," he said. "See, just do a bit of juggling…" He reached over and moved a few things around, took the pizza from her hands, found a spot, and closed the door. "See? We don't need a new fridge. You just have to learn how to make room."

She looked up at him. "Yes, we do need a fridge. Of course we do. I thought we were getting a new kitchen?"

"Well, yes. I mean, new cabinets," David said patiently. "But not new appliances. We can't afford those yet."

Miranda frowned. "But we're not getting carpeting like I wanted; we're keeping the wooden floors. I thought we'd use that money."

"Don't you think we should save that in case something unexpected comes up?"

"Like what?" she asked, her voice getting sharp. "We know exactly what has to be done. You and your dad have been over this place a hundred times. There are no surprises here. But there is a gross and dirty refrigerator, and an equally gross and dirty stove, both of which need to be replaced."

I glanced at Ben. He was carefully scrolling through his iPhone, his brow wrinkled in fierce concentration on whatever was on the screen.

Or not.

"Randi," David said, his voice getting a bit louder, "we really can't spend that kind of money just because you want shiny new appliances. They're going to have to wait."

"It's not a question of me wanting *shiny new* anything. It's a question of you thinking you can call all the shots about how we spend the money, with me sitting here like a good little girl and saying yes to everything."

David's face flushed deeply. "That's a shitty thing to say," he said hotly.

"And it's a shitty way to feel," Miranda yelled, her voice shaking. "And I've been feeling that way for weeks now. I know we don't have lots of cash, I know that, but this is *our* house, and I need to make the decisions too. About everything, not just paint colors and where to put the stupid wall sconces."

David threw open his arms in frustration. "How can you say that? I mean, what about all your spreadsheets? You've listed everything down to the last penny!"

"Based on what you told me. But that's the thing—you told me. We never talked about where the money was going. You never asked me what I wanted."

David ran his fingers through his hair. "Are you kidding? What did you know about any of this anyway? God, I had to explain what freaking ductwork was."

Ben gave up all pretense of looking at e-mails. He was watching them closely, his eyes narrowed. My throat felt dry. I wanted to get up and run upstairs. The scene was too raw for me. I did not want to see my daughter like this, lashing out at the man she loved. I could tell this was new for her—her face was a mixture of pain and confusion. I guessed that they had never fought like this before, and she was hurting as well as angry.

Her mouth shut in a thin line, and tears sprang to her eyes. "I'm just as smart as you are," she said at last. "It's not my fault I don't know anything about houses."

David's shoulders slumped. "I never meant…" He took a step forward, but she backed away from him, turned, and ran upstairs.

I stared down at my hands, feeling my own tears start. I swallowed hard and started to get up, but Ben's hand shot out to grab my wrist. He shook his head at me, then looked over at David.

"Son," he called, "it's time to take a step back and think about what she said. Don't think about your arguments, just hers. Is she right?"

David came over and sat across from Ben. "Dad, you know we don't have that much money."

"That," Ben said, "is not the point. Is what she said true? About you making the decisions?"

David ran his hands through his hair again. "She doesn't understand anything about what's important to get done. There have to be priorities."

Ben sat back and crossed one leg over the other. "Yes, you're right. Did she have any input into those priorities?"

"She wouldn't understand—"

"Sure she would," Ben said. "Think about what she said to you. Was she right?"

David dropped his eyes and stared at the floor.

I was watching Ben. Brian and I had gotten into similar fights over the course of our marriage. And always, Brian would end up apologizing. But unlike Ben, he had never been able to distinguish between what started the fight and what the real issue was. Brian just wanted to end the argument.

Ben, on the other hand, was more interested in fixing the problem.

David took a deep breath, stood up, and shook his head. "I'm a jerk," he muttered.

"Most men are," I told him with mock sincerity. "Remember, recognizing the problem is the first step toward recovery."

Ben threw his head back and laughed. David smiled and went upstairs.

"I really need a hot bath," I said sadly. "Every bone and muscle in my body hurts."

"So go take a bath," Ben said.

I sighed. "They need a few minutes up there alone."

Ben nodded. "True."

We cleaned the kitchen together, Ben turned on the television, and I crept upstairs for a bath. I soaked in the hottest water I could stand, trying to take some of the ache out of my bones. I put on clean sweats and had every intention of going back downstairs to spend a bit of quiet time with Ben, but paused for a moment to just rest my eyes on the futon, and that was all I remembered until I awoke with a start. It was daylight, and Ben was lying beside me, rolled over on his side, head propped up, watching me.

"How do you feel?" he asked.

I blinked. My eyelids did not ache. I considered that a good sign. "I think I'm fine."

"Bend your legs."

I did. It was not pretty. "I'm not fine," I said, trying not to sound feeble.

"Mona, seriously. Why are you here? This is not your usual, ah, venue."

I adjusted myself so that the stabbing pain in my back didn't go all the way down to my ankles. "When Miranda showed me pictures of the house, I was kind of freaked out. I mean, I see the potential, and I know this is going to be amazing, but I didn't want my daughter to be living in a hovel."

"I get that part. But your normal response would have been a big check and a carefully researched list of contractors. Why are you *here*?"

"It's a gesture. A grand gesture."

He looked understandably confused. "What are you talking about?"

"I wanted to show you that even though I'm philosophically opposed to Miranda and David getting married, I support their love and commitment to each other."

"Is that romance-writer speak for something? Because normal people don't think that way."

"Well, Anthony thinks that way. I'm not doing this for *them*. Well, I am, I mean, of course, but...I wanted to show you that even though we disagreed, I love you. And I was willing to do something big to show you. You were supposed to know that I wasn't willing to tear up crappy carpet for Miranda. I was willing to do it for you." My heart was pounding so hard I was sure he could hear it. I felt like I'd confessed to some heinous crime and was now awaiting judgment.

He was very quiet. He closed his eyes and shook his head slightly. "That is the most ridiculous thing I've ever heard." He opened his eyes. "I know you love me, Mona. And I've been trying to figure out what you're doing up here ever since I arrived. But I never in a million years thought that this was all for me. Why in God's name would you let Anthony, of all people, talk you into this?"

I took a deep breath. At least my rib cage wasn't sore. "I was worried about you and Carmella. It seemed like a good idea at the time."

Ben lay back and started laughing. And he didn't stop for a very long time, which I found a bit annoying. Was it really that funny? Finally he sat up. "Mona, you are the most fascinating woman I know. You were jealous of Carmella, so you decided to renovate your daughter's house. That only makes sense in Mona World, but that's okay, because you like it there. Wow. Grand gesture." He was still chuckling as he got out of bed. "I'll bring up some coffee and…what are you taking like candy?"

"Advil," I mumbled.

"Grand gesture," he said, pulling his jeans on over his boxers. "Wait till I tell the kids."

I thanked God he laughed.

And then I wondered why he didn't tell me not to worry about Carmella.

I closed my eyes. This grand-gesture thing was a lot more complicated than I originally thought.

Painting, it turned out, used a whole different set of muscles, and I had apparently never used any of those muscles before. In my entire life. Paint also smelled bad, and it got in your hair and under your fingernails. I spent way too long in the shower trying to rid my body of Bradford Street Beige, but finally gave up. Luckily I had a brown sweater, so I was at least color coordinated.

David treated us to a great steak dinner; then we went back to the house. The newly painted first floor looked clean and pretty. We sat and stuffed envelopes with wedding invitations. Miranda did not consult with me about her selection, but they were nonetheless simple and elegant. The four of us chatted and licked stamps until nine thirteen, at which point I was falling asleep on the floor, so I went upstairs and fell into bed fully clothed.

I don't know what time Ben came to bed, but I was instantly awake as soon as I felt his body hit the mattress. I was exhausted and everything ached, but all I wanted to do was reach over and sneak my hand around his waist to feel the hard muscle beneath smooth skin.

"Mona?" he whispered.

"I'm awake."

He was lying flat on his back. I could see his profile by the faint glow of the streetlight outside the window.

"You did really well today," he said softly.

I smiled in the darkness. "Yeah, I did, didn't I? I'm kinda impressed with myself."

"I have to say, I misjudged you. I apologize."

"Accepted." I had to make a fist to keep my hand from inching over. Did Ben feel it? The very air in the room was charged with… what—lust?

"The kids seem to have gotten over their argument," Ben said.

"I was waiting for it. Miranda is a very…let's say headstrong girl. I knew that eventually something like this would happen."

"But now they know how to do it," Ben said. "They know that even if they disagree, there's a way around it."

I was afraid to move. I felt like if I did and the weight on the futon shifted, we would accidentally touch. If that happened, I would probably end up making a total fool of myself. But…didn't Ben feel this too? Was he made of stone?

"Is there always a way around it?" I asked.

"I used to think so," he said. Then he sat up and swung his feet to the floor. "I need a shower."

I sat up and watched him walk toward the door. "But you showered earlier," I called after him.

"I know," he said shortly.

I lay back in bed. He must have been in there for a quite a while, because the second time he got into bed, I was so deeply asleep I didn't feel a thing.

Sunday I slept late. I woke up only because I could hear them struggling to carry David and Miranda's bed down the staircase. I made myself get up, had lots of coffee, ate my bagel very slowly, and watched Ben and David carry furniture from upstairs and try to cram it all into the small living space downstairs. I wandered out to the back. Miranda was out there with her former college roommates—all lovely and energetic girls who laughed and joked while they dragged junk out of the yard and tossed it into the overflowing Dumpster. There wasn't much left to clear out, and I was happy to see there was a cement patio pretty much intact under all the junk. When it got too cold to just sit and watch, I went back inside. Ben and David were sitting on the steps, finished. David offered to carry my suitcase to the car, but Ben vetoed him and walked me the few blocks over.

"The house looks good," I said.

He nodded. "Yes, it does. It'll take a bit more work, but they can do it. They're a good team."

I nodded. I remembered when he had said the same about the two of us—that we were a good team. I glanced at him. Did he remember?

We got to the car, and he put my suitcase in the trunk. We stood in the cold. For the very first time since I'd known him, I felt awkward. I didn't know how to say good-bye to him. A kiss on the cheek? A hug? We had tried to avoid touching each other all weekend and had been mostly successful. Now what?

"Drive safe," he said.

I nodded. "I'm sure the kitchen will look great," I said.

He pushed his hands into the front pockets of his jeans. "I'll talk to you when I get back."

"Of course." I reached up and gave him a quick peck on the cheek, got into my car, and drove home.

CHAPTER NINE

WHEN I CAME HOME SUNDAY evening, the black Town Car was in the driveway. It was empty—where was Tony? Scouring the neighborhood for possible danger? Sitting on the roof with a high-powered rifle, waiting for the inevitable attack? Writing his master's thesis on *The Idiot* by Dostoyevsky?

Aunt Lily and Vinnie were sitting at the table in the kitchen, finishing what looked to be an intimate dinner of lobster and champagne. Good for Lily. She swept to her feet as I came in, gave me a hug, then kissed me on both cheeks.

"How was it? Are you exhausted? I'm sure you are. Painting? *Walls?* I can't imagine what you were thinking. Would you like a lobster claw?"

"No, thank you. Hello, Vinnie. Hello, Fred." Fred had come shuffling in, tail wagging. I leaned down to pet him and glanced into the den. No Tony.

"So, tell me about the apartment," Lily said.

"It's actually a house. A row house. Kind of small, but when they're finished with it, it's going to be beautiful," I said, sitting down gingerly. Sometime late this morning it became official—my entire body hurt. "Ben was there."

Lily smiled dreamily. "Was he wearing his tool belt?"

"No. But he did some demo and painted. He's installing their new kitchen tomorrow. Luckily they only have twelve feet of wall space to work with, so it shouldn't take him more than a day."

"He seems to be a pretty good guy," Vinnie said. "Carmella had a great time with him."

What? *What?*

"Oh? When they went out to Chester?" I asked, perfectly calm, like I didn't care at all.

Vinnie nodded. "Yeah, Chester. A whole lot of trees out that way. Carmella said it was very nice. Friendly people. Lots of antiques."

I nodded. "Yes. Trees. Well, you two, I'm exhausted, and I need a long hot bath and three days of sleep. Good night." I rose slowly and went upstairs. As I passed the living room, there was Tony. Reading.

I tried not to think about Ben and Carmella and their little trip to Chester. After all, Ben was a grown man, and he could do as he liked, even if that meant spending the day with an attractive widow who was genetically predisposed to lots of touching, hugging, and arm holding. That she was also obviously on the make caused a throbbing to start right behind my eyes. Ben, I knew, was smart enough to see what she was up to. And I'm sure that if I *had* asked him about it, he would have told me everything. I had not asked, however. And he did not offer the information. And why should he? I mean, obviously it was just an extended business meeting, right? Why would he need to talk about it at all?

Except...we had always talked about everything.

But that was before. Things were changing. Ben was changing. He was slowly moving away from me.

It was less than three weeks until Christmas. Had I done any shopping? No. Had I planned any meals? No. Had I baked a single cookie? No.

I was a bit behind my usual holiday schedule.

Sure, I was thrown off because of the whole Ben situation, but even without that, there was just too much going on.

There was my career. Anthony had gotten copies of the backlist titles from Sylvia. That meant I had to reread books I'd written years ago and make whatever changes I thought necessary. Luckily for me, historical romances did not need much updating—it wasn't like Sir Roderick Lambert of Castle Muir had to upgrade from a BlackBerry to an iPhone—but still, there was some tweaking.

Lily, involved in her own wedding plans, which were becoming more complicated by the hour, was not her usual domestic self, happily puttering around the kitchen, making shortbread and peanut butter fudge. Usually I found her with papers, magazines, and pamphlets spread all over the kitchen table. I'd taken to having breakfast on the stairs.

My three daughters, who in the past had hauled down Christmas decorations the weekend after Thanksgiving, were not around, leaving me to stare at my unadorned mantel in solitary guilt, while I pondered the age-old question—did I *really* need a full-size Christmas tree this year?

Oh, and by the way—did I mention that my oldest daughter was getting married?

The usual scenario for this—at least, the scenario I had run through in my head several times over the years—involved an engagement party, a bridal shower with family and old friends, and at least one additional bridal shower with all the bride's young friends—you know, one of those go-all-night things involving lingerie and sex toys. I also envisioned long intimate lunches where my daughter and I would discuss flowers, centerpieces, and the meaning of life.

I had barely two months between engagement and wedding. Something had to go.

Oddly, it was Dominique who stepped up.

"I think I can put together a shower the Friday night between Christmas and New Year's," she told me.

I tightened my grip on the phone. "Really?"

"Yes. A surprise shower is pretty much out of the question, don't you think? Because I already asked Miranda to send me a list. I'm calling Ben next. How many do you figure for you?"

I did a quick count. When I hit thirty-seven, I gave myself a virtual smack in the head. "I'll narrow the list down to under twenty. Where?"

"The house, of course," Dominique said. "It's beautifully decorated. This year I had Ramon do everything in lavender and gray. It's stunning."

That sounded interesting. "Who's Ramon?"

"He's my interior designer. He's also a close personal friend. He does Christmas for us every year."

Imagine that.

"Thank you, Dominique. And give me any out-of-town guests you want at the rehearsal dinner."

"And where is that?" she asked. I could sense the snark in her tone—she was waiting to see what kind of D-list place I got on such short notice.

"The Highlawn Pavilion." Definitely A-list.

She was quiet.

"Dominique?"

"Well. How lucky for you. That place book weeks in advance. Do you know anyone there?"

"No," I said, not mentioning the fact that Patricia ate there at least once a week and was on a first-name basis with the entire staff.

"Hmmm. What color is your dress?"

"Purple. The girls' are both metallic—Lauren picked out something bronze, and Jess is in gunmetal gray." Of course.

"Sounds lovely. Tyler has a tiny black suit. Gray vest?"

"Your call. How is he?"

"Well, we're still trying to talk him into walking down the aisle without his Batman cape."

"Good luck." Wait—were we becoming friends? "Thank you, Dominique."

"No problem, Mona," she said, and hung up.

I wasn't even sure who would be at my house for the holiday, or when. Ben had texted me that he had finished the kitchen, and had even sent pictures, but had made no mention of Christmas day or eve. Miranda, excited and still in love, called to say that she and David would see me Christmas eve. Did that mean Ben and Ethan would be here as well? I wanted to ask, of course, but what would have been a natural question a few months ago now felt intrusive. When were the girls seeing Brian and their brother? I got different answers from each of them—no surprise there. Although our divorce decree had very carefully spelled out who got the girls for what holidays, they were adults now and could go wherever they wanted. Brian had become even less Jewish with Dominique, and had embraced Christmas without so much as a wink toward Hanukkah. I knew that Phyllis would be spending most of her time with Brian. My ex-mother-in-law was not terribly observant either, but I knew her, and I could imagine the Dominique battles now. Oh, to be a fly on that wall…

Were Rebecca and Julian going to Massachusetts again this year? She hadn't given me a definite answer yet. They usually spent time in Amherst with Rebecca's old friends, involved in some Wiccan celebration that sounded way more fun than stockings on the chimney and a ham.

Thank God I didn't have to worry about Lily. She was booked for Aruba. And that meant no Carmella. Gee, what a loss. Although Trev and his cooking would be missed.

Frankly, the idea of being out on an island somewhere sounded good. Lying quietly on a hot sandy beach. Listening to the gentle sound of the waves. Alone. Except for someone to bring me food and pineapple-flavored drinks. Maybe that was what I really needed to figure out: why I didn't want to commit to spending the rest of my life with the best person I knew. Although my brain was so muddled now, I didn't think there were enough pineapple-flavored drinks in the world for me to find the answer to that question.

Maybe I could let Vinnie and his clan take over my house, and *I'd* go to Aruba.

Then Ben called. When I saw his name on my caller ID, I may have screamed out loud. I know that Fred lifted his head, and at least one cat jumped in the air.

"Listen, I know between Christmas and this wedding you're probably too busy to even breathe, but are you free tomorrow night? I thought maybe we could have a nice quiet dinner."

"It would have to be fairly early," I said. I was grinning so broadly I was sure he could see it through the phone.

"Six thirty? I'll pick you up."

Pick me up? Like a *date*? "Lovely."

"Good. See you then." He hung up, and I stared at the phone in my hand as if it were about to lay golden eggs. I looked around. I was alone. But I needed to tell at least forty-three people that Ben and I had a dinner date tomorrow night, and I needed at least half of those forty-three people to help me pick out what to wear.

I closed my eyes and breathed deeply. I needed perspective. This wasn't a first date with some exotic stranger. This was Ben, who knew me and loved me. Who didn't just know me, but who had known me at my worst—naked, with wet hair, suffering from the flu—as well as at my best. Ben was my friend.

However...this was him and me having dinner. Just the two of us. And *he'd* asked *me*. This could be a chance to mend some fences and get us back on track.

I decided I would not go crazy. I would not worry about what to wear or what to do with my hair. Hell, I wasn't even going to shave my legs.

Besides, I didn't have the time. I looked down at my to-do list.

I normally wouldn't even *have* a to-do list, but I had noticed that in the past few years I had trouble keeping track of things. Not forgetting, exactly—more like delayed remembering. So I had started writing things down. My current list was disheartening.

I needed to buy Christmas gifts. For everyone. That was a separate list that was so long it needed its own notebook.

I had to approve the first three of my backlist titles that were finished with editing and had gotten new covers. Anthony had the formatter scheduled, and the announcement had been made on my website that they would be put on sale after the New Year on January fourth.

I had two industry-related parties to attend in the next ten days, both in New York City, both requiring an amazing new outfit that could not be culled from my California wardrobe. No decent East Coast writer would be caught dead in a gauze maxi dress with a statement necklace and a "pop of color" cardi.

Miranda was driving down for the weekend to clean out part of her closet, make the final decision about flowers, choose music for the ceremony, and find shoes and a headpiece.

Lauren and Jessica would both be finished with finals and would be coming home—they were also in need of wedding shoes and possibly something for their hair.

I needed a haircut, a manicure, and to take Joan to the vet—

again—for her digestive issues. The car was making a noise and belonged in the shop. I had to make a Costco run, but without a plan for Christmas dinner I'd be buying blindly, never a good thing in Costco, where I could spend several hundred dollars *with* a list.

Lana jumped up onto the stool beside me and purred. She allowed me to scratch under her throat while I thought about what to do next. I held up my list.

"What should I do first?"

She arched her back in utter disdain.

"Really? That's it? I need help here."

She turned around and gave me her other end. I scratched her special spot, right at the base of her tail.

"I scratch your butt, you scratch mine?"

She jumped down. Of course.

I called Patricia. "I have three thousand, five hundred, and forty-seven things on my to-do list, and Ben wants to take me to dinner tomorrow night," I told her.

"I could book you into my spa tomorrow morning. You'll come out looking and feeling ten years younger."

"Thanks, Patricia, but what about my list?"

"It will still be there, won't it?"

"Yes, but it won't be any shorter."

She sighed. "Mona. What could possibly be more important than having dinner with Ben?"

I ran down the list. "And I've got two parties in Manhattan and nothing to wear."

"Nothing to wear? Oh, dear."

"Exactly. I need to prioritize."

"Yes, you do. I'll book you extra early. Eight o'clock. You can go straight to Nordstrom afterward for a few outfits and all the shoes you'll ever need. I'll book a personal shopper for you."

"Don't you have to wait weeks for one of those? Especially around Christmas?"

"Not when you pay the kind of credit card bills I do."

"That would be a huge help, Patricia, but I haven't bought a single gift."

"Then bring your laptop. You can do all your shopping online while you're getting your toes done. You do know that Amazon will also wrap for you, right?"

"Right."

"Once the girls are back, use Jessica's car while yours is getting fixed. Have Lauren do whatever with the cat. Send them all out together for shoes and hats. You don't need to be there, because they wouldn't listen to you anyway. Spend that time with Anthony and get those books ready. Then call that caterer of yours and tell him you want a Christmas dinner for four to twenty people."

"Oh."

"Anything else?"

And that, ladies and gentlemen, is what a best friend is for.

I must admit, when Ben picked me up, I felt pretty spectacular. Not only had I been massaged, waxed, shellacked, and moisturized to within an inch of my life, I had managed to get free shipping on all my presents.

I slid into the front seat of his truck and gave him a chaste kiss on the cheek. I felt absurdly nervous. Come on—this was Ben. But was this date going to be the brush-off? The you're-right-we-don't-need-to-get-married conversation? He looked at me very seriously.

"Please don't take what I'm about to say too personally," he said.

I sat up straighter. "All right."

"What exactly are you wearing under your coat?"

I laughed. "Basic black pants from the Gap and a sweater."

He pulled away from the curb. "Good."

We ate in town, a great little place that normally would have been half empty during the week. But because of the holiday, we were told there was a wait and pushed toward the bar.

"Martini?" Ben asked. I nodded and tried to find a spot at the bar where we could at least stand together. I saw Ben make his way to the other side, where the (female) bartender immediately dropped six different things to take his order. He stood there, patiently waiting, and when his eyes met mine, he flashed a smile that made my heart tighten.

Why didn't I want to marry this guy again?

He got our drinks and made his way back to me. I had managed to capture about eleven inches of bar space, and although we couldn't stand side by side, if I put my back against the bar, Ben could stand in front of me so we could have a very cozy conversation space.

"Here," he said, handing me my drink. We clinked our glasses. "Here's to a great rest of the year."

I smiled, took a deep gulp, felt the kick in the back of my throat, then took a breath.

"So," Ben said, sipping his beer. "I thought the groom's family was supposed to do the rehearsal dinner."

Oh, so this was a business meeting? "Well, technically, yes, but since the kids insist on paying for the wedding themselves, which is usually what the bride's parents do, I thought it only right that I do something else, you know?"

He nodded. "I get it. But now what about me?"

"Didn't you just give them a brand-new kitchen?"

He shrugged. "That was a wedding present. Dominique is throwing the shower; is there anything left?"

"Bachelor party?"

Ben grinned. "David already talked about that. He wants the entire wedding party to go on the sunset cruise around Manhattan. No wild strippers or drunken debauchery."

"What a lovely idea! So pay for that."

Ben shook his head. "Too late. His old roommate from Yale, his best man, has already claimed dibs."

"Those Yale boys do all right for themselves."

Ben chuckled. "Yes."

Someone pushed Ben, causing him to bump me. We were very close. I could count the chest hairs peeking out from his open shirt collar. He smelled faintly of musk. This may have been a business meeting, but I still rated a bit of primping. I took another gulp of martini.

"Did you do something to your hair?" he asked.

I fluffed it carelessly. "Just a trim." And new color. And highlights. Then a deep protein conditioning treatment, followed by a meticulous blowout and restyle.

"Looks good. How about cars?"

"You want to buy them a car?"

"No. Limos and stuff. Who pays for that?"

"Don't know. You should probably ask Carmella if she has that taken care of." Wait, did I really just say that?

"I imagine she has. She's very efficient."

I kept my voice very casual. "Yes, I'm sure she is. Too bad she won't be around for Christmas."

"She actually has a Christmas eve wedding. She won't be in Aruba with her family after all. Maybe you could invite—"

"No," I yelped. I cleared my throat. I figured he was probably teasing, but I wasn't taking any chances. "No, Ben, I don't think so."

He threw back his head and laughed. "Don't tell me you're jealous."

I raised my eyebrows. "Should I be?"

He ignored my question. "Do you know what she said about you?"

"About me? When were you two talking about me?"

He was grinning. "Chester, of course. And I must say, you've really held your tongue on that."

I ignored the dig. "Oh, yeah, Chester. So, what did she say?"

"That you were a formidable competitor."

"Oh? And what exactly are the two of us competing for?" I asked, keeping my face straight with a great deal of difficulty.

"Do you know what kind of a woman Carmella is?" he asked.

"Beautiful? Successful? Driven?"

He shook his head. "No. I mean, yes, but…" He sipped his beer. "She's the kind of woman who has never *not* gotten what she wanted. Between her father and his money, her own drive, and, well, her personal mission statement, she doesn't know what it means to go after something and not get it."

I tilted my head up so I could look directly into his eyes. "And she wants you."

"Yes."

"Can she get you?" My voice cracked. I couldn't help it.

He leaned in closer. "I've been in love with you for as long as I've known you."

I nodded. "Yes. But that really doesn't answer the question, does it?"

He straightened. "I keep waiting for some sort of compromise to present itself."

"Like me suddenly deciding I want to run off to Vegas and get hitched by Elvis?"

He shrugged. "That would work."

"That's not a compromise," I said.

"No, it's not."

My throat felt dry.

"Cutler, party of two. Cutler, party of two."

We made our way into the dining room, sat down, then opened menus. I had my drink clenched in my hand, and I downed what was left. Ben was still nursing his first beer.

"Did you and David get suits?" It was time to lighten the conversation.

Ben followed my lead. He knew me well enough to know that sometimes, in the middle of a serious discussion, I needed space to regroup. "Yes. And I dragged Ethan, who could not understand why he couldn't be an usher in cargo pants and a hoodie. Are the girls all set?"

I nodded. "Now it's all about the shoes."

Ben lowered the menu. "Shoes? Damn. We need shoes?"

"Don't you own anything besides work boots and loafers?"

He made a face. "Why would I need anything besides work boots and loafers?"

I smiled, the knot between my eyes starting to relax. "You can always rent them."

"Seriously? They rent shoes?"

"They rent everything"

Ben shook his head. "Unbelievable."

Our waitress hurried over. "Can I get you refills?" she asked Ben rather breathlessly.

He drained his glass. "Sure. Sam Adams. Mona?"

I nodded. The waitress turned to me with a slight scowl. "And you?"

"Vodka martini. Grey Goose. Straight up with an olive."

She scurried off.

This part of the restaurant was surprisingly quiet compared to the bar. The walls were dark paneled, with framed hunting scenes and brass wall sconces on the walls. There were candles on white tablecloths and classical music played in the background.

"Carmella had an interesting thought," Ben said slowly.

"Again with Carmella?" I snapped. "What was she talking about this time?"

"You."

I squirmed. "I wish Carmella would spend less time thinking about me, Ben. Why on earth would she find me so interesting?"

He was looking at the menu again. "She said you may have connected with somebody in LA, and that's why you were so, well, distant."

I could feel a burning right behind my eyes, one that had almost gone away, start back up again. "Oh? She said that, did she? What would she know about it anyway? Did you tell her how often you came out to see me?" I blew out loudly in disgust. "I met lots of somebodies in L.A., and I didn't even *like* any of them."

He kept his eyes on the menu and shrugged. I took a deep breath but was interrupted by a martini, plunked down very ungraciously in front of me.

"Have you folks decided?"

"Yes," Ben said.

"No," I snapped.

Ben raised his eyebrows.

"Wait, sorry, I'm ready," I mumbled. "Pork chops. Baked potato. Bleu cheese."

The waitress scribbled, then turned to Ben, her expression of one about to receive a precious gift wrapped in starlight.

"Sounds good. I'll have the same."

She looked slightly disappointed, took our menus, then left.

"I have not," I said slowly, "been distant."

He reached for his beer, took a long drink, then shrugged.

"In fact," I said, gaining a bit of steam, "I spent a great deal of time and money on amazingly sexy black undergarments, specifically for your benefit."

His mouth twitched. "True."

"Just because I am conflicted about the idea of marriage, that does not mean I am conflicted about you. I love you. I want to be with you. In fact, if it were at all possible, I'd be with you right now on top of this table."

He laughed. "I see." He was silent for a moment. "How do you feel about the kids getting married now, after seeing them together? You have to admit they looked like two people heading in the right direction."

I had to think about that for a second. "Yes, they seem very happy together. And they...think alike. I mean, they seem to be working together for the same things. Miranda has changed. For the better, but...she could always turn on a dime into a spoiled brat, and she has managed to put that part of her aside. I don't know if that will last. Once this flush of true love wears away and it's just the day-to-day hard work of being married, she might not find it as easy to stop wanting everything she sees. And I worry about David—sure, he's perfect for her now, but maybe there's something in him that he's changed for her, and once she finds out..." I shook my head. "Which is why I wanted them to wait to get to know each other better. We always put our best faces forward in the beginning. Sometimes that's a bad thing."

"Has anything about me changed?" he asked cautiously. He seemed almost afraid of my answer. "Anything you didn't know about before?"

I looked at him steadily. "I never knew you believed in love at first sight. I always imagined you as more...practical."

"And I guess I always thought you were just as big a romantic as Maura Van Whalen. I had no idea you had such a cynical side."

"I am not," I said loudly, "cynical." I glanced around and lowered my voice. "I didn't realize you thought of me that way. I've always considered myself a realist."

"Based on *your* experience, Mona."

I nodded and sipped my drink. "I know."

The waitress appeared, setting down our salads.

"Everything okay?" she asked Ben.

He nodded.

She looked at me and raised an eyebrow. I nodded, and she left.

"I was hoping," Ben said quietly, "that we could figure out a way for both of us to feel better about things."

I played with my lettuce, pushing it from one side of the plate to the other with my fork. "What things, exactly? The kids' wedding? Or ours?"

"There is no *ours*."

"Right." I looked up at him. He seemed so sad. "Listen, Ben, even if I admit that David and Miranda seem to be made for each other, it will take ten years of them happily married before I agree with you on this. And I'm sorry. I will do everything I can to support my daughter and her choices, but that doesn't mean I'm happy with them. And as much as I love you, I still don't understand why things between us can't stay exactly the same. If it ain't broke, don't fix it, right? And we're not broken, Ben. I don't know why we have to go through a symbolic ceremony to be happy together."

"Marriage is not just a symbolic ceremony, Mona." He ran his hand through his hair. "Just ask your daughter. It's important. It means something."

I pushed away my plate. The waitress hurried over to whisk it away. I had no appetite left. A perfect waste of pork chops and baked potato. I looked over at Ben, who was staring at his empty beer bottle.

I could see no way out of this.

Chapter Ten

Some things had turned around.

Fabulous and comfortable shoes, black patent leather with purple suede accents for wedding number one—check.

Fabulous and less-than-comfortable shoes, ivory with sparkly heels and hot-pink soles for wedding number two—check.

Amazing and fairly sexy pantsuit, as well as smashing plan B outfit, perfect for posh, intellectual holiday parties with the New York literati—check.

Unbelievable black Chanel bag practically stolen from an online consignment shop, my Christmas gift to myself—check.

Wardrobewise, I was on a roll.

Anthony and I finalized three titles that would be ready to launch on schedule. Sylvia had called to say my old publishing house loved both of my manuscripts and were going to make an offer. A good one. I was writing again—no, not a romance, but a modern comedy—with more than a touch of fantasy—about a jaded divorcée who inherits a farmhouse in the country next to a cemetery and finds that she can talk to all the "residents."

Workwise, I was in the zone.

I had hung garland over the fireplace mantel, purchased several wreaths, and bought—and decorated—a smallish, pre-lit tree for the corner of the living room. The cat's digestive issues had ceased. I managed to whip together two batches of homemade biscotti.

Domestically speaking, I was back on the goddess track.

Miranda's new job didn't start until after the first of the year, so she was still reveling in her newfound role as housewife and calling me daily for advice on things like grout cleaning and how to season a cast-iron skillet. Lauren was still moping over her breakup with Justin but confided in me that she realized I had been right when I told her to make a clean break, and had said no to the last booty call. I think she said that to make me feel better, but it really didn't. Jessica's tattoo had healed, and she agreed with me that for her next one, something subtle, like a musical note inside the left knee, was a better idea than a map of the Shire between her shoulder blades.

My parenting skills had never been less needed, but also never more appreciated.

So you'd think that I'd be a happy camper.

I missed Ben so much it was like missing a part of my body. An important part. Like my right arm. Our dinner was only a few days ago, but I felt the distance of one hundred years, and I knew that wasn't good.

But I was getting used to living alone.

I had never done that before. I had gone from my mother's house to my husband's house. After Brian left, the girls and Lily had lived with me. True, I had been living on my own in California, but I was always with *somebody*. I was working twelve-hour days or was in meetings until late at night. When I did have downtime, I was flying home or Ben was there, or one of the girls. It was not like now, with the girls barely home between terms and Lily practically living in Bay Ridge. Now I woke up, one morning after the next, with no one around.

It was a revelation to have to think about no one but myself.

Of course, the dog had to be walked, and the cats had to be fed, and I had a writing schedule. And let's face it, the bills had to be paid on time. But I pretty much could do whatever I wanted. I never had that luxury before. It was liberating.

"So," Anthony asked, "do you dance around the house naked to the Bee Gees?"

"What? Did you do that when you lived alone?"

"No, but I wasn't a child of the disco era."

"Neither was I. Well, not really. What are you and Victor doing for Christmas?" We were over the garage, working through e-mails and cinnamon-flavored coffee.

"New Hampshire. His sister is renting a cabin and we're going to ski and sing carols. And drink spiced rum."

"That sounds nice. Can I come?"

"Ben skis. Ask to go with him."

"We did that once. Spent a weekend up at Stowe. I never actually went on a slope, but I waved at him a few times as he skied by the main lodge."

"I love those shoes, by the way. For Lily's wedding? Louboutin?"

"I have no idea. Carmella found them. The underside exactly matches the color of Lily's dress."

He looked at me steadily. "Why aren't you happy?"

"I am happy."

"But you seem sad."

"I am also sad. I'm allowed to feel more than one thing at once, you know."

"I know. What are you sad about?"

"Ben and I have never disagreed about anything before. It's really hard to take. What if I lose him over this?"

Anthony leaned over and hugged me. "How can you lose a man who loves you as much as Ben does?"

"Love isn't everything, Anthony. And sometimes it isn't enough."

"I refuse to believe," he said loudly, "that you won't get through this. After Miranda's wedding, the two of you need to spend a long weekend alone, talking things out. You'll be fine."

Anthony, just as a point of information, still made Easter baskets for the girls and left them on the kitchen counter, along with a half-eaten carrot. Just so we all know where he was coming from.

"How's Lily?" he asked.

"Doing great. I'm kind of really liking the scenario. Except the part where Vinnie's connected, of course. Maybe when you reach a certain age you're less afraid of failure. Or more willing to take the risk. Whatever. I suppose you reach a point in your life where you know you can trust your instincts. And I'd like to think that I could still find love if I were old and gray."

"When you're old and gray, you and Ben will be sitting together in a front porch somewhere, side by side in matching rockers, throwing things at people who walk by."

I felt a twist in my gut. Would Ben and I grow old together? "Maybe."

"No, certainly."

"I never thought of myself as a rocking-chair type."

"But you're definitely the throw-things-at-people type."

"True."

"I bet she doesn't invite me to the wedding."

"Don't take it personally. After all, she still only knows you as the guy who does stuff around here occasionally."

"What do I do around here?"

"Hold my hand and make me feel better when I'm bummed."

"Oh, baby cakes, I am *so* underpaid."

Who gives a party in the middle of Manhattan the day before Christmas eve? Requiring me to not only take the bus wearing a stunning chocolate-brown pantsuit and very high heels, but also to carry a paper bag filled with canned goods for the local Food Pantry (in lieu of a hostess gift) down 42nd Street?

Amanda Witt, that was who. And for her, I'd do it gladly.

Amanda began writing romance when it was tucked away in the corners of drugstores and stationery shops. She was one of those referred to as a "grande dame," and she not only deserved it, she reveled in it. She had slowed down when she hit her seventy-fifth birthday and was now writing only novellas and short stories for various charity anthologies. But she still had a sharp mind and sharper tongue, and she'd been my friend and mentor for years.

She always rented a suite in the heart of Times Square for her holiday party, and no one involved in the romance biz ever turned down her invitation. Not only did she always have the best food and drink, but certain people at her parties tended to loosen up so much that they could be counted on to open their mouths and let all sorts of interesting things fall out. No one wanted to miss out on that kind of fun. Even though I wasn't writing romance with a capital R anymore, I still rated an invite. I knew what an honor it was. Even during the past two years, when my time home was limited and packed full of things to do and people to see, I went to her party.

She was that kind of friend.

A week earlier I had gone to another literary-type party, this time given by my once and future editor, Francine Welles. She had been an editor for a very long time, and was one of those almost-recognizable names in New York publishing. It was one of those Noel Coward–type affairs, with everyone standing around the piano at the end of the night singing show tunes. It was usually a mix of book people, theater people, and art people, so there was a lot of ego and opinion thrown around.

But at Amanda's little shindig, everyone spoke the same language, and we all checked our pretentions at the door. It took me a few minutes to find her. She was surrounded, as usual, but when she saw me she bumped a younger and obviously star struck author from the seat next to her so I could sit. She kissed me on the cheek and got straight to the point.

"You're really giving us up?" she asked.

"I don't know. Let's face it, I haven't written a romance in almost two years. That's a century in fan-years."

She sniffed. She looked a little tired, but her makeup was perfect, as usual, and not an ash-blond hair was out of place. Nor would it be, even if a tsunami swept through Times Square. "That thing with your backlist—are you really doing it yourself?"

I nodded. "Yes. We release the first three in a few weeks, as a matter of fact."

She raised her eyebrows. "I can't imagine doing all that work, and for what?"

"Seventy percent royalty?"

Amanda was rich enough that she never bothered even calculating her royalty share. "What else are you writing?"

"Paranormal romantic comedy."

"Good sex?"

"Good dream sex."

"Whatever. And where is that gorgeous Ben that you brought last year?"

"He got propositioned so much that he swore he'd never come to one of your parties again," I lied.

"Are you going to put him on one of your covers?" she asked.

I shook my head.

"Oh, dear, Mona. Have I taught you nothing?" She looked at me shrewdly. "What's going on?"

I didn't usually share personal things with Amanda, but I knew that she'd been married to the same man for more than fifty years. "Do you like being married?"

"Of course. It's the best thing in the world. Why on earth do you ask?"

"I can't imagine getting married again, that's all."

"You know, dear, that I rarely give advice, but can I share with you my secret?"

"Of course."

She leaned in to whisper in my ear, "The key to happiness is to make sure your expectations are based on reality." She sat back, looking very smug.

"Oh?"

"Never look at the world the way it was, or the way you want it to be. Look at your life the way it truly is, and make your plans from there. You'll save yourself a lot of heartbreak."

I thought about that for a moment. "That's very good advice, Amanda."

She sniffed. "Of course it is, dear. Now, go forth and be brilliant."

Yes, Amanda.

The girls spent Christmas eve at home. Ben, David, and Ethan came over, as did Patricia. I felt that automatic jolt when Ben came through the door, but I was not as anxious as I thought I'd be. I was trying very hard not to obsess about us and just enjoyed his company. He seemed a bit withdrawn at first, but he soon relaxed. We had been good friends for a long time, and that was where we found ourselves by the end of the night. I had a beef tenderloin with scalloped potatoes delivered, and afterward we sat around the fireplace and talked about Lily in Aruba, the wedding, the

DeMatriano family, the wedding, my new book, the wedding, Ethan's psychotic roommate, the wedding, and, oh, yes, the wedding.

It looked as though everything was set. Carmella's checklist was complete. The first RSVPs were coming in. The happy couple had written their vows. Ben had rented shoes.

It was going to happen.

I sat next to Ben on the couch, just close enough to feel his phone vibrate at least five times during the evening. To his credit, he never pulled it out to check who was texting him so urgently on Christmas eve. My guess was that it was Carmella, and I felt slightly smug knowing he was basically blowing her off in favor of our company.

Basing my expectation on the reality of his not caring what she wanted, I should have felt not just smug, but happy.

So why wasn't I happy?

Because it wasn't enough that Carmella wasn't that important to him.

Okay, then, what *would* be enough? I had no idea.

See my problem?

Patricia left early. We sat and watched *It's a Wonderful Life* until midnight. Then, since Ben and I weren't going to be together on Christmas day, we went into the living room to exchange gifts. He handed me a box. I was afraid to open it up. Last year he had given me a beautifully illustrated first edition of *Lassie: Come Home*, one of my favorite children's books. This year the gift was smaller. It felt like a jewelry box. Most women would be thrilled with jewelry, but I had all sorts of sparkly things—why hadn't he spent time and energy finding something unique and different, just for me?

My expectation should have been based on the reality that Ben and I were not the same couple we were a year ago. In fact, we weren't the same couple we were *months* ago. Just because I had spent hours online looking for framed original blueprints of famous architectural buildings before spending a small fortune on the floor plan of the Thomas Gale House, designed by Frank Lloyd Wright, didn't mean that Ben was still as enthusiastic about shopping for me as I was about shopping for him.

I carefully peeled open one side, prying open the tape with my thumb. I unfolded the silver paper and slid the box out. Plain, white. No name or logo. I pulled off the lid.

There, in a bed of cotton, was a heavy gold bangle, fine engraving intertwined among tiny diamonds. I held it up and read the inscription.

Better Than Your Dreams.

"Oh, Ben."

In the early days of our relationship, I had told him that even though I was a best-selling author of some pretty hot romance, being with him was better than anything I could have dreamed up. A few days later, he found a quote, by Dr. Seuss, of all people, that said, "You know you're in love when you can't fall asleep because reality is finally better than your dreams." It meant so much to me then. It meant even more, now, that he remembered.

He put it around my wrist very carefully.

"It's so beautiful," I whispered. "Thank you."

He just nodded. I handed him his gift, which he opened with the same care and patience he had for everything in his life.

"Oh, Mona, how perfect," he said. "Just perfect. Wow, it must have taken you days to find something like this."

Weeks, actually, but I just shrugged modestly. He leaned over, and we kissed, very softly. I wanted to move toward him, put my arms around him. Maybe ease him onto the floor. The kids were watching *A Christmas Story.* I could hear the television in the other room. It ran with no commercials, right? And I knew there was plenty of popcorn left in the bowl. Those kids were in the Ralphie zone. They wouldn't notice a bomb going off. Maybe Ben and I could slip right behind the tree and...

He sat back. "Thank you."

I pushed those thoughts to the side. "I'm glad you like it. I thought it was really beautiful."

He sat, looking down at the print for a long time. Then he took a deep breath and stood up. "I should go."

I stood up with him. "Right. It's late."

He kissed me on the cheek. It was a good-friend kind of a kiss.

After he left, I sat. Maybe good friends was going to have to be enough.

Christmas day, I had been invited to Brian and Dominique's with the girls and David. By the time we got there, Tyler had already exhausted himself opening several thousand presents, so we had a peaceful dinner while he slept under the dining room table. Christmas night, I sent lots of texts and e-mails. I still hadn't taken off Ben's gift. Not even for the shower. Of course, it wasn't the same as having him there. But at least I looked elegant in my loneliness.

The day after Christmas, David and Miranda went over to Ben's. Both of them were very polite and did not ask questions about what was going on, which I appreciated. They would be spending the night there, but coming back to spend time with me before the shower. Jess and Lauren were off somewhere. The house was quiet. I sat in the living room and looked at my beautiful tree, watched the cats play soccer with a few fallen ornaments, and ran my fingers over Ben's gift over and over again.

CHAPTER ELEVEN

ONCE BRIAN AND DOMINIQUE FIGURED out that a chic two-bedroom condo was not the best place to raise a baby boy—especially since said baby boy would have to share his bedroom with his three half sisters whenever they came to visit—they'd moved west from Hoboken to the 'burbs into a five-bedroom, four-and-a-half–bath colonial on a sweeping half-acre lot, complete with pool, circular drive, and three-car garage. That may have been overkill, since Dominique made it very clear that Tyler was a onetime extravagance. My daughters were pleased that they now had a pool to hang out in whenever they wanted, as well as a very well decorated place to crash if they happened to be in the neighborhood. But their enthusiasm disappeared as soon as they started classes and realized they weren't going to be back from college often enough to sufficiently abuse their own home, let alone their father's.

Still, the Berman manse remained impressive. I'd been there on only a few occasions—holiday events, mostly—and had been quite taken by Dominique's style and efficient housekeeping. My own efficient housekeeping showed up once a week in a little yellow minivan. Hers apparently showed up twice a week.

I arrived early to the shower, mainly to keep Miranda company, but also, quite frankly, to watch Dominique at work. The woman was impressive. Any sort of event that required feeding more than six people put her in her true element—this woman could plan a party like no one else I knew.

Ramon had done an amazing job with his holiday decorating.

The tree in the family room glittered with tiny white lights, silver ornaments, and clusters of dried lavender tied in silken ribbon. Pearly gray garland cascaded down from a magnificent angel wearing the traditional Christmas robe of royal purple and silver. I imagined Tyler had a real blast helping hang all the ornaments.

The rest of the house was just as beautifully and tastefully done —I was particularly impressed when I went into the first-floor guest bathroom, right off the foyer, and found a glass column filled with silver and lavender balls. And the gray bows around the spare toilet paper rolls were an extra-festive touch.

Lily had driven with me. She had returned from Aruba the evening before, very tanned and with splash of purple dye in the front of her silver hair, obviously for the holidays. As she looked around, she murmured, "Look, I match," then let her coat fall over a nearby chair, and marched into the living room, where she immediately grabbed the chair with the most commanding view. The living room, by the way, was massive, with a huge fireplace decked with holly and silver candles, with matching eight-foot sofas, wing chairs, ottomans, and occasional tables scattered throughout. In pale taupe with chocolate and hunter-green accents, it was comfortable and elegant without looking feminine at all.

The girls had followed in Jessica's car. Miranda looked nervous.

"How many people did she invite?" she asked. I shrugged. I had kept out of this completely, other than spending a small fortune on a Calphalon cookware set, and talking Lauren and Jessica out of hiring a male stripper.

Dominique was hanging up coats and playing kiss-kiss with the girls. Tyler came running in, a large truck in his hand. Upon seeing us he dropped to the floor, pushed on the top of the truck, then let go. It shot forward with considerable force and hit a fragile three-legged table standing innocently in the foyer, which promptly fell over, bringing the crystal vase full of white roses down with it. Tyler screamed with delight, threw his arms around my legs, and then tore out of sight. Dominique's shoulders slumped, and she said a very bad word. But in French, so it sounded almost classy.

"Let me," I said, rushing forward. "Point me to a broom." As I moved, I could feel the water from the vase seeping into the soles of my lovely red suede driving shoes. I followed her into the kitchen. As she reached into a large closet, she suddenly turned to me and began to sob loudly.

"Ah, Dominique, it's only a vase. I'll take care of it, honestly."

"I think Brian's cheating on me," she blurted. She turned back to the closet and pulled out a broom and dustpan, which she handed to me, tears streaming down her face. "A salesperson. Younger." She wiped away tears but continued to sob. "And skinnier."

I stared. Younger? And skinnier? True, Dominique was not her former size double zero, but still, who could possibly be younger and skinnier than her? A twelve-year-old anorexic?

I hesitantly moved toward her. "Dominique?"

She waved me away. "Go! That spilled water will ruin the floors."

"I'll be right back," I blurted, grabbing a roll of paper towels out of its tasteful brushed-chrome holder and taking it with me.

Lauren had picked up the larger pieces of glass, and Jessica had salvaged the flowers. We threw down paper towels to absorb the water, and I carefully swept up the glass fragments. Miranda muttered something about Tyler and followed the sound of his shrieks.

"Mona," Lily called from the living room, "is everything all right?"

"Yes, Aunt Lily," I answered. Lauren and I went back into the kitchen, where Dominique was sitting on the floor in front of the broom closet, crying her heart out.

"Mom?" Lauren said, staring.

I knelt down next to Dominique. "Listen, I'm sorry, honestly, and if you don't feel up to this, just let me know. We'll send everyone away. In fact, if we start texting people now—"

"No, I'm f-f-fine," she said, struggling to stand. I stood with her, and she leaned against me for a second. I tried to put an arm around her shoulder, but she straightened up, then grabbed the broom and put it back, closing the closet door firmly. She inhaled deeply, then rubbed her eyes with both hands. "I'm fine." She smiled at Lauren. "I'm fine. Thanks for helping. The broken glass goes in recycling, under the scrub sink. There's another vase right behind you, top shelf, on the left."

Lauren put the broken glass away without a word, then pulled the vase from the cabinet.

I leaned toward Dominique. "Are you sure? Honestly, there are a lot of people coming—"

"Forty-six," she said.

"What? Forty-six people are coming to the shower? That's almost as many people as are coming to the wedding!"

She looked at her watch. "The caterer will be here in ten minutes. People will start showing up in half an hour. I need to fix my makeup. Can you handle this?"

"Of course."

She hurried out of the kitchen.

Lauren, filling the vase with water, immediately turned to me with raised eyebrows.

"Nothing," I muttered.

"Liar."

"She thinks your father may be cheating on her. Don't say a word."

Lauren shook her head and arranged the flowers. "Dad is kind of a jerk-wad."

"Lauren!"

"Well, he is. He dumped you, got her pregnant because he wanted a son, moved her out here away from everything she loves so he could make the right impression on everyone, and now he's doing exactly the same thing to her that he did to you." She shook her head again. "Jerk-wad."

"Where is he? Do you know?"

"With the new girlfriend?"

"Lauren!"

"Well, she told him to stay away from the house for the whole afternoon. Where else would he be?"

Good heavens, the girl was probably right.

The caterer took several minutes to bring in the food, set up the appetizers, and arrange a bar area in the eating nook in the kitchen.

If I had been planning this little soirée, I would have put the bar directly in the middle of the living room, but, hey, that's just me.

Dominique came back downstairs, her face recomposed, and took charge. I went into the living room, where Lily, Miranda, and Jessica all looked at me with practiced innocence.

"Lauren, you've never heard of discretion? You couldn't wait, what, twenty minutes?" I sat down heavily. "Forty-six people."

"Forty-six people where, dear?" Lily asked.

"Here. Today."

Miranda frowned. "Do I even know forty-six people?"

Jessica rolled her eyes. "High school friends? Boston people? David's cousins? Mom's friends? Who knows, maybe Dominique has a friend. Seriously—you know forty-six people."

Miranda's own cousins, I knew, were not in the mix. Marsha the Bitch had two children, both of whom fled home as soon as humanly possible, and as far as I knew, had not returned. My own sister, Grace, lived in Oregon on a commune with the same sitar player named Shadow she ran off with back when sitar players were sexy and a good catch. Her offspring, five sons, stayed close to the commune, three of them working with their father, who now made handcrafted string instruments that commanded thousands of dollars each. I had gotten to know all of the boys and even flew out to a few of their weddings, but I did not expect to see their wives here with wrapped presents of towels and bake ware.

Ben's sister Marion, ten years older, had eight children, which was why he often chose not to spend any holidays with her, as that particular branch of the family had pretty much exploded with small children. I had met Marion—one of those tiny, frail-looking women who constantly complained about vague, annoying health issues, but who could put together a meal for seventy-five in an hour using just pantry ingredients.

Tyler slunk in, obviously threatened to within an inch of his little life, and snuggled next to Jessica on the couch. She immediately pulled out her phone and started doing something on it that had the little boy in giggles. Lily had grabbed a plateful of cold appetizers from under the caterer's nose and was examining them closely.

"These look amazing," she said. "Are these the same people you're using, Miranda?"

Miranda nodded and snatched what looked like crab salad nestled in a tiny green leaf of something. "Yes. Mom's suggestion. Those people from Madison."

"I always forget about them," Lily said. "Carmella said she had someone in mind, but I'm going to have her talk to these people when she gets here."

My head swiveled. "Gets here? Is she coming to the shower?"

"Of course, Mona. After all, she's going to be family, isn't she?"

I should have been paying more attention to all of this. I grabbed a green apple slice topped with Brie and mango chutney and thought dark thoughts.

Phyllis arrived next, sadly without Rebecca. Rebecca was snowed in, in Amherst. Apparently even the most powerful Wiccans cannot control the weather.

Marion arrived with three of her daughters. She looked like Ben —same dark hair and amazing eyes, but he got all the beauty. Poor woman. To grow up looking back at a younger brother as dazzling as Ben must have been hard, but I knew they were fairly close.

There was a flurry of noise and laughter as two or three groups of Miranda's friends arrived all at once. These young women all blended together in a whirl of short skirts, long hair, and very high heels. How did they walk anywhere? And phones—none of them had a purse, but they all held on to their phones as if they were their most glamorous accessory, which, in a way, I suppose they were.

We had hit the halfway point, guestwise.

Patricia and MarshaMarsha arrived with Anthony. I had tried to explain to Anthony that it really was all about the women, but he had spoken to Dominique directly and had been added to the list. Miranda, of course, was delighted—they were each other's number one fan.

A few women arrived whom I recognized from Brian's office— among them his executive assistant and another I recognized from HR. They greeted me vaguely, as if I were someone they had met on a cruise rather than the woman who had been at Brian's side for every work-related party, dinner, or event for years.

A few more from the Cutler cousins, Miranda's roommates from Boston, and someone who was introduced to me as David's aunt on the Calhoun side—Ellen's sister.

Carmella was among the last to arrive, and she brought her sisters, Assunta ("Call me Suzi") and Vincenza ("Enza, darling, *pul-eeze*"). The three of them were cut from the same cloth—beautiful, dark-haired, with curves that left little to the imagination. They turned heads completely as they entered, lots of gold flashing and breasts bobbing. They had matching tans, although I knew that Carmella had not been with them in Aruba. Had she stopped for a spray tan on her way to see Ben? Patricia, martini in hand, raised her eyebrows upon their entrance.

"Good Lord, three of them?"

I nodded as Lily embraced them. She had spent the last few days in a private villa in Aruba with the two other sisters, so of course there was much hugging and kissing. Lily introduced us, and I had to brace myself—they hugged and kissed me as well, welcoming me to the family before they drifted away, leaving me in a cloud of Shalimar.

Patricia laid a hand on my arm. "Are you sure you're not drinking?"

I shook my head. "I can't. I have to drive. Besides, Dominique could cave any minute, and if she does, someone is going to have to run this party."

Patricia raised an eyebrow again, but did not question me further. She knew she'd get the whole story behind that remark and was quite prepared to wait.

I looked around. The crowd began in the living room and spread into the dining room and on through the family room. There was a separate cluster in the kitchen. Dominique was working the room like a pro, being the perfect hostess, not a single blond hair out of place. The mountain of gifts by the fireplace would take hours upon hours to go through. And there was hot food coming.

We could all be here for days.

Two hours later, a few token gifts had been opened.

There had been a great deal of food eaten and various types of beverages consumed. We had played a few very inventive games, including Best Advice/Worst Advice, Name That Fictional Husband and Wife, and, my personal favorite, the team challenge Mother-Daughter What Would You Do?

Anthony, who managed to find a nickname for anyone and everyone, immediately tagged Carmella and her sisters "Act Four, Scene One." Anthony, being a very literary kind of guy, was alluding to the scene in *Hamlet* where the three witches made their appearance. Patricia chided him, claiming the reference was too obscure. He agreed, instantly renaming them Nina, Pinta, and Santa Maria. Every time I looked over at one of them, however, I imagined all of them hunched over a bubbling cauldron.

My daughter, Miranda, was overwhelmed. This was a girl who, for most of her life, expected that the earth would revolve around her every whim. A few months with David Cutler and she was humbled and grateful by everyone's obvious good wishes. She did not spend all her time huddled with her sisters or gossiping with her friends. She talked to everyone—even David's family, whom she had never met before. Miranda was by no means shy, but talking to strangers had always been hard for her.

"Maybe Ben is right," I said to MarshaMarsha.

"Of course Ben is right," she answered. "About what?"

"Maybe they will live happily ever after. Maybe I'm totally wrong, and I should stop overthinking this."

She sighed. "Well, Mona, I wouldn't want any of my boys to marry somebody they had only known for a few months. But I have to admit, these two seem really right for each other."

"Yes, they do, don't they?" I was finding myself more and more accepting of them as a couple. How could I not? They were disgustingly adorable together. As a *married* couple—that still seemed fairly unacceptable, but the idea was creeping up on me.

"Are the presents going to be opened?" she asked. "Because as it is, we'll be here until Tuesday."

Jessica came up beside us. "No, it's not about the gifts. She'll open them at home with David."

MarshaMarsha made a face. "What about the bouquet?"

"What bouquet?" Jess asked.

"You know, made from all the trimmings?" MarshaMarsha explained. "All the bows and ribbons are saved and taped to a paper plate, and that's the bouquet she uses during the rehearsal."

Jess looked stunned. "People do that? That's the stupidest thing I've ever heard of." She raised her voice. "Hey, Miranda! Guess what?" She trotted over in obvious delight.

I looked at MarshaMarsha. "Are we really that old?"

She shook her head. "Apparently. When did that happen?"

Aunt Lily still maintained control of the living room. In her immediate orbit were Nina, Pinta, and Santa Maria, my ex-mother-in-law, the Cutler contingent, and Ellen's sister.

The dining room was filled with the twenty-something crowd. For a group of young women all so thin as to make my own stomach ache from hunger, they stayed close to the food and seemed to be in constant grazing mode.

Brian's coworkers were huddled in the kitchen with Dominique, where there was really no comfortable spot to sit, but it had the obvious advantage of being right next to the liquor.

I held the foyer with Anthony, MarshaMarsha, and Patricia. Patricia had obviously bribed one of the waiters, because although we were relatively removed from the crowd, there was a constant stream of food and drink coming our way.

"Well, here's a question," Patricia said. "If she doesn't open any gifts, how do we know when this is over?"

Anthony frowned. "No clue. Let me see what I can find out." He squared his shoulders and headed for the dining room.

Dominique had been circulating like a pro. She spent several minutes with Phyllis, and things looked heated at one point, but Carmella said something to defuse the situation, and Dominique moved on.

"I don't normally enjoy this sort of thing," Patricia said, "but this seems to call for lawn chairs and a cooler."

I nodded. "Dominique thinks Brian is cheating on her," I said.

"Oh, no," MarshaMarsha said. "That's terrible. And with Tyler so young!"

"Where is the little beast, by the way?" Patricia asked.

"Upstairs. She got a babysitter for the afternoon. She was crying on my shoulder earlier."

"Well, that's rather cheeky," Patricia said.

I shrugged. "I feel bad for her."

"Of course you do," MarshaMarsha said. "It's not her fault Brian is a cad."

Patricia looked over at MarshaMarsha. "Cad? Is that really the best you can come up with? He's beyond cad. He's a complete and utter—"

There was a loud knock behind us, and the front door opened cautiously. David's head peeked in.

"Hey, Mona, Is it okay for me to come in?"

I pulled the door wide and kissed his cheek. "I'm clueless here, David. So come on in. Hey, Ben."

He was wearing his dark wool coat, not his work jacket, with a red wool scarf wrapped around his throat. His cheeks were slightly flushed from the cold, his hair was tousled, and there was a faint shadow on his jaw.

Oh, m'gosh.

He touched my cheek and gave me a light kiss on my forehead. I resisted the urge to drag him into the guest bathroom and scatter some silver and lavender balls around. After all, we weren't those two people anymore.

"And how are things?" he asked, pulling off his gloves.

"The kids are going to have to buy another house just to fit all this stuff. The food is amazing; make sure you grab a plate. Lily is behaving, and Carmella brought her sisters. The three of them are kind of hard to miss."

He chuckled. "Yes, I can see that. They certainly look a lot alike, don't they?"

Anthony, honing in on Ben, returned from the dining room. "Now that David is here, they're going to say a few words, then get the bulldozer in here to collect their presents. Hey, Ben, you're looking quite dashing."

"You too, Anthony. I've got my truck, and I'll take most of this back to my place." He shrugged out of his coat and hung it in the closet. "I'm going to grab some food." He headed for the dining room. I narrowed my eyes as Carmella casually rose from her chair, making a subtle "follow me" gesture to her sisters, and headed after him. Nina and Pinta followed smoothly. Lily, deep in conversation with Phyllis, lifted an eyebrow as they left, glanced around, found Ben, then shot me a look. She returned to Phyllis, barely missing a beat.

The noise in the dining room was pretty intense. The long table had been pushed against one wall opposite a huge breakfront, and all the food was laid out. The dining chairs, along with pretty folding chairs, were grouped in twos and threes around small round tables covered with gray tablecloths. The young women were all sitting, standing, leaning—some were stretched out on the floor, texting. The noise was interrupted—kind of a wave of silence—as Ben made his way toward the food and was noticed by every single female in the room. Yes, he was old enough to be the father of most of them, but his kind of looks were ageless.

I watched Carmella. Man, she was slick. She didn't touch Ben, but introduced her sisters, manipulating herself so that her boobs never bumped his arm, but he was very aware of her trying to avoid the collision. Her sisters were showing no such restraint. Ben was getting a big-boob massage from both of them.

He stood, half-filled plate in one hand, a spoonful of spring peas in cream sauce in the other, with a very faint smile on his face as he nodded, often, and tried to move. The man was trapped. Those three women closed in around him and had him as helpless as if he'd been surrounded by iron bars. He caught my eye.

Half of me was screaming obscenities at Carmella and her vile and obvious plan to hijack Ben right in front of my nose. But the other half of me kind of enjoyed seeing Ben in a completely new situation—uncomfortable around a woman. Or rather, a trio of women. He recognized a superior enemy and was actually awaiting rescue.

I squared my shoulders and walked over.

There were a few square inches of Ben's back that were not covered by one of the sisters, but that was all I needed. I slid both of my arms around his waist and brought the palms of my hands up the front of his shirt, bringing my head over his shoulder. "Ben, darling, here you are. I was afraid you'd been shanghaied."

Ben turned his head toward mine, his eyes dancing, a smile playing around the corners of his mouth. "Almost."

The sisters fell back a step, and I slid in under his arm, taking the spoonful of peas and putting it back in the bowl. "Not those, Ben." I reached over and plucked a tiny crab cake off a platter. "These were amazing," I cooed, holding it up in front of his mouth.

He leaned forward and took it from my fingertips, chewed, swallowed, then smiled appreciatively. "Yes. Amazing."

I made a little pouty face and held up my thumb. A stray bit of crab cake clung. He bent his head, took my thumb in his mouth, and when I drew it out, the stray bit was gone.

"The best part," he said.

Luckily I was sort of leaning against him, because I swear my knees buckled just a little.

Behind me, Nina, Pinta, and Santa Maria breathed a collective sigh.

I beamed at them. "Isn't the food marvelous?" I asked.

They all nodded, perfectly synchronized.

I focused on Carmella. "Do you think you'll use these folks for your dad's wedding?" I asked, keeping a fixed smile.

Her eyes narrowed, but she pasted on her professional face. "Yes, I think so. Being local helps."

"Yes," I agreed. I could feel Ben relax a little.

"I'm going to get more food," he said, and moved away.

I stood firm, blocking any attempt Carmella might have made to follow. I turned to the other sisters. "Are you ladies getting excited?"

Suzi was wearing a dark blue scarf, distinguishing her from Enza, who was wearing a black-and-gold scarf. "Yes. Carmella seems to be doing her usual fantastic job," she said.

"And on such a short timeline," Enza added.

I nodded. "She's a very fast worker."

We all smiled.

I saw that Ben had made it over to the Lily zone and was seated next to his sister. I grabbed another crab cake, popped it in my mouth, and backed away slowly.

Miranda and David made a glorious couple. David was not quite as handsome as Ben, but he was still rather a stunner. Miranda had always been pretty, and as I watched her laughing with Marion, her arm through David's, I realized what was different. She was a woman in love. She *did* shine. She was radiating happiness. Suddenly, placed next to this lovely young man, she reflected his obvious devotion.

Wow, I thought.

Ben was leaning in to hear something his sister had said. He glanced up, caught my eye, and nodded briefly—*Thanks*.

I felt the usual jolt—first in my throat, then down to my belly.

When I stood next to Ben, was I equally transformed?

Carmella appeared at my shoulder, watching Ben. "Do you want him or not?"

"Of course."

"Then do something quick, sister. Because I will take him if I can."

"But you can't, Carmella. He's in love with me."

She turned her head and looked at me. "And how stupid are you to think that's enough?"

Then she walked away.

CHAPTER TWELVE

ANTHONY CAME OVER. AS OF 12:01 a.m. on January fourth, three of my books went on sale. We had discussed a preorder option, and then decided against it. We had sent out a newsletter informing readers what was coming up. Anthony had launched a huge Facebook campaign, and a few of my favorite reviewers and bloggers promised to give a shout-out. I tried to write. Anthony went from one retail site to another, hitting the refresh button, trying to track sales. This was big. Actually, it was huge. Was I going to be one of those self-publishing success stories that would rise to the top of the best sellers list all over again, or was I going to sink slowly into who-was-she-again oblivion?

"Am I rich yet?" I asked him—again—around one in the afternoon.

Anthony sighed. "Why won't you show me what Ben got you for Christmas?"

"It's just a piece of jewelry."

Anthony turned away from the computer. "The words *just* and *jewelry* never appear in the same sentence. It's a rule."

"Is not." Anthony was right. It was not just a piece of jewelry. It was something beautiful that also said a lot about Ben and me in just a few words. "Anthony, how many books have I sold?"

He'd been writing things down. He frowned at his notebook, then smiled. "Probably enough for a bauble."

"Really?"

"Yes. Now show me that present."

"It's in the house."

"I can wait." He sat back, folded his arms across his chest, then raised his eyebrows. "I got nowhere else to be, baby cakes. I can wait here all day."

I glared at him, got up, went down the stairs, then ran into the house.

Ben's gift was back under the tree, right next to the beautiful cashmere shawl Lauren and Jess had gotten for me. I grabbed the shawl and Ben's little box and went back out to the garage.

Anthony had—seriously—not moved an inch, but his eyes lit up as I got to the top of the stairs. "That shawl is gorgeous! Who?"

"Thing One and Thing Two," I told him. "They're getting much better at gift giving. Remember the year they gave me Zumba lessons?"

I handed him the bracelet, and he turned it over carefully in his hands, reading the inscription out loud. "What does it mean?"

"It's from a quote that Ben found. 'You know you're in love when you can't fall asleep because reality is finally better than your dreams.'"

"Oh, how beautiful! Who said it? Robert Browning? I love Browning."

"Dr. Seuss."

His face fell. "Are you kidding?"

"No. Seuss was a very smart man."

"Sure, if you're a red fish or blue fish."

"I once told Ben that being in love with him was better than anything I could have written. Then he found that quote."

"See, I told you the two of you just needed time. Let's face it—the man is crazy for you."

Oh, Anthony, I so wish that I could believe you.

Miranda called me—again.

So far, in one week, she had called me to tell me that she loved her job, hated her job, hated Boston snow, made a friend at work, loved her job again, and had cooked a roast chicken for dinner that took her only three and a half hours.

And it was only Wednesday.

"Mom, I just got an RSVP from Aunt Grace."

We had sent my older sister, Grace, an invitation to the wedding as a pure formality. Although I had flown out for the weddings of three of her five sons, Grace had not left Oregon in more than twenty years, and as far as I knew had never gotten on a plane to anywhere. She had driven to Florida once a year when our mother was still alive, but she had often voiced her contempt for the East Coast. New Jersey, in particular, was full of idiots, religious conservatives, money-mongering opportunists, and Republicans. She would remain on her commune, surrounded by like-minded liberal, environmentally correct, nonmaterialistic animal lovers, thank you very much.

"Well, honey, we knew she wouldn't come out here."

"Yeah? Well, that's the thing. She *is* coming. With a guest."

"Really?"

She giggled. "Uncle Shadow."

Let's face it, "Uncle Shadow" is a little tough to say with a straight face.

I stared out my kitchen window for a moment, focusing on a left-hand corner of my garage, trying to collect my thoughts. Was she really going to drive all the way out here? What could have prompted such an outburst of family loyalty? She'd certainly never shown any before. "Really?"

"Yes. She asked for the names of hotels in the area."

"Really?" That was still the best I could manage.

"Mom?"

"Yes. I'm here. I'll send her an e-mail." There were no phone lines at the commune, and no cell phone service. But three times a week one of her sons drove into town with a laptop, as most of Shadow's business was now conducted online. An e-mail was better than snail mail, the usual means of communication between my sister and myself.

Lily was home—Vinnie had flown out to Las Vegas for the week, and Lily had declined to go with him. She had been sitting across from me, and looked concerned. "What, dear?"

"Grace and Shadow are coming to the wedding."

Her coffee mug hit the tabletop. "Really?"

See—it wasn't just me.

"Yes. And she was asking for names of nearby hotels."

"Really?"

"Yes." I sat back down and my eyes met Aunt Lily's.

"You know, I'm practically moved out of my rooms," Lily said. "You could ask her to stay here."

I leaned back. "How is that going? Playing house with Vinnie?"

She smiled a slightly wicked smile. "I'm having the time of my life. It's nice that he's away right now—you know how I enjoy my private time—but I miss him. He's a darling man."

I would not go so far as to call him a darling anything, but I had to admit he'd grown on me a little bit in the past few months.

"Grace and I…" I began. I stopped. Grace and I what? Were never close? Had absolutely nothing in common? Lived on opposite sides of the country for a good reason?

"Exactly," Lily said. "It's time for you and Grace to reconnect."

"That statement implies that there once *was* a connection. I don't think that was ever true."

"I remember you as children. You adored her. And she once told me that she thought you were the sweetest person on earth."

"How old was I when she said that?"

"Six. But still, family ties are very strong. This is a wonderful opportunity for you both."

"For us both to do what?"

She leaned forward and grabbed my hand. "I'm old, Mona. And I have learned a great deal in my life. Family is the most important thing there is, whether it's the family you were born into or the family you create. If you have a chance to make a real connection with your sister, take it. Who knows when you'll have another opportunity."

So I sent Grace an e-mail inviting her and Shadow to stay with me for as long as they liked.

And I got an e-mail back, saying they accepted.

The week before Miranda and David's wedding, the entire bridal party, as well as their friends and family members, got on a private yacht docked off South Street Seaport, and sailed around the island of Manhattan as the winter sun was setting. There was food and champagne and soft music.

David's roommate from Yale, a serious young man named Roy Smith, had landed some sort of stock market job in his father's firm. It must have paid very well, because in addition to the yacht, food, champagne, there were several white-jacketed waitpersons buzzing around, replacing half-empty champagne flutes with brisk efficiency. Lauren and Jessica got tipsy right away. I knew that their demographic was used to warm vodka, straight, so I could only blame their condition on the unfamiliar bubbles.

It was a lovely evening. The bridal party had filled out to include a few young people who would be doing readings during the ceremony. Also included was the harp player (a friend of Miranda's from Boston), a few young Yale types (extra ushers), and Father McLaren, who would be marrying the couple in a week.

Brian looked happy and relaxed. Dominique did not. Dominique walked back and forth between the food table and the bar, while Brian charmed the few younger women who had not been forewarned by Miranda.

Ben asked me to dance, then suggested we go to the empty upper deck. My whole body tingled. Dancing with Ben was one of the best things ever. His arms around me, my head on his shoulder —even on a damp and cold night like this one, I knew it would be the highlight of my day.

"This," I said to him, "is so much better than separate bachelor and bachelorette parties."

"I agree. Although I haven't had a lap dance in a while."

I tilted my head up to his and arched my eyebrows. "Maybe later?"

He did not laugh. He didn't even smile.

"What?"

He tightened his arms around me. "I've got a job. Luxury condos. *Very* high-end. Waterfront."

"That's great. Where?"

"Maine."

"The state of Maine?"

"Yes."

I tucked my head back against his shoulder and didn't say

anything for a while. Finally: "When?"

"They want me there now. I told them right after the wedding."

"Ah."

The music changed, something Latin and upbeat. Ben stepped back. "I'll probably be gone for two or three months."

I stared at the decking. "How often will you be coming home?"

"I don't know."

I took a deep breath. "I thought that after the wedding, you and I were going to talk things out. Isn't that what you said we'd do?"

"I thought it would work out that way. But let's face it, Mona, we're both dug in. What could I possibly say to you that would make you marry me that hasn't already been said? Besides, this job is...well, it's an opportunity."

"Of course." I looked up at him. It was cold and his breath was visible in the pale light from inside the yacht. "What do you want us to do?"

He shrugged. "We're still friends, Mona. We will always be friends."

I nodded, but my brain was screaming, *No!* I did not want us to be friends. I wanted us to go back to what we'd been before, lovers, partners, two halves of a glorious whole.

"I will always love you."

I nodded again, feeling suddenly cold and empty.

"I'll be back in time for Lily's wedding. I would not miss that for the world."

"Of course not," I said, my voice cracking a little. "You know, it's getting nasty out here. I think I want to go inside now."

He took my arm, and we walked down the stairs and into the closed lower deck. People were still laughing. Miranda and David were engaged in a deep conversation with Father McLaren. Jessica and Lauren were both dancing with Ethan, and he was blushing from exertion. Brian caught my eye and nodded.

It looked like the world had continued on after all.

My sister drove from Oregon, leaving on Sunday and taking the southern route to avoid any snowstorms in the Midwest. She arrived early Thursday morning. Very early. In fact, I was still asleep, and only woke at all because Fred shot off the bed, barking like a mad thing, alerting me to the fact that someone was knocking on my front door at 6:23 a.m.

I stumbled downstairs, pulling on my robe. I knew it was Grace, of course. She had called the night before, telling me they were driving the last leg straight through because of a predicted snowstorm Thursday evening. And I'm sure I heard "sometime after six," but I probably went to sleep in a state of denial.

I had not seen her in almost six years. When I opened the door, she looked so much like our mother that it was a shock. But she hugged me hard, picking me up off my feet and swinging me around in my foyer.

"Mona, you look the same. How did that happen?" she cried.

"And you look just like Mom!"

She laughed as she shrugged off her coat. Shadow came in behind her, carrying two pieces of luggage. He smiled crookedly at me.

"Mona."

"Shadow, your hair!" I cried, hugging him. "What happened?"

Shadow had maintained his waist-length ponytail since the seventies. Now he was completely bald, his beautifully shaped skull gleaming under the hall light.

He shrugged. "Started losing hair. Friar Tuck with a ponytail. Looked all kinds of stupid."

I laughed and hugged Grace again. "Come on in, you two. I'll make coffee. And eggs? Toast? I have fruit salad." I had no idea what they were eating these days. They had already cycled through vegetarianism, no red meat, homegrown only, organic homegrown only, commercial organic, no wheat, and no dairy. The last time Grace and I talked food, she was making a Tofurky for Christmas, with gluten-free cheesecake. I had no idea where they currently fell in the food pyramid, so I just hoped for the best.

"Coffee sounds great. And eggs, please. Scrambled's fine. Can I help?"

"No, sit. Tell me, how was the trip?"

She made a face.

My sister had always favored my mother—pale skin, strawberry-blond hair, and freckles. People didn't believe we were sisters, as I had the dark hair and eyes of our father, not to mention a slightly olive complexion. We were even built differently—I was short waisted with boobs and no butt. She was much taller and willowy —reed like, although this morning she looked more treelike. Her waist had noticeably thickened. Her hair was cut short, in a simple bob, and it was turning white, lightening her hair color to almost... pink?

Shadow, on the other hand, must have had a pretty bad-looking portrait stashed away somewhere, because his face was unlined, his teeth flashed, and he was still thin as a rail. He was wearing what he had always worn—jeans, a denim shirt, and cowboy boots. The same outfit he'd worn on his wedding day. Grace was in a long gray skirt of a thickish material—hemp?—and a woolen dark green obviously hand-knitted sweater. And I mean obviously in a not-so-good sort of way.

The coffeemaker started making noise, and Grace was looking around the kitchen. "Beautiful, Mona. What a pleasure it must be to cook in a kitchen like this."

Her own kitchen, I knew, was a low-ceilinged room with only one window, a stove that ran on propane, an icebox—with ice— and running water that depended on solar power to heat. Living in Oregon, she took a lot of cold showers, I knew, and washed her dishes by hand in water heated on the stove.

"Yes, well, the evils of modern capitalism. There is an upside."

Grace never minded my having money, because I was a writer. Brian, as a greedy corporate drone, had a paycheck stained with the blood of the proletariat, but I earned my money honestly, through my own effort and imagination.

I scrambled eggs and started making toast. Shadow went off to use the bathroom. Grace rummaged through my drawers and set the table. When Shadow returned we were sitting down, eating. I was almost awake.

"How are the wedding plans?" Grace asked, turning over the toast to see if side A was as evenly browned as side B.

I shrugged. "Running perfectly. Lily engaged a wedding planner, and I must admit the woman has been a marvel."

"And who is the lucky young man again?" she asked. "Did you tell me he's the son of your boyfriend?" Toast was approved. She took a bite.

I chewed my toast a little slower. "Yes. I mean, no. That is, Ben and I are taking a break."

Her brown eyes were as shrewd as ever beneath her pale brows. "I'm sorry. You two had been together awhile, yes?"

I nodded.

"So what happened?"

"We had a disagreement."

"Are you kidding? A disagreement? Shadow and I have a disagreement at least once a week."

Shadow, his mouth full of breakfast, nodded.

"Yes, well, this was a kind of big disagreement. About love and marriage, and what it takes for two people to spend the rest of their lives together."

Grace nodded and sighed. She ate a few bites. "I'm sorry, Mona. I'm sure he was a lovely man. And Lily's wedding? The last name of her fiancée sounded familiar, so I had Sinclair Google it." All of Grace's sons were named after authors who, in Grace's opinion, were game changers in the writing world. They were, in no particular order, Sinclair, Harper, Fyodor, Edgar, and Raymond. For all her deep thoughts and feelings, she had a soft spot for the hard-boiled detective novel.

"Really?" Oh, this was going to be good.

"Did you know that there was a very notorious crime family with that very same name?"

"No!"

"Yes. From Brooklyn." She arched her eyebrows. "No relation, I'm sure, but interesting."

Now, what were the chances that she would drive out for the second time in just a few months—after avoiding Westfield, New Jersey, like the plague ever since I'd lived here—to attend Lily's wedding? And if she did attend, would she notice all those black Town Cars? And young men with sidearm bulges under their dark suits? And the machine gun nests in the oak trees?

"Vinnie is retired," I told her.

"From what?"

"Selling shoes."

Shadow frowned. "Same family."

"Yep."

Grace leaned back in her chair and glanced over at Shadow, who shrugged. "How could you allow that to happen, Mona?"

Ah, yes. And here it came. "How could I allow what, Grace? How could I allow a grown woman with a life of her own—and some *very* strong opinions on how to run that life—how could I allow her to meet someone and decide to marry him?"

"She was living in your house."

"While I was out in California. Even if I wasn't, she was never on a leash. She's been running rampant for years, and you know it. *You* try talking her out of something once she's decided on it."

Grace shook her head sadly. "Mona, I must admit I'm rather disappointed that you couldn't handle something like this."

Of course she was disappointed. She always was. Which is why we got along so much better when we were living on opposite sides of the country.

Shadow, always a man of very few words, said, "Mph." Profound as ever.

Something that I recognized as her martyr face appeared. "I'll talk to her."

"And say what? Aunt Lily, even though you're a fairly sane, financially independent, and thoroughly emancipated woman, I forbid you to marry that man?"

"Well, obviously you never said anything to dissuade her."

Oh, my God. "No, I didn't. If she's happy, I'm happy for her. And now, if I ever want anybody knocked off, I have a guy I can call. More coffee?"

Grace nodded. I poured. Shadow shrugged and finished eating in silence.

"I assume there will be some sort of bachelor party?" Grace asked. "Not that Shadow would go, but I'm curious."

"No bachelor party. Or bachelorette. We all went on a sunset cruise last weekend and blew off lots of steam. Food, drink, dancing—it was great fun." Except for the part where my world caved in, of course. I was still getting used to the idea that Ben and I were no longer a couple. It was like trying to get used to breathing rock.

"What a wonderful idea."

"David is a wonderful young man. I always thought so, even before he decided to marry my daughter."

"And what does he do?"

Oh, blast. "He's in finance," I tried to bury my last word behind a slurp of coffee, but she caught it anyway.

"How sad. Couldn't your poor daughter find a man with a more worthwhile occupation?"

"No. And she started work at a bank."

Grace closed her eyes as a shudder ran through her body. "Oh."

There was a moment of silence.

Shadow got up to put his plate and coffee mug in the sink. "Show me?"

I nodded, and he followed me up the stairs, then up to Lily's now empty suite. He dropped the suitcases with a thump. "Nice."

"This was where Lily stayed. You and Grace should be very comfortable. How long are you staying?"

He half smiled. "As long as the two of you can stand to be around each other," he answered.

It was the longest sentence I had heard come out of his mouth since 1983.

I never had a very good relationship with my sister, and it looked like it was beyond repair at this point. She was smug and condescending, criticizing everything from my shallow, materialistic lifestyle to the total lack of social responsibility in my children, obviously a result of my poor parenting. I reacted badly to all of that of course—she was not my mother, therapist, or priest, so where did she come off passing judgment? Whenever we were in the same room together, I reverted back to my snotty thirteen-year-old self.

It got ugly.

But Grace and my daughters? Well, that was another story. Miranda, growing up, was not at all curious about her West Coast family, and her few visits out to Oregon remained memorable in her mind more for the airplane rides and any occasion that required new clothes. The last time the twins had spent time with Grace, they actually looked like twins. As they had grown older, Miranda grew more detached, but Jessica had become more fascinated. She had once asked to fly out to stay with Grace, while Lauren barely remembered her existence.

Grace, for her part, was torn. Jess, with her tattoos, piercings, and longtime record of wreaking havoc as a matter of course, was a natural fit for Grace. However, attending a liberal private college? As a math major? Now, if Jessica were looking forward to teaching mathematics to struggling inner-city school kids, Grace might have had a different attitude. But people with degrees from private colleges rarely landed on the inner-city side of anything. More likely Jess would end up working for a large corporation, a think tank, or—gasp—the government. So, what was a dyed-in-the-wool liberal near-anarchist to do with a rebellious niece obviously heading toward life in the establishment lane?

Jessica arrived home Friday by noon. It had snowed the night before, as predicted, almost six inches, but by midday the roads were clear, and the temperature was rising, melting pretty much everything. Grace and I had spent a fairly peaceful twenty-four hours together. Shadow had slept almost continuously. The only obvious conflict came when Grace lit up a joint at the dinner table, and I had to inform her that no smoking—of any kind—was allowed in my home, but she was more than welcome to sit out on the back deck. She made a face. Shadow took the joint and braved the cold, snow, and wind alone, came back inside, and went immediately back to sleep.

Jessica came into the kitchen and sniffed. Her face lit up. "Aunt Gracie smokes?"

I hugged her. "Yes. Can we not spread it around? So far, *don't ask, don't tell* has worked pretty well around here."

She shrugged out of her jacket and dumped her backpack on the counter. "When is Miranda due in?"

I glanced at the clock. "Now. The snow was a bit thicker up there, but she and David were leaving early. Lauren is taking a later train, but should be here by three. Can you pick her up?"

She nodded. I noticed that her nose ring had been replaced by a tiny gold stud, and all the hoops in her left ear matched. Her left ear, by the way, was more visible than her right ear, because she had shaved a graceful arc on the left side of her head back in September, and it had not grown back in.

"Where's Aunt Grace?" she asked.

"Walking back from town. They wanted to see Westfield. They're bringing something for lunch."

She sat. "How is it going?"

"My sister thinks I've failed as a responsible relative because I did not prevent Lily from finding Vinnie."

"Oh. So, how is it your older sister never met Aunt Lily?"

I laughed. "I know. You'd think she'd remember something about Lily, but no, she'd rather assume this was a preventable disaster that I sat back and watched."

She was watching me carefully. "That boat thing last weekend was great."

I nodded. "Yes, it was. A terrific idea. I think everyone enjoyed themselves very much."

"Except for you. What happened?"

I looked at Jessica. She and Lauren both had my father's eyes. In Lauren, I always found comfort looking into them. With Jessica, I always found that pressing, probing need-to-know look that was the other side of my gentle, loving father. "Ben is leaving for Maine right after the wedding. He has a big job up there. We're sort of broken up."

Her jaw dropped. "But I like Ben! Mom, this sucks. Why don't you just marry him? I bet he'd cancel Maine if you said yes."

"No, honey, he wouldn't. This is his career, and it's a big step. Just like I wouldn't have canceled LA."

"You're not Ben."

"I would not ask him to do that. It means a great deal to him." And it did. And knowing that, I would have followed him up there as a loyal camp follower if he'd asked.

"So do you. You mean everything to him. I know that Dad really sucked as a husband, but Ben is a very different kind of man.

He wouldn't make you miserable. In fact, you'd probably like being married to him."

I walked over to her and put my arms around her. "When did you get so smart?"

"Third grade. Where have you been?"

I started to laugh. Grace and Shadow came through the kitchen door, and Jessica jumped up in delight. There was a spurt of activity, and by the end of lunch—roasted veggies on gluten-free artisanal rolls, with quinoa salad—alliances had been forged. The three of them announced another walk, and I could imagine all my neighbors looking out their windows and seeing my daughter sharing a joint with her aunt and uncle. I tried blocking out the visual by going upstairs and finding something to wear to the rehearsal dinner.

Miranda arrived. David came in with her carrying three suitcases.

"Honey, your dress is here. Your shoes and veil are here. Your going-away dress is here. You're spending one night at the Pierre before going back to Boston. Why do you need three suitcases?"

Because Miranda had been at her new job less than two weeks, she did not ask for time off for her honeymoon. She had negotiated a leave in May, when she and David would fly to Paris, on my dime, for ten days. But it looked like she'd packed *way* early.

"Rehearsal dinner, remember?"

"The Highlawn Pavilion is fancy, but you don't need a formal gown and train."

David just grinned and carried her luggage upstairs, then drove off to Ben's.

I sat with her as she dragged clothes out of her suitcases and hung them in her now-empty closet. She had taken the last of her clothes with her after the shower, and I had occasionally come up here just to gaze in wonder at the empty space. But in five minutes she managed to replace eighty percent of the clutter.

She talked nonstop—her job, the drive down, David's boss— before she threw herself down on the bed and gave a long sigh.

"I'm getting married tomorrow."

"I know, baby. How does it feel?"

"Amazing. How does it feel for you?"

Tears came in such a fierce rush I surprised myself. Miranda was getting married. A handsome young man had swept her off her feet, and tomorrow they were going to announce in front of the world their love and commitment to each other. How did this happen? Last week she was still a baby.

"Mom, are you crying? You're supposed to be happy for me. I really hoped by now you'd have changed your mind."

Tears were in her eyes as well, and I grabbed her and hugged her tightly.

"I am happy for you, Miranda. I know how much you and David love each other, and that's *so* important. It's just...this is such a huge step. You don't even know. And I want you to have a good marriage. I just wish I could tell you how to do that."

She nodded against my shoulder. "I know. But don't worry, okay? David knows."

I pulled away and looked hard at her.

"He does?"

She shrugged. "It's fine, Mom. Growing up in this house I learned what it meant to be a hardworking, independent woman. You showed me everything I needed to know about going it alone. Not so much about what a good marriage was all about. I know—Dad was the jerk. But—you let him be the jerk."

Oh. "Miranda, I'm so sorry."

"Don't apologize, Mom. If I hadn't met David, I probably would have been the most successful single person of my entire generation, thanks to you."

"So, where did David learn about what a good marriage is?"

"From Ben, of course."

Of course.

There were noises downstairs. Jess was back. Fred was barking. I gave Miranda another hug.

"You're going to be an amazing wife."

"Yeah. I think so too."

The Highlawn Pavilion holds a special place in my heart. Not just because it's a fabulous restaurant with incredible food, impeccable service, and a view to die for, but it's also where Patricia and I had our first martini together. Patricia ate there on a regular basis, and I often met her there on a weekday afternoon, just for another perfectly made vodka martini.

The rehearsal dinner was scheduled for 8:00 p.m. on Friday evening, the rehearsal itself starting at six. I was worried about checking on the dinner space beforehand, but Patricia called to tell me she would go over there herself and make sure everything was perfect. Having rich friends was a wonderful thing.

The church in Montclair was beautiful, one of those old stone buildings that looked like a Scottish castle, with stained glass and a dark, polished altar. Father McLaren was a rather tense sort, but he ran a good rehearsal. Everyone learned where to stand and how fast to walk. The usual complications—bouquet handoffs, candle lightings, getting to and from the podium—were ironed out with little fanfare. I sat in my designated pew and got teary every time Brian walked Miranda down the aisle.

Tyler refused to take off his cape, and relinquished his laser gun only when he realized he couldn't carry it without dropping the all-important rings.

Father McLaren suggested that Ben and I walk down together and, upon arriving at the altar, turn and walk into our separate pews. The symbolism was too much for me, so I walked down the aisle escorted by Ethan.

The organist was there, and so was the choir. They would sing in the guests, and sing them out again. They gave us only a sample, but they sounded magnificent. The harpist would play during the ceremony after the vows were said and during the candle lighting.

There is absolutely nothing as useless during a wedding as the mother of the bride. I was grateful to Dominique, because as partner to the father of the bride, she was the only one lower than I in the pecking order. In fact, she didn't even get a special escort. She took it quite gracefully.

Of course, Carmella was there. She was recording the entire affair on her iPad to incorporate it into the final wedding video. She also double checked with the harpist and the choir. She had extra copies of the readings in case anyone forgot to bring theirs.

She insisted that she would take over Tyler duty so that Dominique could walk down the aisle with the other guests.

She also gave Ben a lingering hug and spent a few minutes whispering in his ear. He leaned down into her, nodding, and finally breaking into a smile.

Something twisted in my gut. That had been my job, making Ben smile.

Grace and Shadow, as honored out-of-town guests, hung out in the back row, watching. I knew that their attitude toward organized religion was one of general contempt, but they remained quiet and respectful throughout.

Three run-throughs and we were finished. We piled into our cars and drove out to the Highlawn Pavilion.

I had been worried that Shadow would not be appropriately dressed for the occasion, but he cleaned up very nicely in a double-breasted navy jacket and a subtle red tie. For what I was paying for this little dinner, I presumed he could have arrived naked, and no one would have blinked, but it was nice of him to put in some effort.

Fortunately, Patricia was there as we arrived. She took one look at me and drew me into the ladies' room, where she gave me a long, hard hug.

"You're going to be fine," she insisted, handing me paper towels to blow my nose.

I nodded. "I know. I apologized to Miranda for not being able to tell her how to have a good marriage. She said it was okay, that David knew how."

Patricia folded her arms across her chest. "Where did David garner all his wisdom?"

"From Ben."

"Ah. Yes, that makes sense. But from you she learned how to stand up for herself, and how to get things done."

"How is that going to help her be a good wife?"

"You can't be a good wife if you're a bad person. Fix your makeup."

"Ben is leaving for Maine after the wedding. He said we'd always be friends."

She had been pulling my mascara from my purse to hand to me, but froze. "Mona, tell him you've changed your mind, and you don't want to be friends. Are you crazy?"

"It was his idea, not mine. He didn't think that any more could be said. Or done."

Her face softened. "Mona?"

I grabbed the mascara. "Yes."

"Oh, Mona."

I sniffed and concentrated on my face in the mirror. After a few moments I turned to her. "Better?"

She nodded. "Yes. Do you want me to stay? I can hang out in the bar."

I smiled. "Yes, I'm sure you can. But I'm fine. Can you come over early tomorrow? Help out?"

She nodded again. "Of course." She ran her fingers through her elegant bob and kissed my cheek. "I love you, Mona. You're going to be just fine."

"I know."

Chapter Thirteen

It was a beautiful wedding.

I did not cry.

The ceremony was equal parts solemn occasion and joyous celebration.

Tyler ran down the aisle wearing a cape, holding the pillow with those precious rings attached high over his head, screaming, "*Yaaay!*" The entire church burst into applause.

The choir sang "Hallelujah Chorus" as the married couple left the altar.

At the reception, David's best man Roy, that rather wealthy young gentleman from Yale, gave a funny, poignant, and altogether amazing speech. So did Ben.

I was incapable of speech. But I did not cry.

Brian and Miranda danced together to "Girls Just Want to Have Fun." They had practiced in secret—God knows when—and did something that looked like the jitterbug. They brought the house down.

Carmella, working the event, had toned down her sex appeal. She had worn a gray smock like dress and remained out of sight most of the time. I've got to say, everything went beautifully. There was not a misstep all day.

Ben and I danced just once. He came up to me halfway through the wedding and simply held out his hand. The last time we had danced, he had broken my heart. This dance could not fix that, but I let his arms go around me, and we moved slowly together, not even speaking, and the joy all around us kept some of the sadness at bay.

I did not cry.

Anthony caught the bridal bouquet. Ben caught the garter. I thought Anthony was going to hyperventilate himself into the ER, but Patricia managed to talk him down.

The food was delicious, and I sipped champagne and managed to enjoy myself by watching all the guests. Everyone had a wonderful time. The bride and groom radiated the kind of happiness that frequently appeared in bridal magazines. People laughed and cheered and danced. Lily and Vinnie tore up the dance floor with a polka that had the whole room up and clapping. Tyler curled up and fell asleep under the bride's table. My sister and I led the limbo.

Did I mention Ben and I danced?

Miranda changed into her going-away dress. She and David got into one of the many limos that Ben had hired for the day, and drove off to New York City, leaving their guests to dance and eat for another hour before Carmella had to ask the deejay to stop playing music.

We were a small crowd, but mighty.

Ben and I were the last to leave. We sat together in the empty, littered room. Finally he stood up and offered me a lift home. I shook my head.

"Stay warm in Maine," I said to him. My voice was steady. How could I sound so calm and reasonable? I wanted to race around the room, lock all the doors, and never let him leave.

He exhaled loudly. "I'll be too busy to feel the cold. Take care, Mona. I'll see you in a few months."

We did not kiss good-bye. We didn't even shake hands. I just sat there as he walked across the room, his rented shoes echoing throughout, until he was out the door and gone.

My house was empty by Sunday afternoon. We all had a lovely breakfast out, Grace and Shadow, with Lauren and Jessica, and we all got along just fine. The girls headed back to their respective schools, and my sister and her husband headed west. Miranda texted me from her honeymoon night at the Pierre—they had enough money for a washer, dryer, and a new futon, so the next time I came up to stay with them, I'd be much more comfortable. The rest of the money would be put into savings. That, I knew, was David's idea. Miranda alone would have been buying designer sheets and fifty-dollar scented candles for the powder room. But my daughter's text was full of hearts and happy faces. That's why it was called a "honeymoon phase." I prayed it would last for her.

Ben texted me to say he had just crossed over into Maine and would be spending the night in Portland.

Patricia called to ask if I wanted company. I said no.

MarshaMarsha came over from next door and brought a baby casserole dish of her homemade macaroni and cheese and asked if I wanted company. I said no.

I ate the mac and cheese, took Fred for a very long walk in the cold January darkness, came back, put on my favorite flannel pajamas, then went to bed very early.

And cried myself to sleep.

There was a lull.

February has always been my least favorite month. Luckily it's the shortest, because twenty-eight days is about all I can take of February. Leap years, I just slept through the whole extra day.

My self-pubbed titles had taken off, and the next three titles were ready to launch. Sylvia had gotten a contract for the new books. A new publishing house, a new editor, and an amazing advance, so I took myself down to Florida for a long weekend with Patricia. We stayed on Longboat Key, because I loved the Gulf of Mexico. I spent four days lying in the sun, shopping, eating too much, and drinking. *Way* too much. By the time I returned back home, March had arrived.

Luckily, the DeMatriano/Martel wedding went into full five-alarm mode, leaving me little time to sit around and miss Ben.

Carmella started calling me. First—what about a shower?

"Bridal shower? Are you suggesting that, as matron of honor, I throw a bridal shower for Lily? Doesn't your father have sheets at his house?"

"Of course, Mona. But Lily *is* a bride."

"She is also a woman with three different china services for twelve, and enough sterling silver to sink the USS *Enterprise*."

"Well, you could always do a lingerie shower."

Oh, my God. "No, Carmella. I am not throwing a lingerie shower. Why don't I talk to her and see what she wants, okay?"

Aunt Lily, as I had guessed, was completely uninterested. "Mona, that's very thoughtful, but I can't think of one single thing I need."

"That's what I thought. But since I'm your matron of honor..."

"Mona, dear, your only duty is to make sure I don't get too drunk on my wedding day to say my vows. Got it?"

"Got it, Aunt Lily."

Next Carmella called to ask when it would be convenient for the masons to come over.

"What masons?"

"The ones who are working on your lighted fountain. They have to take apart what's there so it can be wired."

"Seriously? I thought you'd just throw up a few spotlights." I had no idea. After all, that had been her project. With Ben.

"No. Mona, it's a bit more complicated than that."

"Okay...anytime next week? Have someone call me."

"Pasquale."

"Who's Pasquale?"

"He'll call you."

Pasquale did not have a tortured accent. He just showed up at the designated time and place with two assistants and started to take apart the top of my perfectly fine fountain. I thought that Ben should be here, supervising. After all, it was his idea. But Ben was up in Maine. He'd probably forgotten all about it. And me.

I watched for the first fifteen minutes, then went back to work. I still went to my office every day, leaving my empty house and making the long trek across the driveway. Anthony came by twice a week, but the other three days I spent writing alone. My jaded divorcée was coming alive in a way that hadn't happened in a while, and as her relationships with the neighborhood dead grew, so did her story. I was completely involved in my writing, which kept my mind off other things—like missing Ben. Wanting to talk to Ben. Wanting to tell Ben how the book was coming along. In fact, I wanted to pick up the phone that very afternoon and tell him all about the fountain, and Pasquale, knowing he would love the name and tell me to put it in my next book.

All that writing was why I hadn't bothered to check on the fountain progress until I heard the loud noises of equipment being rolled onto the truck. I ran downstairs to take a look.

My fountain was gone. In its place was a pipe protruding from the ground and a pile of stones.

"Pasquale," I yelled. "What did you do to my fountain?"

He looked at the pile of rocks, then at me. "I'll put it back together."

"When?"

"After the electrician does his wiring."

"I thought you were just going to put some spotlights around."

He shook his head, reached into his truck, and pulled out a manila folder. He shuffled some papers, then handed me a photo. "It will look like that."

I had to admit it was beautiful. Soft light glowed from the main basin, and the spout of water was lit in a golden hue. "How long will this take?"

He shrugged. "Depends. Do you want to get permits?"

I had experience with getting permits. After all, there had been a lot of renovation done over the years. "Do we have to?"

He grinned. "No."

"Okay, then," I said, envisioning a midnight visit by some unlicensed electrician. "Somebody good?"

He nodded and made the of-course face, complete with hand motions.

I sighed. "How much is this costing me?"

He suddenly looked very concerned. "No, you're not paying. This is a wedding gift, for Mr. DeMatriano."

I nodded, and it occurred to me I could mention that Mr. DeMatriano also wanted a new patio, front walkway, and oh, how about repointing the chimney?

"Thanks, Pasquale."

I went back inside the house, fed the dog, then made myself a plate of scrambled eggs for dinner.

With no one around to cook for, or even get dressed for, I had fallen into a rather lazy routine. Days that Anthony worked with me required a shower, fairly decent yoga pants, and at least a shirt that did not have a cartoon or silly saying on it. The other days of the week were something of a crapshoot. If I was having lunch or running specific errands, well, that rated jeans and a bra. But you know that old joke? About the best thing about working from home is walking to your desk in your pajamas? Yeah, well, that was me. Some days I didn't brush my teeth until lunchtime. And while part of me enjoyed the idea that I had no one to primp for, I really wished I had a reason to shave my legs and put on some makeup. More specifically, I wished I had Ben to primp for. I was actually dreading the warmer weather, because now all I had to do was throw my long winter coat over my jammies to walk the dog. Those days would soon be over, and then what would I do?

I started thinking about selling the house and living permanently at the shore. I had owned, for many years now, a little Cape Cod-style home on Long Beach Island. The rather tall and annoying dune that stood between my block and the beach had prevented Hurricane Sandy from leveling the homes on my street, so my house had suffered no more than missing shingles and torn screens. I loved it there and felt alive and happy so close to the ocean, but I also knew that out of season, the place was like a graveyard, filled with empty homes and the ghosts of summer past. I was already feeling a bit too lonely for comfort. That much solitude I didn't need. Besides, Ben and I had spent some wonderful times there. I needed to find somewhere with no ghosts.

I thought about getting a condo somewhere, not like Patricia's, of course. I didn't have that kind of money. In fact, very few people had that kind of money. I could see myself as a cosmopolitan kind of person, spending time on a balcony instead of a patio, but then I thought about those cold or snowy or rainy days when I just opened the back door for Fred. In a high-rise condo, I'd have to not only take him out in all weather, but I probably couldn't get away with the old coat-over-jammies trick.

As much as I loved all the freedom of living completely alone, I kind of didn't want to be *that* alone. That was why, if Ben and I had continued as we had been, my life would have been perfect. I could do exactly as I pleased, but anytime I wanted I could pick up the phone, and he would be there.

As it was, maybe a smaller space would mean a less empty space. I was clicking my way through Zillow when Aunt Lily called.

"Mona, dear, I have a tricky question for you."

"Okay, Aunt Lily. I'm sitting down. Go."

"Should I send Ben an invitation?"

"Ah…" I hadn't thought about Ben since I put my silverware in the dishwasher that morning.

"Yes. Exactly. You know how I feel about him. I love him dearly. And the sight of him in a suit on my wedding day will make me the happiest bride ever. But I also love you and don't want to make you feel uncomfortable. Have the two of you talked about this at all?"

"No, Aunt Lily. I haven't spoken to Ben since he left."

"Oh, dear. Really? What is wrong with you, Mona? Did you know that Carmella has been talking to him on a regular basis? In fact, I think she went see him up there last weekend."

"To Maine? She went up to Maine to see Ben?"

"Well, I can't imagine her going up to Maine for any other reason."

Carmella had been to *Maine!* I saw red for a second, then realized I had no right to be angry anymore.

"I thought all you young people were constantly texting and things."

"That's younger people than myself, Aunt Lily."

"Well, can't you Tumble him?"

"I don't think so."

"Oh. Too bad. Well, what should we do? I need to send these invitations out this weekend."

I took a deep breath. "Send him one, Aunt Lily. I know how fond he is of you. He was really looking forward to your wedding." Which was true. But more important, he'd be right in my backyard. For a whole afternoon. And at a wedding, all sorts of things could happen.

"All right, Mona."

"So, what was the final total?"

"For guests? Just under one hundred."

"*What?* Aunt Lily, there isn't room for one hundred people in my backyard."

"Carmella says there is, and she's the expert. Besides, this all became rather complicated. Vinnie has lots of friends, and he doesn't want anyone to feel slighted."

No, I didn't want that either. The last thing I needed was a disappointed mobster taking revenge on Vinnie in my backyard because I was getting finicky about square footage.

"By the way, she'll be stopping by next week with someone who's doing something with the tents. And heaters."

"Heaters? In my backyard?"

"Well, what if it's cold? Not to worry, Carmella has everything under control."

I hung up the phone.

Carmella had everything under control. Of course she did.

Aunt Lily's wedding to Vincent DeMatriano was beginning to look like something that normally took place around Buckingham Palace. The midnight electrician came and went, and my fountain was put back together. With less than month to go, Carmella went into that mythical sixth gear.

She kept hinting about replacing all my shrubs and plants with pre-blooming versions, but I was resistant. Then she mentioned power-washing my patio, driveway, and sidewalks. I was waiting for her to arrive with exterior paint colors for my house, and some ideas for changing out the banisters on my front porch.

Our conversations were all by phone, of course, and she was unfailingly polite and considerate, but all I could think of was her driving up to Maine, where Ben had been staying all alone in a cold, isolated cabin, starving for company and more than ready to accept her eight-armed embrace.

The truth was that Miranda had spoken to him, and he was staying in a very comfortable hotel in the middle of town, worked most nights until very late, and had become good friends with the general contractor, spending most of his spare time with him, his wife, and four kids. Miranda did not mention Carmella's visit, but that might have been because Ben didn't mention it. So I was left stewing, with my romance writer's over imagination placing the two of them regularly in various erotic situations, often involving bearskin rugs and blizzards.

I kept telling myself it was no longer my concern. My self was not getting the message.

I spoke to a Realtor about putting my house up for sale. Since I'd lived there more than twenty years, of course I'd make some money off the sale. After all, a five-bedroom, three-and-a-half-bath Craftsman on almost half an acre of landscaped lot, including a garage with living space (not to mention Lily's amazing third-floor suite) in one of the most desirable neighborhoods in northern New Jersey was still worth a pretty penny. But the real estate market was on a fairly slow upswing, particularly in the price range I was looking at. Still, I kept all the information and would regularly look around, trying to decide which pieces of furniture I'd keep and which pieces I'd try to sell or give away. I kept telling myself I should wait until Lauren and Jessica had at least graduated. But I was haunted by the idea that if I still had that great big house when they got out of school, they might be tempted to return to living in it full time.

Carmella kept calling. Keeping me in the loop, she told me. After all, I was the matron of honor. A videographer had been engaged to preserve every precious detail of the ongoing plans. She warned me that she'd given him my address, and he might show up for some preliminary work.

"What kind of preliminary work could he do?" I asked her.

"Well, before and after shots, for one thing."

"Before and after of my yard? Carmella, I don't know what Brooklyn looks like, but it's still winter here. My backyard is covered in snow."

"Well, still. So don't be surprised by a stranger walking around with a video camera."

For Miranda's wedding there had been a photographer, of course, and he had also taken lots of video. Carmella had also videotaped all sorts of vignettes to include in the final album or whatever. But for her father she had found a real pro. He first appeared in my yard when the fountain was turned back on, and the newly installed lighting was put through its paces. He stood next to Pasquale with a very official-looking camera perched on his shoulder and filmed the turning on, the various colors, then the turning off. He even filmed Pasquale getting back in the truck and driving away. Then he wandered around the yard, which was still partially frozen in most spots, with snowdrifts everywhere.

April in New Jersey could easily bring warm breezes, chirping birds, and outbursts of greenery and flowers. But there had been plenty of cold, snowy Easters in my memory. The wedding was the Saturday after Easter, the last April weekend, so odds were good that there would at least be no snow left on the ground.

I watched him and his camera as he wandered around my yard. He was, by the way, a very attractive man. Older, I guessed, close to sixty, with curly gray hair and a tall, lean body in jeans, boots, and a down vest. I finally grabbed my long coat—it was one of those sweatshirt-but-no-bra days—and went outside.

"Are you videoing anything specific," I called, "or just casing the joint?"

He dropped the camera from his eye and laughed. "Carmella wants before and after. What can I say?"

I stood next to him and looked around. "Couldn't you at least wait for the snow to melt? It won't look quite so bad once the grass can be seen."

He put his camera in the large leather bag hanging from his shoulder. "I just do as I'm told," he said. He stuck out his hand. "I'm Alex."

I shook it. It was strong and graceful. "Mona."

"Oh? You're Lily's niece?"

I nodded and looked sideways at him. "You've met Lily?"

He threw back his head and let loose a long laugh. "Oh, my God," he said at last. "That is one crazy old lady."

I felt a smile. "Yes, she is."

"She's keeping old Vinnie on his toes; I'll give her that. She may even get him to give up the game."

I stopped smiling. "Game?"

He noticed the change in my tone and looked apologetic. "No, listen. Vinnie has been square for a long time now. But he still likes to play the horses, you know?"

I shook my head. "No, I didn't know."

He started laughing again. "Well, Lily didn't know either, and boy, was she pissed off when she found out."

Who was this guy? "Are you…related?"

"Sort of. My younger brother was married to Carmella."

"What!" Oh, gosh—the one who ended up in a river. "I'm so sorry."

He shrugged. "Thank you."

"So. You're a photographer?"

He shook his head. "Not really. I'm retired now, but I was a producer. I made documentaries for National Geographic. I still freelance now and then. Usually not weddings, but Carmella asked, so…here I am."

"You're a good ex-brother-in-law."

"And I can use the money. Carmella has opened her father's coffers pretty big for this thing. She was always very good at spending other people's money."

I shivered. "Want some coffee?" I could use a second cup, and I could also use company. I was starting to have long conversations with the cat.

He nodded. "Thanks." He followed me into the house, where I was reminded, as he took off his vest, that under my coat I looked like the suburban version of the Little Match Girl. I'm not one of those types who need to look glam at all times, but an attractive man in my kitchen called for at least a bra and hair that wasn't bunched up in the back. Even if I never dated another man again in my life, I didn't want to become one of those women who didn't care about her appearance. So I excused myself as I shrugged out of my coat, ran upstairs, threw on a bra and jeans that fit, then combed my hair with my fingers as I raced back downstairs. I eased into the kitchen just as the machine was finished with his cup of coffee. A new world's record, I was sure.

"Cream?"

He smiled "No, just black, thanks."

I slid the coffee mug across the counter. I felt a little nervous being in the company of a strange man for the first time in a very long time. An attractive, appropriately aged man who, despite a tenuous connection to Carmella, Vinnie, and the entire assorted DeMatriano family, was also an interesting guy whose job had been to make elephant movies. I mean, how cool was that? Besides, his eyes were big and dark, with very nice laugh lines, and his eyebrows weren't all wonky and gray. He also had a sexy smile. Since I still thought about Ben most of my waking days, I knew I wasn't ready to start seeing anyone else, but it was nice to practice—keep the skills sharp, you know?

"You're a writer?"

I nodded. "Yes."

"Lonely work?"

"Very. Of course, I have lots of imaginary friends, so that helps."

He grinned. His teeth were large and slightly crooked. "Of course."

"So, what was the scariest thing you filmed?"

He thought a moment. "There was this spider in Guatemala."

I held up my hand. "Enough said."

"Exactly. But to do what I did for as long as I did it, you had to be a bit of an adrenaline junkie. I really loved the scary. And the dangerous. And unpredictable."

"Well, you're at the right wedding then."

He nodded. "Oh, yes. You seem almost normal, though."

I had made myself coffee as well and stirred in sugar. "I'd like to think I'm mysterious and fascinating, but normal is probably closer to the mark. And the older I get, the happier I am with that."

"Are you married?"

I shook my head. "Not anymore." Not even remotely attached. I found myself having to concentrate on keeping my voice light and even. "You?"

"No. Never. It's hard to commit to one person if you're going to spend half a year in exotic places, surrounded by young and nubile women who think that because you're a producer, you can cast them in Justin Timberlake's latest video."

"Ah. You're a hound."

"I *was* a hound. Now I'm just a tired, lonely old dog."

I smiled and sipped my coffee. There was a nice, comfortable silence.

Since Ben had left, I had thrown all of my love, anger, passion, and pain into my newest character, Maria Demerest. Ria was my age, divorced, and had inherited a two-hundred-year-old farm with its own cemetery. She'd moved up there with her two teen daughters and discovered that all the women in her family had a special gift—they could talk to the dead. Only the dead in their particular cemetery, but hey—pretty cool, right? Ria was falling in love with Walden Moore, who had died in 1965 when his motorcycle crashed into a nearby tree. No one at the time knew who he was, and he had no identification, so the family just buried him next to all their departed loved ones. He was charming and funny, and they began to talk regularly. In daylight, his spirit could not leave the confines of the cemetery. This brought a whole new meaning to the phrase "long-distance relationship." But although Ria and Walden could not touch, when she slept he could enter her subconscious. Ria was having lots of great sex, but only in her dreams.

Which was exactly my situation. Sometimes I woke up from dreaming of Ben and found myself embarrassed.

Alex smiled at me, and I felt the sudden urge to brush my teeth and shave my legs.

"Where to from here?" I asked.

He shrugged. "Who knows?"

"She may want you to check out the tents," I suggested.

"Yes. All rolled up in a warehouse somewhere."

"Or chairs. The before—folded up—and after."

He laughed again. "How about the flowers? I'm sure there's a vast field of unpicked roses somewhere that I could get on tape."

"And the band? Catching them in their homes?"

He grinned. "And here," he said, his tone perfectly hushed and announcer-like, "we have the elusive bongo player, roaming his natural habitat of Queens."

I giggled.

"If we watch closely," Alex continued, "we may chance to see him engaging with one of his fellow band mates—wait, is that a bass player? Could it be—yes. Let's see how they interact."

"You could *so* sell that," I told him.

"Yes, I probably could. I hear YouTube calling as we speak." He got up and walked over to the sink, putting his mug down. "Would you consider having coffee with me again? Maybe, you know, out somewhere?"

What? I don't know what my face looked like, but apparently it scared him as much as the spider in Guatemala.

"I'm sorry," he said quickly. "I didn't mean—"

"No. Alex, I'm fine." I cleared my throat. "I'm just, well, I'm wrapped up in this book right now. In the zone, so to speak. But you'll be at the wedding?"

He nodded. "Yes. Although, I'll see you much sooner than that."

"Oh?"

He pulled on his vest. "Well, there's the rehearsal dinner to be filmed, and if I know Carmella, she'll want the whole transformation of your yard preserved for posterity. Not to mention all that pre-wedding bride-and-matron-of-honor stuff. By the time the actual wedding takes place, we'll be old friends."

"You're probably right."

He smiled and shut the door behind him.

Okay, then. A real live man just asked me out for coffee. He was not up in Maine. He was not haunting my dreams. And I would be seeing him again. Soon.

I kind of liked that idea.

When Anthony came up the stairs the next day, carrying a box of cupcakes from Crumbs, he took one look at me and almost dropped the whole half dozen. "You brushed your hair."

"I brush my hair every day, Anthony."

"Yes. But it's usually stuck up on the top of your head like Pebbles Flintstone. You've been in a bit of a funk lately, remember?"

"So?"

He walked around to where I was sitting at the worktable, typing furiously. "And you're wearing shoes instead of slippers."

"It's twenty-seven degrees outside."

"That meant nothing to you before. What happened?"

"I think I have to call Sylvia. This needs to be a trilogy." I stopped writing, hit save, and pushed myself away from the keyboard.

"Mona, you don't do trilogies."

"Maura didn't do trilogies. I can do whatever I want."

He got himself a cup of coffee, opened the box of cupcakes, and handed me a miniature red velvet. "I thought Walden was going to ask the witch to send him back for good."

"No. Ria is going to meet someone else. A real person. And there's going to be a triangle. Walden will always be her true love, but she'll have to decide between loving what she can't have, or trying to be happy with someone in the real world."

"Oh, Mona. Who did you meet?"

I stuffed the entire cupcake into my mouth. That's not as disgusting as it sounds, by the way. The mini cupcakes from Crumbs are the perfect size for me to do that without choking or looking too gross. "No one," I said when I swallowed.

He raised his left eyebrow. "Try again, baby cakes."

"Carmella sent her former brother-in-law out to video my yard for the Technicolor production that will be this damn wedding. He successfully captured the fountain changing colors before it was shut back off until the thaw. He's a very nice man."

"Is he, ah…"

"No. He's not part of the DeMatriano family. He was a producer for National Geographic. He was an adrenaline junkie, never married, now retired. We're going to meet up again on the next film-worthy event."

"Why wait that long? Oh, was he ugly?"

"No. Think David Straithorn, but more Italian looking."

"What's his last name?" Anthony asked at the laptop, typing like crazy.

I spelled it for him, very slowly. He was frowning in concentration.

"Okay. Alexander Ciavaglia, born 1953 in Nutley, New Jersey. He's won awards! Lots of them. He's practically famous, if you're into wildlife filming and photography. And he's kinda hot for a guy almost sixty. Good job, Mona."

"He's nice, Anthony. Don't start."

"Don't start what? Just says one brother, deceased, no mention of the details of his demise. Well, we have a daughter, Hailey, from his relationship with former model—I've never heard of her. She was probably not pretty at all."

"Anthony, stop."

"Stop what?"

"I know how you get."

"About what? Just passing on a little information here."

I got up and looked over his shoulder. As a young man he had striking good looks. "The daughter is a knockout. Her mother was probably gorgeous."

"Who cares? Out of the picture, right?"

"It doesn't matter, Anthony."

He turned away from the laptop and grabbed my hands with both of his. "Of course it does. Everything you do matters to me, Mona. Every person you meet matters."

"Anthony, how sweet."

"Besides, you need to move on and start having sex again. You're always more generous when you're getting some, and my birthday is coming up."

"I love you too, Anthony."

Chapter Fourteen

So far, March had come in like a lion and stayed there. The morning after the fifth snowfall of the month, Brian knocked on my front door. He stood on the porch, a scarf wrapped around his face, and asked to come in. I looked past him—no Dominique or Tyler following up the newly shoveled walk. I let him in, and he followed me into the kitchen.

"So, how are things?" I asked as I made him coffee.

"Great, just great. But I have a favor."

"Sure."

He took a long drink of coffee, leaned back, and smiled. He still had a charming smile, and for most of my adult life, when I looked at the smile anything I had was his. "Can I camp out here for a while?"

I looked down into my own coffee mug and ran the words over in my head a few times. "Is the house getting fumigated?"

"No."

"Quarantined?"

"No. Mona, I just need a place to stay for a while."

"Just you?"

"Yes."

Silence hung in the air.

"Because?"

"Mona, I'm asking a favor. Yes or no?"

"Did you cheat on Dominique?"

"I don't think my relationship with Dominique has any bearing on this. I'm asking a favor."

I raised my head and looked him in the eye. "No."

His eyes widened in surprise. "What?"

"No. Obviously you learned absolutely nothing in the past five years. I can't abide stupidity, Brian. I never could. Find another place to crash."

He threw his hands up in the air. "Dominique has a bee up her butt. There's nothing going on, but she doesn't believe me. She's still going through that postpartum thing; her hormones are all over the place, and she's totally irrational."

I choked back a laugh. "Postpartum thing? Hormones? Really, Brian? How about you're cheating on her, just like you cheated on me, and she figured it out a lot sooner than I did, because she knew from the very start that you were a miserable SOB who can't be trusted."

I watched him as he went from battle mode to wheedling mode in a heartbeat. "Mona, it's snowing outside; the roads are a mess—how about just tonight? I'll start looking for a place tomorrow morning."

"Why don't you stay with your mother?"

He actually flushed. "She's not speaking to me."

"Wow, Brian. Even your mother? How big a screw up do you feel like right now?"

"You know what, Mona? There are two sides to every story. Why are you automatically assuming I'm at fault here?"

"Personal experience?"

He leaned forward and buried his head in his hands. I saw his shoulders rise and fall. When he looked up, his face looked old. "I've really made a mess of my life, haven't I?" he asked quietly.

I sat back. He'd never, in all the years I'd known and loved him, said anything like that before.

"Yes, Brian. You have. But you're right; there are two sides to every story. Including ours. I loved you, Brian, and I wanted so badly to be happily married that I let you coast along while I did all the work. I did us both a disservice. I spent so many years thinking I knew what marriage was, and I was wrong all along. I think our daughters were smart enough to know that what we had wasn't the way things were supposed to work. I wish I had been that smart. I wish had thrown you out much sooner."

"Thanks."

"No, Brian. I'm not trying to kick you while you're down. We both learned some very bad lessons. And we're both suffering for them now."

"You?"

"Yes, me. Everything I thought I knew about marriage came from one place. A wrong place. I should have been willing to look beyond you and me. I should have been able to realize that marriage is not about the institution itself. It's about two people coming together. Different people have very different results. You and I brought out the wrong things in each other. That's why we failed."

"But you think we can succeed? With the right person?"

"The trick is finding the right person. I thought I had. In fact, he might have been the *only* person for me. But taking another leap —that was the scary part. Very scary. As for you, I don't know, Brian. Maybe if you learn to keep it in your pants."

"So you think you and Ben can have one last happily-ever-after?"

"I hope so." I thought about Ben. Was it even possible we could somehow be together again? "God, I really hope so."

"Tell me again why Brian is living here?" Patricia asked.

Brian had been up in Lily's old suite for almost a week now. "Because I'm a marshmallow, that's why. And I actually felt sorry for him. I think he finally realized how badly he's screwed up. He's looking for a place to live. In fact, he's signing a lease this weekend and will be out by the wedding."

We had finished lunch and were watching a group of non-English-speaking men in hoodies clear every stray leaf, twig, and dead flower stem out of my backyard. We stood on the deck. The sunlight was feeble, but with no wind it was almost pleasant.

"I think it's very kind of you," MarshaMarsha said. "He's obviously going through a rough time."

"Why can't he just move in with the new paramour?" Patricia asked. "That's what he did last time." Five years ago, just about this time of year, I had found out about Brian and Dominique. He had moved from our house into the condo he had bought with her the previous fall.

I shrugged. "I think the new paramour is still living with her parents."

Patricia made a very rude noise. Even MarshaMarsha registered disapproval.

I had called my usual yard guy and asked for an early cleanup. They had arrived three days earlier and did what I thought was a very respectable job of removing all the winter leftovers. But this crew really took it to another level. They had raked the whole yard twice, and were now going over it again, picking up stray bits by hand.

The wedding was ten days away. The azaleas were not going to be in bloom, but the bank of forsythia that spread across the back of my property looked ready to burst. The daffodils were up, and the tulips were right behind. The grass was turning green, and the hostas were peeking through. If we didn't get a major snowstorm in the next week, we'd be in great shape for a wedding.

"When is the rehearsal dinner?" Patricia asked.

"Next week. Wednesday night. The bishop was busy with Easter this weekend, so they pushed it into the week. At a restaurant in Manhattan, one of those places where you have to know the owner to get in," I told them.

"But don't you have to rehearse first?" MarshaMarsha asked.

"Carmella worked it all out," I said. "She's going to re-create the setting. How much practice are they going to need?"

"Oh, my goodness," MarshaMarsha said. "Look at that—he's using the leaf blower like a vacuum cleaner. I wonder if my leaf blower can do that?"

"Wait—is he actually picking those leaves off the tree?" Patricia asked, obviously impressed.

"Well," I said, "they are all brown and ugly. Can't have brown and ugly on Mr. DeMatriano's big day."

"Isn't it Lily's big day?" Patricia asked.

"Not as far as Carmella is concerned," I told her. "I invited Lily to spend the night before back in her old rooms, and Carmella got upset. She wanted to stay here so she could supervise."

"So, who's staying?" MarshaMarsha asked.

"Both of them. Lily's getting the third floor, and Carmella is staying in Miranda's old room."

"Well, now, that should be interesting." Patricia looked at me with raised eyebrows. "And the girls?"

I sighed. "Lauren and Jessica were invited to the wedding, of course, so they'll be here as well. And my sister is flying in to attend. She sent me an e-mail. She had such a good time at Miranda's wedding, she's coming out to *continue rebuilding important familial relationships.* Lily is thrilled. She's considering it her bachelorette party. She wants pizza and popcorn, but declined Jessica's offer of a stripper. I'm thinking back to when the girls were in grade school and had slumber parties, but with more vodka."

"Dear God," Patricia said. "Are you sure about this?"

"Of course she is," MarshaMarsha said. "It will be a terrific bonding experience for all of them."

Patricia shivered delicately.

I shrugged. "The whole weekend is going to be a circus anyway, so why not? After all, I owe Lily so much—she's been a great help to me; you know that. As for Carmella, well, since it looks like we'll be in each other's lives from now on, I should at least get to know her a bit more." And find out who—if anyone—she'd been dating. "She'd be here all day anyway; after all, she's in charge of this show. And it will be good for Grace to be here. We kind of got along when she was here, and it's important that the girls get to know their only aunt."

"Well, when you put it like that," Patricia said, "it almost makes sense." She shot me a look. "Was Ben invited?"

"Of course," I told her. "So were David and Miranda. In fact, the kids are staying at Ben's for the night."

"Ahh," she said.

"Ahh what?" I said. I looked at the both of them and threw up my hands. "Yes, Ben is going to be at the wedding, and we haven't spoken in months, and I miss him like crazy, and I don't know what I'm going to do about it."

"You know," Marsha said slowly, "the back window of my bedroom overlooks this yard perfectly. If anyone wanted to be a fly on the wall..."

Patricia grinned. "It's a date."

I was going to drive myself into Manhattan for the rehearsal dinner. After all, I could park my car at the Port Authority and take a cab downtown. But Lily offered a car and driver, and how often does that happen? I felt slightly guilty and pleased at the same time. Then a car showed up, and it was Alex Ciavaglia.

"I wasn't expecting you," I told him.

He shrugged. "I live in Mendham. I'd be driving out there myself anyway, so I asked Carmella. She was going to send somebody to get you, but since I already knew where you lived, I offered." He opened the car door for me. "Hope you're not disappointed."

I waited until he got into his car and backed out of the driveway. "Well, to be honest, I was hoping for a big, silent type with scars and a lisp."

He glanced at me and grinned. "Louie 'Let-me-at-'em' Lombardi?"

I nodded. "Or maybe Bennie 'Break-a-leg' Bonanno."

"I think I've met Bennie. Very nice guy."

"I'm sure. You know that Lily, as well as Carmella, will be spending the night before the wedding with me?"

He nodded. "Yes. I've been assigned to cover Vinnie, unfortunately. I'm to follow him from breakfast, across the bridge, and stay with him until the very end. I offered to follow the bride. My feeling is that anywhere Lily is has to be more interesting than anywhere else."

"You're right about that. I think she expects some giggly girls' night, right out of *Gidget*. Has she settled into the Bay Ridge house?"

"I haven't been there myself. Rumor has it she's repainted everything lavender."

Alex must have had excellent directions or had been to the restaurant before, because two seconds after turning off Broadway,

I was lost. Little Italy was a warren of tiny side streets, most of them one way. He parked the car in a small lot, and we walked four short, crowded blocks. Number 732 was a plain blue door.

"Please tell me you need a secret knock," I said.

He laughed and turned the knob. To my disappointment, the door opened easily, and we walked down a narrow hallway, turned a corner, and the space suddenly opened into a vast single room, low ceilinged, with the entire back wall opened to a dimly lit courtyard. One long table was in the center of the room. No corny accordion music playing or fake ivy dripping from brass chandeliers. I looked around quickly and was disappointed that there was not a corner table of old men, all wearing slouch hats and drinking red wine from juice glasses. Wasn't that how it had been whenever Tony Soprano went out to eat?

There was a lone waiter who looked up from folding napkins and hurried off.

"We have the whole restaurant?"

He shrugged. "Probably. Vinnie has some very good friends."

I was not comforted. "Perfect."

"We're here a little early," he said. He had brought his leather case in with him, and he pulled out his video camera. "I have to work. Do you mind?"

I shook my head. "Not at all."

A short, bald man came running out. He clasped Alex's hand, then hurried to take my coat.

"And you are?" he asked.

"Mona Quincy. Matron of honor."

He bowed. "A pleasure. I am Nick. You are early, yes? But please sit, and I'll bring you wine."

I nodded. "Yes."

Alex disappeared. Filming the arrivals of all the major players, I assumed. What was Carmella going to do with all of this footage anyway? Maybe she was putting together a pilot for a reality show. I could imagine that a show based on the life of a wedding planner who also happened to be the niece of a known kingpin would be considered a hot property. Add in a home life that included stepmom Lily, and you had a real winner.

I wandered over to the wall of glass and saw that the courtyard was set up in a reasonable representation of what my yard would look like, at least the area where the actual ceremony would take place. Very clever, Carmella. I had to give her credit. Nick brought out a single glass of wine on a silver tray, serving me in silence. I slid open the glass door and stepped into the courtyard. It was cool, no breeze. I looked up. The stars were peeking out. It was all just beautiful.

"You must be Mona," a low voice behind me said.

I turned and found myself looking at Joseph DeMatriano, longtime head of DeMatriano crime family and shoe salesman extraordinaire. He was short and powerfully built, salt-and-pepper hair brushed back from his high forehead, eyes very black and narrow. I knew he was fifty-four. He was in a perfectly cut gray suit, and at his side was a striking woman, maybe my age, in an obviously designer outfit.

He held out his hand. "I'm Joe DeMatriano."

I shook his hand. It was surprisingly soft. Obviously he didn't do too much hard work himself. He probably just pointed and spoke in a whisper.

"And this is Angela," he said.

Angela nodded, but kept her hands folded over her Hermès bag.

"A pleasure," I said. My voice cracked a little, so I sipped some wine. "It looks like the weather for the next week is going to be perfect." Weather? I was talking about the *weather*?

That must have been good for Joe. "Yes," he said. He turned slightly to take a glass of wine off another silver tray, which had silently appeared. Angela also took a glass, but did not drink. She glanced around.

"I'm going in and sitting down," she said, and walked off.

Joe and I stood in the courtyard. "Your aunt," he said, in a voice like silk, "is quite a character."

"Yes." My voice was back to normal. "She's always had her own, ah, compass."

His thin lips turned slightly. I assumed that was his version of a smile. "There aren't many people I like the way I like Lily," he said. "And it's not often I welcome someone into the family with such enthusiasm."

I smiled brightly. Yes, I could imagine.

"My uncle," he continued, "is a good man. They're well matched."

I nodded, still smiling. Where was Lily anyway? This was her rehearsal dinner. Shouldn't she be here by now?

"And of course, Carmella is doing her usual amazing job. That woman can accomplish anything she puts her mind to."

I stayed smiling. "Yes, she certainly seems to know what she's doing." I forced myself to look at Joe, rather than search the room behind him for someone—anyone—else.

He sipped his wine. "It's very generous of you to host the wedding. You have a lovely home."

My smile froze. He had seen my home? When had he seen my home? "Ah, yes. Well, Lily is family, after all."

Lily, my family, finally came in. She threw her arms around me. "Mona, what is that asshat of an ex-husband doing at your house?"

She looked bright and happy, her gray hair slicked back, makeup perfect.

"He needed a place to stay. Not to worry. He's moving out tomorrow." I nodded at Tony, then gave Vinnie a kiss on the cheek.

"Joe!" Mona cried. "You've finally gotten to meet Mona. Isn't she wonderful?"

He flashed a quick smile. "Wonderful." He turned to me. "You're still having problems with your ex?"

Years ago, when Brian first moved out and was planning a trip back to reclaim some of his belongings, Aunt Lily had called her good friend Joe because she didn't feel comfortable being alone with Brian. Joe had graciously sent a knee-breaker named Mickey to protect Lily from harm. Luckily Mickey's services were not needed, but Brian was apparently still on the radar.

I shook my head quickly. "No. He's just taking a bit longer to move on than I had hoped."

Joe raised an eyebrow. "I might be able to help you with that."

My heart froze in my throat, and I pasted on another smile. "No, thanks, Joe. It's good." I turned to Lily. "Tell him it's good."

Lily put her arm through Joe's and walked him back into the

main room, laughing. I stepped back and leaned against the cool brick wall of the courtyard.

"Another glass of wine?" Tony asked me. He looked very solemn, but there was a tiny smile around his lips.

"No, Tony. Thanks."

"Can I offer you a piece of advice?" he asked softly.

I nodded.

"Be very careful about what you say. Mr. DeMatriano takes things very…seriously. If he thought that you were in any way uncomfortable because of a certain person, well…"

"Got it, Tony. Thanks."

In a matter of minutes the bishop arrived, as well as Carmella and the rest of Vinnie's immediate family. Trev I knew, but Paulie had flown in from France for his Pop-Pop's wedding. Suzi and Enza were also there, with husbands and various grown children, all of whom blended together in a blur of dark hair, dark eyes, white teeth, and obvious opulence. Alex hung back, his eye glued to the camera as the bishop (call me Francis) walked us through what was a very short and straightforward rehearsal.

Francis, Vinnie, and Joe would walk up the aisle first. Suzi's daughter, an obviously beautiful and gifted young woman, would sing "Ave Maria" a cappella. Then I would walk down, followed by Lily. Words would be said. Rings would be exchanged. The bishop would raise his hands, and bingo—man and wife.

Suzi burst into tears. Carmella and Enza hugged her as she sobbed.

"Really?" Lily said. She looked at Suzi in disgust. She leaned over and whispered in my ear, "That damn woman cries at everything," then grabbed Vinnie's arm and dragged him into the dining room.

It had gotten cold enough that we were all glad to be back inside.

I sat next to Aunt Lily, of course. The table was odd. We all sat on the same side, rather *Last Supper*ish. I would have liked to have been a bit closer to Alex, but Trev sat on my other side, and he kept a running commentary about the food, all of which was delicious. Joe DeMatriano was not a very bubbly or boisterous guy, but Vinnie had lot to say, and with Lily doing counterpoint, it was quite a show. In between listening to Aunt Lily and trying *not* to listen to Aunt Lily, I played the if-this-were-my-rehearsal-dinner game. I'd definitely serve the fish. I wouldn't bother with three different wines. Absolutely change the music. But I had blown the chance at *any* rehearsal dinner of my own. I shrank back in my seat a bit more and went back to being a spectator.

This was a very different kind of rehearsal dinner from David and Miranda's. For one thing, my emotions weren't open and bleeding like raw meat. For another, this family was…well, loud. Not angry loud, but there were a lot of opinions expressed in raised voices, accompanied by hand gestures and exaggerated eye rolling. Despite the constant interrupting, everyone had a chance to put in their two cents' worth.

Vinnie's grandchildren ranged in age from sixteen to twenty-something, and were all very well behaved. They did not have cell phones on the table to be checked every thirty seconds, and they listened to the conversations with apparent interest. Lily knew them all by name, and they seemed enchanted with her.

Vinnie's daughters were a bit more reserved around Lily. I could understand that, but surely by now they knew that she had a very tidy sum all her own that she had invested nicely, and it was more than enough to keep her in pin money until 2023. Maybe they just realized that Lily would now be whirling through their family occasions like a dervish. I was beginning to think that Vinnie DeMatriano's becoming a member of my family was actually the better end of the deal.

Alex finally put the camera down to eat. The rest of us were finishing the coffee and cake, so he nudged Trev out of his seat so he could sit by me with a plate of pasta. I glanced at Carmella, who was watching us with interest. Was this a setup?

"What happens next?" I asked him. "The Tarantella? A few arias from *Carmen*? Does the ghost of Frank Sinatra croon a few numbers?"

He shook his head. "No, I think they'll all go back to Brooklyn. I'm sure there will be a line of black cars heading west, like a funeral procession."

"Your nephew is a delight, by the way."

"Trev? Yeah, he's a good kid. Paulie is the real pip, though. Try to get him talking at the wedding. Very shy, but once he opens up, he's a treat. It's late. Do you want to head to Bay Ridge, or should I take you home?"

I was surprised. "Bay Ridge?"

Lily, on the other side, leaned in. "Yes, Mona, why don't you come back with us? I'm sure we can get somebody to take you home tomorrow. You can get to know all the girls better, and if we're lucky, Joe will start telling stories about the good old days."

"You know," I said slowly, "that sounds really fun. But I should probably get back to Jersey. There are still lots of things to be done."

Vinnie nudged Carmella. "She could stay with you, no?"

Carmella smiled brightly. "Of course. What do you say, Mona?"

What *could* I say? Did I really want to insult a single person at this table? No. Did I want anyone to think I was not perfectly comfortable around a man whose face was in every FBI office in the country? Of course not.

Alex cleared his throat. "Actually, Mona and I were going for a drink. Uptown. We thought we'd take in a little jazz."

I turned gratefully to Alex, who smiled innocently.

"Well," Carmella said, her perfect eyebrows disappearing under her bangs, "have fun, you two."

Alex stood. "I'll get the car."

I stood with him. "No, I'll walk with you."

We said our good-byes. Everyone seemed very happy for us. Lily, as she kissed my cheek, whispered to me, "Really?" She was one sharp old lady.

I followed Alex back down the long hallway and outside. Once the door was closed behind us, I let a nervous giggle escape. "Thanks, Alex. I was feeling a little uncomfortable there."

He nodded and tucked my arm into his. "That's what I figured. But I do know a great little jazz place uptown. What do you think?"

What *did* I think? Hmmm. I had not seen Ben since the kids' wedding. For all I knew, he and Carmella had been canoodling under bearskin rugs up in the wilds of Maine. And here was an attractive man asking me to have a drink and listen to some jazz, two of my favorite things to do.

"That sounds lovely. Thanks."

We got into his car and started up Broadway

"That was quite a nice time," I said. "I don't know why I'm surprised, but I am."

"Vinnie really did try to make life for his family as normal as possible," Alex said. "Mike, my brother, had a degree in business. He didn't have to join the family, but he was like me, in a way—craving danger and excitement. He thought the whole thing was a game. Stupid mistake on his part. When he was killed, Vinnie pulled out of everything and sent his daughters and their families as far away as he could. Carmella went back to Brooklyn when her mother died—to be near him, of course—but none of those kids have followed in Joe's footsteps. Vinnie would never allow it. So they really are just like any other Italian-American family—very close, and crazy when it comes to food and wine."

"That sounds like my family."

"See? We're all pretty much the same."

"Joe isn't."

"You're right there."

He found a space to park on a side street, and we walked to a tiny club with an excellent trio and equally excellent martinis. We did not talk much, mostly because the music was so good. When we did talk, it was about jazz and old movies. He loved old movies. So did I. That was enough to carry the night.

We drove back to Jersey in silence. As he turned the corner onto my street, I got a quiver of butterflies. Would he ask to come in? Would I say yes?

He stopped the car, threw it into park, and turned in the seat, facing me. "See you Saturday," he said.

He was very close. I could feel that quiver again, but I opened the car door and smiled. "Saturday."

Then I slammed the door behind me and went into the house alone.

CHAPTER FIFTEEN

CARMELLA ARRIVED VERY EARLY ON Friday morning. I was awake, drinking my first cup of coffee and talking to Lana. Lana always listened to me as though she were fascinated by every single word, but I knew she was just waiting for me to turn my back so she could put tiny paw prints all over my shiny granite countertops. I had never caught her in the act, but I had often heard the thump of her landing on the floor as I approached. She was one sly cat.

Fred started barking, and I could see strange men carrying rolled-up tents walking past my kitchen window. I wandered out to watch.

In addition to the tents, they carried in a portable dance floor, and a small army of young girls started draping white fabric around the inside walls of my garage. I had arranged to park in MarshaMarsha's driveway for the festivities, leaving Carmella plenty of space to work her magic.

Suzi and Enza soon joined Carmella, and the three of them pointed, shouted, and argued all morning. I sat on my deck, drank more coffee, smiled, and waved.

Before lunchtime, I took off to pick up Grace at Newark airport. Her plane was due in at 12:47 p.m., and was on time. I sat on the stairs outside of the security area, waiting for her. And waiting.

At 1:15 p.m. she still had not appeared.

She didn't have a cell phone, and I wouldn't be permitted past the screening area, so I couldn't go to her gate and track her down. I waited some more, looked at Pinterest on my phone, and tried not to get too worried.

She finally wandered into sight, her hair slightly disheveled, a loopy smile on her face, pulling her carry-on behind her.

I ran over and gave her a hug. "Grace, are you okay? How was your flight?"

I looked into her eyes. She was obviously stoned out of her mind.

"Bumpy," she said at last. "We went through a storm, and there was lightning. Everywhere. And they won't serve you alcohol during the bumpy parts. Or during landing."

We walked slowly to the escalator and through the parking garage. "No, they won't. But did you have a drink before the storm hit?"

"I had three. Straight vodka," she said. "And a Xanax. And I smoked a joint before I even got on the plane. It didn't help."

Poor Grace! I knew she hadn't flown in years, but I always thought it was in protest of one thing or another. I never realized she was afraid of flying. "Well, you're on solid ground now, Grace. You're fine. You should have tried to sleep. It always makes the time go faster."

"No, Mona, I couldn't sleep," she said very seriously. "If I had stopped praying, the plane would have crashed to the ground."

"Grace, you were praying to God? I didn't think you believed in God."

"I prayed to Him. And Allah. And Zeus. I prayed to everyone."

I threw her suitcase in the trunk and got in the car. Her hands were clenching the dashboard, her entire body braced for impact. "Grace, you're not on the plane anymore," I told her gently.

She nodded and sat back. "I don't suppose you have any of those little bottles of vodka here, do you?"

"No, I don't. Sorry."

She nodded. "I'd take another Xanax, but I need to save them for the flight home." She closed her eyes and was asleep in three minutes.

When I got back, Jessica had joined the party and was helping to set up chairs. She saw me and ran over to the car. She opened Grace's door.

"She's asleep?"

"We'll go with that for now. Let her alone. How are things here?"

"Nina and Pinta have returned to Brooklyn. Aunt Lily has arrived and taken back the third floor. A bunch of food got delivered for lunch if you're hungry. And Dominique is here. She was looking for you, but is now Carmella's best friend. Was Daddy really staying here?"

I nodded. "Yep. Can you take Grace's suitcase upstairs? I'll find Carmella."

My backyard had been transformed. A white arbor had been set up at the far end of the yard, and against the backdrop of yellow forsythia, it looked lovely. Port-A-Potties arrived, looking like tiny Victorian garden sheds, and were tucked behind the garage. Workers had squeezed the dance floor between the deck and the patio, and had scattered small tables everywhere. There was another tented area along the back, with more small tables and chairs for sitting and eating, as well as a long table for the wedding party and other VIPs. Carmella really knew her stuff, and her army had accomplished a miracle.

Carmella and Dominique were standing by the arbor in deep conversation. They were so different—Carmella tall, dark, and statuesque, Dominique tiny, blond, and almost sticklike, even if she was still in her stuffed-sausage stage. As I approached, Carmella was flailing her arms around, and Dominique was nodding furiously.

"What's up, ladies?" I asked.

Carmella grinned. "It looks like I have a business partner."

I stared at her, then at Dominique. "What?"

Dominique actually hugged me. "Isn't it marvelous? Carmella is going to expand her wedding planning out to Jersey, and I'm going to set things up for her and run the office here."

"Well, that makes sense, Dominique. You are the best organizer I've ever seen at this kind of thing, and Carmella, you've done wonders here. This is just beautiful. I wouldn't have believed it."

She tried to look modest. "Well, you had the perfect space. I usually don't get such a big and beautiful yard to work with."

Something caught her eye, and she hurried off.

Dominique cleared her throat. "Thanks for giving Brian a place to stay."

I sighed. "I'm so sorry, Dominique. I had hoped that you and Tyler would be enough for him."

"Nothing will be enough for him," she said quietly. "But now I can leave that ridiculous house and find someplace for just Tyler and me. And I have a new career."

"You and Carmella are going to be quite a pair. You complement each other. But I think you should bring back that accent of yours. Add a touch of class?"

"Yes," she agreed with a grin. "I'll do that."

"Is Tyler with Phyllis? Why don't you stay? It looks like we'll be having one heck of a girls' night here, and you'll fit right in."

She smiled gratefully. "Thanks, Mona." She took a deep breath. "I really loved Brian," she said.

I didn't quite know what to say, so I just nodded.

"And he told me that his marriage to you was over," she went on. "I didn't know what he'd done to you. I didn't realize I was tearing apart a happy marriage."

I looked at her. "Dominique, you and I will never be friends. Not really. But I'm starting to like you, so I'll tell you the truth. You didn't tear apart a happy marriage. I thought that's what it was, but I'd been deluding myself for a long time before you came along. You can't tear apart something that's not badly broken to begin with."

We headed back toward the house. I saw that Miranda and Lauren were walking Grace through the maze of chairs. Lauren had taken the train to Boston and driven down with the newlyweds. They must have just arrived. Grace was rather unsteady on her feet, and as I got close enough I could hear her saying over and over again, "Bumpy, bumpy, bumpy."

Miranda held the chair as Grace sat down. "Mom, maybe we should get her a drink?"

"God, no. She's already toasted." I knelt down and tried to make eye contact. "Grace, honey, would you like to lie down?"

"Bumpy," she whispered.

I looked up at Lauren and Miranda. "I don't know how we'll ever get her on the plane going back. We may have to make an illegal drug run somewhere."

I stood up and gave Miranda a big hug. Although we talked all the time, I had not seen her since her wedding. "How's married life, my sweet?"

"It's the best thing ever."

"I'm beginning to think that with the right person, it can be. Grace, how about coming into the house?"

Grace nodded, and we walked her inside. She turned toward the den, went straight for the couch, then sat. She closed her eyes and leaned back.

"Aunt Grace," Lauren asked, "can I get you something to drink?"

Grace's eyes flew open. "Wine?"

"How about a nice cup of tea," I said quickly. "With honey?"

She nodded and closed her eyes again.

Jessica appeared and sat at the counter. Miranda got down the mugs as I set the kettle to boil. Lauren found the honey and sliced a lemon. There was food on the counter in foil containers, remnants of lunch, and I grabbed a sandwich. Miranda and Lauren helped themselves to a few of the salads. Jess had taken a sandwich and was picking it apart very carefully, separating the bread from the meats, and eating in very small bites.

"So, Mom," Miranda said, "David mentioned that Carmella had been up to visit Ben."

I focused on the kettle. "Oh?"

"Yeah. How could you let that happen?"

"How could I stop it?" I said shortly. I checked the heat. The gas flame was on high.

"I don't get it," Lauren said. "You spent a year and a half doing everything you could to be together, and as soon as you were back, you guys called it quits. What happened?"

"It's complicated," I told her. What was with this water? How long did it take to bring a kettle of water to boil?

"So we're all grown up now, Mom," Jess said. "Explain it to us. Because I thought that you and Ben were great together."

"We were." At last, steam. I removed the kettle and poured the boiling water into my favorite teapot, breathing in the scent of Earl Grey. I waited.

"So?" Lauren prompted.

"Ben felt that we needed to be married. I didn't. End of story." I poured the tea into four mugs, hovering over the fifth. "Do you think she'll even drink it?"

Jessica shook her head. "She's out. What was that about, anyway?"

"I guess she's afraid to fly. She loaded up on false courage." I took a sip of tea, closing my eyes, feeling a warm trickle down my throat. When I opened my eyes, my daughters were all staring at me.

"Are you happier without him, Mom?" Lauren asked.

Interesting question. With an obvious answer. I shrugged. "You make your own happiness, Lauren."

"Sometimes," Miranda said slowly, "it's given to you. I don't think that Daddy ever made you happy. Not the way he should have. Not the way David makes me happy."

I leaned forward, curious. "And how does he do that, Miranda?"

She looked into her tea. Jess and Lauren were watching her as well, all of us waiting. What words of wisdom could this new bride possibly offer?

"Well, it's like, your family has to love you. At least, good families. Like ours. I know that no matter what I do, even if it's something really stupid, you guys will never let me down. You will always love me. Right?"

I nodded. I felt my throat tighten.

"Right. And the world is this big, scary place. We don't know what's going to happen next. The only thing you can count on, really, is your family. But when you marry somebody, well, you've got that person too. And that person *chose* you. The world is still scary, but now there's someone in your life who wants to take your hand and go into the great unknown *with* you. And even though you guys will always be there for me, it's David who's stepped up to say, 'Hey, from now on, you're with me. We're in this together.'" She looked around. "We've chosen each other. That's my happiness."

Oh.

The back door opened and Lily and Carmella came in. Lily was flushed and glowing.

"Did you see what Carmella has done? Everything is so beautiful. I can't wait until tomorrow!"

"I can't either, Lily. By the way, Grace is here—in body, at least. And I hope you don't mind Dominique staying for your little party tonight?"

Lily waved a hand. "Now that she's free of that dreadful man, she's more than welcome." She looked at the girls. "I know he's your father, but…"

Jess jumped off her stool. "No offense, Aunt Lily. Tea?"

"Oh, is it too early for a glass of wine?"

"Not for the bride-to-be," I said. "Just don't wake up Grace."

Grace emerged from the den looking like five miles of bad road but perked up at the sight of us all in the kitchen, picking at trays of food and drinking. She refused to talk about her flight, after the first, tentative attempts, but instead began telling us all about what she really thought of living in a commune when you were no longer twenty-three.

"For one thing," she began, "all the young men who join up think they're going to have sex all the time with any woman they want."

Jessica, of course, was all over this. "But they don't? Can't? What?"

"It's not a brothel," Grace explained. "It's not about sex."

"If I remember correctly," Lily said, "that's why you went out there in the first place. What changed?"

"Aunt Lily," Grace said hotly, "I did not go out there in the first place just to have sex. Shadow and I were looking for a place where we could freely express ourselves without being tied to the middle-class conventions of our parents."

"Yes, dear, I'm sure," Lily said. "That and the fact that your father cut you off when you asked him if Shadow could move into your dorm room." Lily smiled. "Isn't that what happened?"

Grace made a rude face and gulped wine. "Whatever. That was then." She pointed a finger at Lily. "It meant something back then. There was the war and civil rights and all sorts of injustices in the world. We needed a place to feel safe and to try to make changes for the better. Now? Now there are still wars and injustices, but instead of trying to fix anything, it's a bunch of spoiled ex-hippies who want to fool around and not pay taxes. And they think that just because Shadow makes six figures a year, they can be just as successful tie-dyeing hemp prairie skirts."

Carmella raised an eyebrow. "Is he your husband? Six figures? Good for him. And you."

Grace may still have been feeling the effects of the various drugs she had ingested earlier. "Yeah? What's so good about it? You know solar hot water heaters? Good for the environment, blah, blah, blah. In Oregon, it rains frickin' all the time, so I get a hot shower maybe once a month. A whole lotta good six figures does me when I'm dirty and need to wash my hair." She had perched herself on a stool at the counter, but now got up and started weaving around the kitchen. "Don't you think I'd like to be able to go on the computer whenever I wanted to, instead of having to drive thirty miles for a crappy Wi-Fi signal?" She threw her arm around Jessica's shoulders. "I hate quinoa."

Jess's jaw had dropped open at that point. "Sorry, Aunt Grace."

"If I couldn't get high whenever I wanted," Grace whispered loudly into Jessica's ear, "I'd have probably hacked up a few people with an ax by now."

"Oh, dear," Lily murmured. "Somebody get that poor woman some more wine."

Dominique hopped up to oblige. "But it's very beautiful there," she said, pouring.

Grace slumped against Jess. "Trees. Lots of trees. You know what you can't do where there are lots of trees? Get a manicure. Or try on new shoes." She stared mournfully into her glass. "No MTV."

"Ah, Aunt Grace," Lauren said cautiously, "if you want to watch MTV, I'll turn it on for you."

Grace waved a hand and drained her wineglass again. "Nope.

Thanks. I think I'll just go back in there and sit on that nice comfy couch." She made a face. "No comfy couches there, either."

By now Carmella and Dominique were both choking with laughter, and Miranda had her head down, shoulders shaking. Lauren jumped up to help Grace back around the corner to the den. I just kept my head down as long as I could before I burst out laughing.

"Your sister," said Carmella, "could probably use a vacation from her life."

Lily had been nibbling on sliced salami and provolone cheese. "My God, Mona. Is she on anything?"

I shook my head. "Several things. I'm hoping that's what's wrong with her, and that tomorrow she'll feel a little better about the world."

Lauren had returned. "Let her have my manicure appointment tomorrow, okay?" We had booked an entire salon in town for various manicures, pedicures, and hairstylings.

"That's very sweet of you, honey."

"I'll go with her for new shoes," Miranda offered.

"And I'll make sure she has plenty of pot," Jessica said.

"No, Jess," I said, "that won't be necessary."

Dominique, fanning her red face with her hand, finally choked out, "Are you kidding? What if she comes after us with an ax?"

She and Carmella dissolved into giggles again.

Lily looked at Jess. "Get on that, darling. Right away."

I always felt that, given a common goal, friend, or enemy—not to mention a few bottles of wine—any group of women, even complete strangers, could come together. So I wasn't too surprised that I found myself thinking, by the third bottle of wine, that Carmella Ciavaglia was the most wonderful person I'd ever met, instead of the evil vixen who had stolen the man I loved. After all, it wasn't my fault that I had not stepped forward, knocked Ben on the head, and dragged him into my cave when I had the chance. I was an idiot.

Carmella, on the other hand, was smart and funny and had a fairly cynical outlook on life that I really appreciated. She was not just some old gangster's daughter—she'd raised two sons, started her own successful business, and maintained a fairly close relationship with both of her sisters. All rather admirable. I found myself liking her more and more as the night wore on in spite of myself.

I was not a terribly religious person. I never had been. If you're raised a Catholic, you're either in it all the way, or you fall to the wayside and occasionally wave as the parade passed by.

I was a waver.

But there were moments in my life when I knew that God loved me and that he was taking care of me.

Like when I woke up the next morning and did not have a hangover.

Fred had developed a bit of a snoring issue as he got older, and he was snuffling on his side of the bed. Other than that, the house was very quiet.

I glanced at my bedside clock.

Well, no wonder. It was barely six in the morning. Why on earth would I be up so early on a Saturday?

Oh. Right. Lily was getting married today.

And Ben would be there. I felt myself smile. I'd be seeing Ben.

I rolled out of bed and into the shower, threw on jeans and a sweater, and went downstairs. Whom should I wake up first?

Carmella was off the list, because as I came into the kitchen, she was dressed, eating a container of yogurt, and on her iPad. She looked up as I padded in.

"How's the head?"

"Amazingly, fine. Yours?"

She nodded. "I'm good. What about Lily?"

I watched as the coffee dripped into my cup. "She could drink a longshoreman under the table." I glanced out the window. All the tables and chairs had been covered with sheets, to protect them from the gentle fall of pollen that had, overnight, covered everything in pale green. "When do the drones return?"

"They'll be here by nine. The flowers arrive first, then the plates and glasses. By two the wait staff should be here. Food arrives by three thirty, ceremony's at four, music starts at five."

"You're good at this. Did I mention how much I admire you? I mean, you did an amazing job for Miranda, and all of this...well, thank you."

She shrugged. "Hey, how often do you get to plan your own father's wedding? This has been a real blast for me. Let me know when you're ready. I'll give you a discount."

I sat down across from her. "And what makes you think I'll need your services?"

She looked up from her iPad. "I went up to see Ben in Maine, you know."

I nodded. "Yes, I know."

"And can I tell you, I hate the cold? And I hate driving by myself in the snow, and there was traffic like you wouldn't believe, and there is absolutely *nothing* to do in Portland."

I sipped my coffee and nodded. "Lucky for you Ben was there to entertain you," I said calmly.

"Yeah, well, he didn't. I mean, look at me. I'm not used to men saying no."

My chest tightened, and I felt the blood start to pound in my ears.

"You know what he said to me?" she asked, leaning forward.

I shook my head.

"He said he was flattered, but he had too much respect for himself, and the woman he loved, to sleep with me just because he could." She sat back and shrugged. "He also said it would be disrespectful to *me* if he used me just because he was lonely. Who says crap like that? I mean, seriously? Too much respect? And he was talking about you, Mona."

"How do you know?" I asked, my voice shaking.

She rolled her eyes.

"Because there's no one else for him; that's how I know."

I tightened my hands around the coffee mug. "That ship has sailed, Carmella."

"Only if you want it gone, Mona." She spread her arms wide. "Men don't turn *this* down lightly."

I cracked a smile. "I'm sure. Thanks."

"No problem. So, is Dominique going to be a pain in my ass?"

I shook my head. "She'll be great. Really."

"Hope so. And about Jess and Tony. You okay with that?"

My eyes widened. "Jess? And Tony the Bodyguard?"

She rolled her eyes. "Listen, he's not a bad guy. He drives my dad around, but he's not exactly tied to the DeMatrianos in a, uh, business sense. He's going for his master's at Columbia. He's a smart boy."

"Jess?"

"I guess she didn't tell you? Oh, well." She drummed her fingers against the table. "I never wanted my husband in the business. I begged him to work in a bank. My kids stay clear. So do my sisters' kids. It's not glamorous. It's brutal. Tony knows that. He's going to end up teaching anthropology at some private college someday. Don't worry, okay?"

I nodded. "Okay."

"Now, let's wake these women up and get them started. There's a whole lotta shit happening today."

I drank more coffee. "Let me get some toast first, okay?" She nodded, and I started to go about the business of possibly eating something when Lauren wandered in.

"Mom, I think Aunt Grace needs help," she said.

I shrugged. "Probably feeling the effects of yesterday."

"Well, maybe," she said slowly. "But she was crying."

I put down the toast and went upstairs.

Sure enough, on the other side of the door I could hear not-too-stifled sobbing.

"Grace?" I opened the door. "Grace, honey, are you okay?"

"No!" she wailed. She was sitting up in Miranda's old bed, her hair sticking out in all directions, wearing a sleeveless T-shirt with "Springsteen '92" emblazoned across the front.

I crossed the room, sat on the edge of the bed, then reached for her hand. "What's the matter, Grace?"

"I h-h-hate my life."

Oh, dear. I put my arm around her and gave her a hug.

"You know, you had an awful lot of, ah, stuff in your system yesterday. Do you think that's why you're a little down?

"No, I don't." She sniffed. "I'm a little down, as you put it, because I've been stuck in 1978 for most of my life, and I've got nothing to show for it but a collection of handmade marijuana clips."

"You have five amazing sons."

"Shadow has five amazing sons. I have five grown men in my life who can spend three weeks carving a single piece of wood into something beautiful and exotic, but can't find five minutes to make me a cup of tea. Can I just stay here with you?"

I let go of her. "Grace, you've spent most of your adult life disapproving of pretty much every single choice I've ever made. Why on earth would you want to live with me?"

"Because I don't know where else to go," she said, and started sobbing again.

"You've had a home with Shadow since I was a little kid."

"Shadow is a selfish bastard. He didn't even want to give me the money to fly out here. I had to borrow from Harper. And he sleeps with a new girl every spring. I'm tired of putting on a brave face. I want to live a nice life. Like here."

I looked up. Lily and Jessica were crowded in the doorway.

Lily raised her eyebrows. "Well, this is certainly a blow for flower children everywhere. Grace, dear, how long have you felt like this?"

Grace wiped her face with the hem of her T-shirt, showing us all pale pink underwear. "Since 1997."

"Oh, Grace." I hugged her again. "I'm so sorry. You've been unhappy for so long. Why did you never tell me?"

"Because I didn't want you to think I was a failure."

"Gracie," I said, shaking her slightly. "Failing at something that makes you miserable is nothing to be ashamed of. It just means you made a wrong choice. Everyone makes wrong choices." I had made a bad choice, too. But the problem had never been choosing marriage. It had been choosing Brian.

She sniffed. "Now what do I do?"

I kissed her cheek. "Make some different choices."

"You make it sound so easy, Mona."

The words came out of my mouth so naturally, I didn't even have to think about them. "It is easy. All you have to do is know what you want. Then make the choice that gets you there."

She shook her head and wiped her face again. "I'm sorry. Aunt Lily, this is your day, and I'm acting like a spoiled child. My life has plodded along this long; it can wait another day."

I could see Lauren's head bobbing up behind Lily. I made shooing motions with my hand, and they all faded back.

"Grace?"

She looked up.

"We will talk about this. I promise. Tomorrow. But about today…"

She nodded. "Lily is getting married."

"That's right. And a major crime boss is the best man. A few of his cohorts are guests. We don't want to do anything to piss them off, do we?"

She shook her head.

"Good. Now, we're taking you for a manicure. You can get your hair done as well, maybe add some highlights. Then Miranda will help you buy new shoes. If you want, you can get a whole new outfit. And I promise you, Brian's money won't pay for any of it. Okay?"

She nodded again.

"No drugs, okay?"

She paused. "You know, a Valium…"

"No, Grace."

"Wine?"

"Later."

"Okay."

She got up and headed for the bathroom. I sat on her bed. Could it really be that easy? Making a different choice? And then I knew that unless I was willing to do that, I would never have Ben in my life again.

There was really no choice at all.

I don't know if Grace felt any better after spending three hours in one of the poshest salons in Westfield—which is a pretty posh place anyway—but she certainly looked better. Her hair had been colored and cut, and she looked ten years younger. She'd been mani-pedi'd and even had the hot-rock treatment to help her de-stress. Miranda whisked her off to buy a new outfit for the wedding and promised her pizza for lunch.

Apparently there were no pizza ovens at the commune.

I also looked and felt pretty good, although I was terrified to even touch the steering wheel of my car for fear of smudging my nails. I left Lily at the salon—she was also getting her makeup done—and drove back to the house.

Grace wasn't the only thing transformed.

There were pots of white azaleas lining my driveway and scattered all over the patio. Sprays of pink orchids, the exact color of Lily's sash, were on every table. White and pink roses had been woven into the arbor. There were white and pink bows on the backs of the chairs. The grass looked as though it had been raked.

Yesterday the inside of my garage had been draped in white fabric, hiding all the rakes, tires, and forgotten sports equipment. Today there was a miniature kitchen set up in the half of the space that was not taken up by a very well organized bar. White-coated staff persons stood like soldiers in a line, waiting for the next command.

I went into the house.

Carmella had also found time to do her hair and makeup. She was dressed in well-fitting jeans and a blouse, frowning at her iPad.

"Everything looks amazing," I told her.

She glanced up and smiled. "Thanks. Love the hair! You look great. Lily?"

"About a half an hour behind."

She nodded. "Alex is wandering around somewhere. He asked where you were." Her voice was very noncommittal.

"Oh? I though he was covering your father."

"Well, how interesting can that be? Last night there was a bit of a thing, but today, what? He puts on a suit, gets in a car, and drives across a bridge. A lot more going on here."

"You realize you'll have enough footage for a trilogy."

She grinned. "The wave of the future. All those kids taking movies on their phones? It's a whole new industry. I'm trying to get Alex to commit to doing this for me full-time, but he doesn't like getting tied to anything."

"So he said."

She put her iPad down. "He liked you, though."

"Meaning?"

She shrugged. "Just saying. I have to talk to a man about a car."

"Yes, where is everyone going to park?"

"At the high school. We're going to have four limos shuttle them back and forth. Don't want to block the street. Have to keep the neighbors happy, right?"

"Right." I watched her leave. It was two o'clock. I had at least an hour before dressing. I grabbed a yogurt from the fridge and went outside.

Alex was talking to the man behind the bar, and smiled when he saw me. He was dressed in slacks and a white button-down shirt, the first few buttons undone, revealing a very neat little triangle of dark chest hair. Not that I was into anything like that. Just reporting.

"You look a little casual for the official videographer of the wedding of the century," I told him.

"I've got a very nice navy blazer in the car. And a tie if Carmella gets in a snit."

"It's a perfect day," I said, and it was. Clear blue sky, barely seventy, no humidity. Being the end of April, it could have been ninety-seven degrees, snowing, hailing, or all of the above.

The man behind the bar, whose nametag read "Stan," nodded as he polished a wineglass. "Last one of these we did was in a freaking monsoon. The tent blew over, and we got drenched. I thought Carmella was gonna have a cow."

"Not even Carmella can control the weather," I said to Stan. He gave me a look that made me, for just a moment, doubt everything I thought I knew about Mother Nature.

Alex laughed. "Come on; give me the tour."

We walked around the yard. I pointed out where Miranda's first swing set stood, where the sandbox had been, and the apple tree, just now blooming pale pink and white, where Jessica had fallen from a high branch, resulting in a black eye, a twisted shoulder, and a visit from the Division of Youth and Family Services.

"They thought you'd beaten her?" Alex asked.

"You have to understand my daughter," I explained. "When the ER doctor asked her what happened, she told him I'd thrown her from the second-floor window to see if she could fly."

Alex burst out laughing. "I want to make sure to meet her."

"She'll be the one hanging out with Tony the Bodyguard," I told him.

"Vinnie's driver? Nice kid. Takes things a bit too seriously, but he'll get over it."

"So, you don't take things seriously?"

He shook his head. "No. Not so much. I'm the perfect example of what women don't want—a real Peter Pan."

"Some women like the idea of a man who won't tie them down too much," I said.

He shrugged. "And if I ever find her, we'll live happily ever after."

I laughed. "If I find her first, I'll send her your way."

Someone was yelling for me, so I waved a hand and trotted back to the house. Miranda and Grace were back. Grace was beaming. Miranda gave me a quick kiss before heading back to Ben's to get ready.

Grace whirled around, her newly cut hair shining. "Your daughter is a treasure, Mona. I don't know why I ever thought she was a spoiled, self-absorbed little brat."

"The last time you saw her, she was fourteen. All fourteen-year-old girls are self-absorbed brats."

"Yes, but I always figured your daughters would stay that way forever. You know, because you're so indulgent."

Well, it didn't take her long to get back to her old, charming ways. "I'm not indulgent."

"Whatever. Wait until you see the dress I found. I may never go back to tie-dye again." And she scurried upstairs.

Carmella coughed discreetly from the den. "I didn't mean to eavesdrop," she said. "But just for the record, I think your sister is a first-class—"

"I know." I held up both hands in surrender. "But she's family. Can't live with her, can't kill her."

Carmella raised her eyebrow. Right. I forgot. In her family, killing *was* an option.

"Maybe," I suggested, "we should start getting dressed."

"Good idea," Carmella said. "Because I think Lily is going to need both of us."

I took a final look in the mirror. The ivory dress fit perfectly. My hair looked great—a messy updo with pink orchids and a few loose curls around my face. The gorgeous shoes made my legs look ten miles long, but I knew that they were coming off as soon as no one was paying attention.

Guests had been arriving in long black limos. I watched as they came up the drive, and saw the expressions of delight and surprise as they turned into the yard. But I was not watching just to keep score of who was thrilled and who was not impressed. I was looking for Ben.

I saw Miranda and David first. Then right behind them was Ben. My heart jumped into my throat at the sight of him. I had not seen him in almost ten weeks. He was still the handsomest and best man I'd ever known.

I casually went out the back door, just in time to meet them as they turned the corner. Miranda hugged me, as did David, and they hurried off, leaving Ben and me alone in the driveway.

"It's good to see you," I said, a little breathlessly.

He smiled. "You too, Mona." He looked around. "I can barely recognize the place."

"I know. It looks great. If this writing thing ever falls flat, I'm thinking about turning the place into a yard for hire. You know—weddings, bar mitzvahs, family reunions."

He grinned. "Great idea." He was dressed in the same dark blue suit he'd worn to David and Miranda's wedding, and his blue eyes sparkled. It didn't hurt me anymore to look at him, because I finally knew how our story had to end. All I needed was the courage to do what had to be done.

"How did you like the limo ride over?" I asked him.

"Are you kidding? It was great! There was even champagne in the backseat, for that long, dry ride over. Lily sure knows how to impress her guests."

"I actually think it was Vinnie's idea. The champagne, I mean."

He nodded. "With ideas like that, he'll be a great addition to your family."

I laughed. "Yes, well, I've done a lot of thinking about what my family should look like, and I have to admit I'm making a few changes to the original blueprint."

We'd been standing a few feet apart, and he stepped closer to me, leaned forward, and kissed me gently on the cheek. I swallowed hard, inhaling the scent of him—clean, with a hint of musk. His lips felt cool and dry. He drew back, and our eyes were inches apart.

"I'm so glad you're here," I said softly.

"I would not have missed this for the world," he said, and as I looked into his eyes I knew we would be fine, that we knew each other too well to ever be less than the best of friends, and that today we would slip into old roles. No matter what happened to us in the future, he would always be my gentle, loving Ben.

He squeezed my hand, briefly, then turned and walked off, leaving me standing in my lovely ivory dress.

I may have looked vaguely bridal, but Lily had been right—there was no way I'd be mistaken for the center of attention. Lily's dress was dark pink lace on top, with an elegant boat neck. The satin sash around her waist was a darker pink, the exact color of the bottoms of my silly, expensive shoes, and the skirt consisted of yards of pale pink tulle, tea length, like a perfect ballerina dress. The colors were just perfect for her.

She looked so beautiful.

She carried masses of pink orchids and white tulips. I carried a single stem of the palest pink. We walked down the grassy aisle to the traditional "Here Comes the Bride," even though there was very little else traditional about the ceremony. What other wedding, presided over by a Catholic bishop no less, had the seventy-something bride reciting from the *Rubaiyat of Omar Khayyam*, with the groom responding from Tennyson?

Joseph DeMatriano and I stood as witness as they did *not* vow to love, honor, and obey. Lily swore to give comfort. Vinnie promised to remind her daily of his love. Both agreed to ease each other into the golden twilight with grace, humor, and patience.

When the ceremony was over, I handed Lily back her bouquet, but she reached past it to take my single, slender stem. She had stood up with Vinnie for one reason, to become his wife, and she'd gotten all she had wanted. She didn't need to take anything else with her back down the aisle.

After the ceremony, there wasn't the usual receiving line. Instead, the happy couple, as well as Joe and I, walked to each table and greeted every guest. I recognized some of Lily's old Brooklyn friends, as well as some of her more recent Westfield posse. Joe didn't shake hands with very many people, bowing gracefully from the waist instead. Those he did deem shake-worthy I looked at closely, but didn't recognize anyone from old episodes of *America's Most Wanted*. My feet were killing me in those beautiful shoes, but I was stuck in them at least until the official pictures were taken.

Alex had videoed the ceremony, of course, but there was another photographer who took countless pictures under the arbor and beside the forsythia. Finally, Lily looked at Vinnie and said, "Enough."

With a wave of Carmella's hand, the photographer was gone.

The band was excellent, and the happy couple danced to "When I'm Sixty-four," the irony of which was not lost on anyone. Suddenly the party started. Trays of hors d'oeuvres and glasses of champagne appeared from everywhere.

I was suddenly ravenously hungry, and champagne would not do.

Stan made me an exquisite martini, and Jessica appeared at my elbow with a plate of goodies. Tony was right behind her, and as we ate he filled me in on some of Vinnie's guests. I finally held up my hand and begged him to stop.

Joe made an early exit, right after he made a touching and obviously heartfelt toast. A few other older gentlemen and their mostly much younger wives left shortly thereafter. Once the politically significant guests left, I relaxed, feeling that the threat of a gate-crashing team of FBI agents was diminished.

I ate four little marinated shrimp in a row, and came dangerously close to following the waiter around just to steal the whole trayful.

The sunlight shifted and the yard took on a golden glow.

What a wonderful wedding.

At six o'clock, the fountain lights were turned on. I doubt anyone really noticed. The dance floor was packed, the white-coated waiters were running ragged, and the noise level had risen considerably. The bar setup in my garage was so efficient and practical, I wondered what it would cost to install permanently. I'd probably have to get rid of the tulle and ribbon, and I doubted the flowers would last forever, but the keg and outdoor fridge could stay, along with the portable wooden bar with its white marble counter.

I had a place at the head table, but other than conceding that the bridal party needed its own designated space, Lily had refused to assign people to tables. She claimed that she could not afford to get anyone in this particular crowd mad at her for any reason, and I had to agree with her there. So the tables were set for four or six people, and like found like without any drama. I spent some time with Nina, Pinta, and Santa Maria and their various appendages. I hovered around the "kids' table"—Jessica and Lauren, Tony, Trev, and Paulie. They were arguing some obscure point in one of the *Matrix* movies. I was beginning to realize that any worries I had about Vinnie's grandkids were all a result of too much time I'd spent watching old movies and cable TV.

Grace sat with Miranda, David, and Ben. Miranda, with her usual good sense of style, had outfitted my sister in an ice-blue sheath dress and nude heels, and Grace looked surprisingly elegant. Very surprisingly, because she spent most of her time flitting around the party like a homegrown, one hundred percent organic butterfly. She drank champagne, and danced with Ben, Trev, David, and several dark-suited gentlemen who were probably too polite to tell her to get lost.

"Mom," Miranda said in a low voice, "is she really going to be living with you?"

What? "Did she say that?" I was sitting between Ben and Miranda, and we were watching as Grace and David danced to a very snazzed-up version of the Hokey Pokey.

"Yes. She said that she was leaving the commune, moving out here, and finding a job. I kinda thought with Aunt Lily gone, you'd be looking forward to being alone."

"She told you she was going to find a job? Doing what? All she's done for the past thirty years is can vegetables and keep bees. Not exactly the job skills needed in this market."

Ben chuckled. "Lucky for you that whole third-floor suite is going to be empty."

I looked at him. "Ben, what am I going to do? We'll be at each other's throats in a week."

"But, Mom," Miranda said, "she was so sweet and friendly yesterday."

"I know. But I can't keep her pumped up on drugs forever. To be honest, I was thinking about downsizing."

Miranda sat up. "You'd sell the house?"

"Why not? You're gone. Lauren and Jessica will hopefully be gone as well in the next two years. Why would I want to keep rattling around in that big old house by myself?"

Miranda frowned, thinking hard. "I guess. Where would you go?"

I shrugged. "I was thinking about just moving to the shore house."

"I could see you living there," Ben said. He was sipping his beer.

"How was Maine?" I asked him.

He shrugged. "How *is* Maine, you mean. Going fine, but much slower than expected. I'll be going back up for at least another month. I need to take care of a few things down here; then I'm going back."

"Do you like it up there?"

He nodded. "It was lonely. And cold. But they tell me spring is lovely, so we'll see." He tapped the side of his beer glass with his fingertips. "Lots of interesting characters. I found myself wanting to call you and tell you about them. They'd be great fodder for your next ten books."

I smiled. "I missed you too," I said.

Something softened around his eyes. "Yes. Missing you was

pretty much the hardest part." He dropped his eyes and played with his spoon.

Miranda cleared her throat nervously. "So, Mom, about Aunt Grace?"

"You know, maybe Carmella can help you out," Ben said.

"Oh?" Enough already with Carmella, okay?

He nodded. "She told me that she and Dominique were becoming business partners?"

I made a face. "Yes. Is that a combination or what?"

He grinned. "I can imagine a few sparks there, yes. But Dominique will need somebody to sit in the new office and answer phones and do paperwork, right?"

I nodded slowly. "I bet Grace could do that."

"But would she still have to live with you?" Miranda asked.

I thought a moment. "I have no idea what she's going to do. This morning she was miserable, and now she's dancing around like a queen bee. Let's just wait and see. Maybe she'll get over this whole thing and fly back to Shadow after all."

"Mom," Miranda said, very seriously, "I don't think there's enough Xanax in the world to get her on a plane again."

Hmmm. True. I smiled and got up. I needed to mingle.

I also needed another martini, but on the way to the bar Alex asked me to dance. I immediately looked for Ben, but he was talking to David, and didn't even notice as I slipped by.

Alex put his arms around me, and we moved easily. "Have you found her yet?" he asked.

"Found who?"

"The woman who could love a Peter Pan." He was smiling, but his eyes were serious.

I shook my head. "Sorry. I thought you might get lucky, but I think she's already left."

"That's too bad. We might have been pretty good together. If she could have ever gotten over her old love."

"That obvious, huh?"

The music changed, something vaguely Latin and upbeat. Boy, he could really dance.

"Well, Carmella filled me in, of course. But I've been watching you. You can't take your eyes off of him. Some habits," Alex said, "are very hard to break."

I shook my head. "More than a habit," I told him. "I can only hope he feels the same way."

When the music stopped, he looked at me with a smile. "You know how to find me," he said. I walked away from him and caught a glimpse of Carmella, watching closely. I waved, and she dropped her eyes.

It took me another twenty minutes to make my way to the bar. Stan saw me, winked, and went to work.

I took a long sip and felt the familiar jolt. I looked up and over at MarshaMarsha's house. There, high in the back window, I could see MarshaMarsha and Patricia. I waved. I was glad they got to see the show.

Patricia opened the window, leaned out, then pointed to something. Several times, in an incessant stabbing motion.

I followed her finger with my eyes. There, standing alone on a tiny patch of quiet green lawn, was Ben.

I glanced back at Patricia. She made an exaggerated motion with both her hands—*Go, go!*

Yes, I did have to go. The wedding was winding down. I'd been around Ben all afternoon, and never once did I manage to get him alone. And there were things I needed to say to him that could only be between the two of us. I gulped my martini and set the empty glass on a passing tray. I bent down and eased my feet out of those ridiculous shoes, and walked across the yard to Ben.

He watched me as I walked to him, his eyes crinkled with pleasure, a smile on his delicious mouth. "Hello again. Did I mention that you throw a great party?" he said as I came up.

I nodded. "Thanks. But the credit all goes to Carmella. The woman really knows her job."

"Yes, she's very good. It was a very lovely ceremony. Moving. I was surprised."

"Me too. In fact, this whole experience has been a surprise to me."

"You look beautiful, by the way."

I felt myself blushing and looked down at my dress. I twirled on my bare toes. "You mean this old thing?"

He laughed. "Yes. In fact, you could be the bride."

"Think so?"

"Oh, yes."

"Then I should probably think seriously about getting married again."

He did not speak. His eyes narrowed very slightly. "I thought," he said at last, "you never wanted to get married again."

I took a deep breath.

"I thought so too, mainly because I really didn't like being Brian's wife. But I've been thinking that maybe I would be a *different* wife the next time around."

"And what kind of wife do you want to be?"

"Yours."

He stuck both of his hands in his pants pockets and looked at the ground.

"The thing is," I said, my voice cracking a bit, "I love you. And I really missed you. There were so many times I wanted to talk to you or ask your advice, and it was awful not having you there. I finally got used to the being alone part, but I still missed the *idea* of you. And I know that, no matter what happens to me in the next fifty years, my life will be better if you're in it."

He looked up, but not at me. His eyes squinted against the setting sun as he looked past me. Was he going to say something? Anything? No—he was not going to make it any easier. I couldn't really blame him.

"I've had to look at what marriage really means," I went on. "Not just to each other, but to the world. It means you're willing to put everything on the line. You're willing to take risks for each other. To be unhappy for each other. It means both of you are willing to do the hard work."

"I know what marriage is, Mona," he said quietly. "I've always known."

"But I've never known. Not really. Which is why I was so terrified about Miranda and David. They took this giant leap of faith. Their whole lives were about to change, and they weren't afraid. At all."

He looked straight at me. His eyes were very dark and still. "Everything *does* change, Mona. That's kind of the point."

"Yes. I know that now. I got a piece of advice a while ago, about expectations and reality. Which is why I think you're the only person I ever *could* marry. I'm willing to do the work. I'm willing to face the changes. I'm willing to risk everything to be with you. That's my reality. So I think I can expect us to live happily ever after."

He was quiet.

"Unless it's too late."

He took a deep breath. Then he looked away, shaking his head. He made a bit of a face, like he was having some sort of conversation with himself. His shoulders lifted, then fell.

"Will you marry me, Ben? I'd get down on bended knee," I said, "but if I got grass stains on this dress and Carmella wanted more pictures, she'd probably have me killed."

Finally he smiled. "Well, we can't have that. I don't think bended knee is required." He reached to take my wrist. There, under the flower corsage, was the bangle he'd given me for Christmas. "Better than your dreams?"

I stepped forward, right into his arms. My silly shoes dropped onto the grass.

His body was long and lean against mine, his arms around me strong and tight. My head fit perfectly against his shoulder.

Was that a chorus of bluebirds bursting into song?

Did the band suddenly start playing "Hallelujah"?

Did a flock of white doves fly by in a hushed flurry of wings?

No.

It was the sound of happiness, and my own heart singing.

Author's Note

As always, I have to thank my agent, Lynn Seligman, for her encouragement and guidance. More thanks to Tiffany Yates Martin for her excellent editing, and Cheryl Murphy, editrix at Inkslinger, who always manages to make my books look perfect. It's great to have a team I can count on as my career moves forward.

Also—thank you to all you readers who asked for a sequel. I had thought that Mona and Ben were done. I hope you all aren't disappointed in how things turned out.

CPSIA information can be obtained at www.ICGtesting.com
Printed in the USA
LVOW06s2109260215

428495LV00028B/1679/P

9 780985 985462